D1423308

THE PAWNS OF KINGS

When Henry I usurps the throne of England, he coldly casts the Princess Nesta, his beautiful Welsh mistress, to the furthermost corner of his kingdom.

Forcibly married to the Constable of Pembroke, Gerald of Windsor, an unknown Norman mercenary, Nest believes that her future life will become pale and uneventful. But Gerald, far from being the battle-weary middle-aged soldier that Nest expects, proves to be a highly unusual young man and an unexpectedly acceptable husband and lover.

Together, Gerald and Nest create a brilliant and exceptional dynasty – the famous fitz-Gerald family, who are to hold positions of power and prestige throughout the Old World and the New, for over eight hundred years.

In this book the author sketches a colourful tapestry of twelfth-century life, its turbulence, pleasures and disasters. And throughout, Gerald and Nest shine through as perhaps one of the most attractive pairs of lovers of all time.

THE PAWNS OF KINGS

MARGARET MACKINLAY

WOLVERHAMPTON PUBLIC LIBRARIES

LOCATION	CLL GR	
CLASS No.	W.M.	
I.S.B.N.		
RESERVED STOCK		
INVOICE No.	C0920	CHECKED

ROBERT HALE · LONDON

© Margaret Mackinlay 1981
First published in Great Britain 1981

ISBN 0 7091 9201 0

Robert Hale Limited
Clerkenwell House
Clerkenwell Green
London EC1R 0HT

Photoset by
Specialised Offset Services Limited, Liverpool
Printed in Great Britain by
Clarke Doble & Brendon Ltd., Plymouth, Devon
Bound by Garden City Press Ltd.

Contents

'Tis all a Chequer Board of Nights and Days.
Where Destiny with men, for pieces plays,
Hither and thither, moves and mates and slays,
And one by one back in the closet lays.

The Rubaiyat of Omar Khayyam
(Infidel Persian poet and philosopher
c. 1100 A.D.)
Translated by Edward fitz-Gerald

Prologue

Apart from the usual background noises, the only other sound that broke the peaceful warmth of that pleasant August morning was the raucous brawling of two scavenging crows, a disreputable pair, who noisily mauled a piece of offal beneath the courtyard wall. I plied my needle in desultory fashion to the tapestry upon my knees, only remotely aware of the pastoral scene that lay before my eyes, which I attempted to reproduce upon the canvas. In spite of the many comforts of Gloucester Castle, I was bored and a trifle ill at ease. It was now two whole weeks since Prince Henry had ridden in haste from Winchester to London, after securing the Royal Treasury. Fourteen long days since his successful coronation, which had speedily followed his brother's untimely death, while hunting in the New Forest. And twelve days precisely, since I had arrived at Gloucester from Winchester.

I paused, holding my needle still, watching the two crows as they struggled beneath the wall beside the postern gate. Suddenly, the larger of the two, having wrested the coveted piece of meat from his brother, flew triumphantly over my head, carrying his prize far away, out of sight beyond the oak trees.

Beneath the tree which sheltered me, my son lay contentedly asleep in his wooden crib, untroubled by the fact that his father had so very recently snatched the throne

WOLVERHAMPTON
PUBLIC LIBRARIES

of England from the outstretched grasp of the heir apparent, Duke Robert of Normandy. I moved away to lean my elbows upon the parapet which surrounded the courtyard. That arrow loosed from the unruly bow of Walter Tyrrel in the New Forest, but two weeks ago, was certain to change the course of many lives. It was whispered that the Conqueror's eldest son, Duke Robert, was already wending his victorious way back to Normandy from a crusade in Jerusalem and that the wife who returned with him was both rich and beautiful.

The baby stirred suddenly and opened his eyes. I leaned over him and smiled. Instantly, two small fists rose in my direction. It was not a gesture of supplication, but one of demand, for like his father, his intentions were always deliberate and unmistakable and could not be denied. I lifted him from the cot and his warm plump body merged with mine blissfully. For a child of such tender age, he showed remarkable energy and enterprise. I disentangled his small fingers from my coif and held him closer. In the seven months since his birth, I had become increasingly fond of this small rotund rascal. He was a fortunate child, who had inherited not only the august blood of the kings of South Wales, but also that of the present King of England. The realization of all that this implied, instilled a curious excitement within me. Would Duke Robert invade England this very autumn, I wondered. Then, when he was successfully defeated in his bid to reclaim the English throne, would his brother, the victorious Henry, then marry me and make this small scrap which I held in my arms, legitimate? The sun, at that moment, chose to return from its temporary refuge in the clouds and its benevolent warmth assured me that all would be well. For although Henry had had many women and numerous other sons, had he not restored me as his favourite, as soon as I had sufficiently recovered from the birth of our child?

My musing was abruptly called to a halt by the arrival of a large host of armed men, at the main gate of the castle. All became bustle and pandemonium. I directed my son's nurse to investigate and she obediently sped away, returning a few minutes later to tell me that the new arrival was Earl Hugh of Chester, he whom they called "the fat", and that he had news of the King, from London. It was but a brief minute later that Earl Hugh came to seek me out, wheezing slightly with the effort of ascending the grassy bank to the rampart walk on which I stood. He was a man of vast proportions and it was said that it involved the work of many armourers, for many months, to contrive each of his massive coats of mail. The nurse, receiving the child from my grasp, rapidly scuttled away. Like most servants, the girl was patently terrified by the awesome bulk of the most premier earl of the Marches. Earl Hugh I noticed, refrained from meeting my eye and giving me but a vague obeisance and a perfunctorily muttered, "Princess Nesta", he lowered himself heavily upon the stone bench. His white surcoat was covered by a fine film of dust and the helmet which he had removed when he dismounted, looked equally travel-stained. He appeared to have ridden with speed and as he had latterly been far from fit and was a man who fast approached middle age, the journey had left its mark upon him. This haste with which he had ridden alarmed me. "Pray give me your news of the King, my lord," I begged, "for here at Gloucester we have little but rumour to mitigate our fears for his safety."

"The King is well," he growled. "Aye, at present the King is very well, for both citizens and garrison of London alike make little secret of the hatred they held for his late majesty, William Rufus." He rubbed the back of a grimy paw across his sweating brow. "So, they have welcomed Henry as their new king readily, putting few constraints in his way. For has he not recalled their saintly Archbishop

Anselm?" He let out a cynical guffaw. "He says that he will offer his people York, or even London if they require it," he murmured, "but it seems unlikely that he will have to resort to such lengths."

"Then the news you bring is good," I ventured, albeit guardedly, for seven years as a hostage at the court of the Red King had bred caution within me.

"For the King yes, all is well," he agreed. "Until such time as Duke Robert sees fit to try to wrest his crown from him." He paused and the silence lengthened ominously. With mounting apprehension, I realized that the Earl of Chester had not, as I had hoped, come to summon me to the King's side in London. "The King has many problems in defending his new realm," Earl Hugh resumed at last. "The Northern border being one of his most acute anxieties." I became painfully aware that he was deliberately avoiding my gaze, for Earl Hugh and I had been on excellent terms when we had previously met at court in Winchester, but now his manner was aloof. At last I could bear it no longer.

"Tell me in plain terms what you have come to say," I directed tersely.

"Spoken like a true daughter of the ancient house of Deheubarth," he complimented. "So you realize that for you my child, the news is not good?" I nodded, sick at heart. "If Duke Robert invades England from Normandy, the King has to be sure that his border with Scotland is secure," he explained. "The only way he can be really certain of this, is to make a treaty of peace with Edgar, King of Scotland. Now King Edgar, has a marriageable sister, Edith or Matilda, call her what you will – ."

After the blow had fallen I felt quite cold, remote from the world.

"You do not need to tell me more," I cut in quietly. "So Prince – ," I corrected myself, "King Henry, is to marry the daughter of Queen Margaret and Malcolm Canmore of Scotland and not Nest, daughter of the Prince Rhys ap Tewdwr of South Wales." I faced him resolutely.

"What is to become of my son and me?" I asked, attempting to rid my voice of emotion, for I knew Henry too well to believe that any detail would have escaped his efficient mind.

The Earl heaved himself to his feet and sweating objectionably, he began to pace the terrace. "You are to return to South Wales; Penbroc in your father's old kingdom of Deheubarth, is to be your new home. There, the King has arranged a suitable marriage for you."

"A suitable marriage," I interrupted. "At Penbroc – Why, that is the new fortress of Arnulf, son of Roger de Montgomery." My mind flashed rapidly back over the years. Somewhere at some time, I had met Lord Arnulf. The Montgomerys were an evil brood and I did not trust them. Vaguely I recalled Arnulf, a black browed effeminate who had slouched around the homosexual fringes of the unsavoury court of William Rufus, clad in padded mantle and ridiculously elongated slippers.

"Lord Arnulf is not, unfortunately, to have the pleasure of being your husband," Earl Hugh announced in cold tones. "Lord Arnulf has expressed the wish that he should not be asked to marry at this season," he advised me. "Your husband will be the Constable of Penbroc, chief officer to my Lord Arnulf, an able and efficient commander." His voice tailed off, as at last his eyes accidentally met mine. He veered away and resumed his pacing.

"Not Lord Arnulf!" I exclaimed, almost speechless. "So the King actually believes that I, the Princess Nesta, daughter of the royal house of Deheubarth, can be cast away into the farthest corner of his kingdom and forced to marry a common castellan. I will not be condemned thus!"

My body trembled, as the full force of my rage consumed me.

"Take care," Earl Hugh warned. "When one is dealing with a King, and not merely the King's brother, tongues must be guarded. What you say could well be deemed a treason. Take care, my lady, lest others hear you."

"That I and my son should be banished to such a paltry fate," I raged. "I tell you, I cannot! I will not!"

"Your son is not to accompany you," Earl Hugh said quietly as I paused for breath. "I am to rear your son at Chester, on the King's express orders and he may not be gainsaid." With this new blow, I could no longer hold back the tide of tears which had been threatening to engulf me.

"My son!" I swallowed convulsively. "You cannot, Earl Hugh," I cried piteously. "I beg you will not take my baby from me. He is all I shall have left." I approached him urgently. "You cannot take him from me. Say you will not?"

"My lady, I have my orders," he said, with a stony resolution which even in my despair, I knew I would never move. "It is the King's command," he declared, "and neither you nor I can alter 'Royal Writ'. You are young, my lady." He attempted to coax me now, his voice becoming a little more kindly. "Why, you are not yet eighteen years old. You have the rest of your life before you. Would that I were young and virile still, for if I were, you would want for nothing. Had you been like other women, the King could have kept you unobtrusively by his side, but you are renowned through court and countryside alike, for your outstanding beauty. King Edgar's sister, a plain enough girl from all accounts, is hardly likely to tolerate the 'fairest of them all, the Helen of Wales', as her open rival at court. The King knows this and that is why he has decided thus."

As I cast myself face downwards upon the green sward, and gave up my soul to the bitterness of anguish and despair, Earl Hugh paced the terrace uneasily, leaving me to rid myself of the first rush of unrestrained emotion. After a while, I was aware that he came to stand beside me.

"You are young," he repeated quietly, "and very beautiful. Life is full of compensations. The fact that you are to be married to this lackey of Lord Arnulf, is of no consequence. A girl like you can take whomsoever she pleases. Find the most attractive man at Penbroc and take him. There is no need for tears!"

PART I

As we neared the castle of Arberth, our last overnight halt on the long road from Gloucester to Penbroc, the distant tinkling of a cow bell made me aware that we were once again within the sphere of organized Norman influence. From over the narrow river I could hear the working song of villeins labouring amongst the ripe corn, as they scythed and bound their lord's harvest, on an outlying manor farm. Their song was, by the very nature of its rhythm, a slow sad air and as the notes reached me across the valley, I sank even deeper into the gloom which had overtaken me, a full week before.

Any hopes which I had nourished of an ambush and subsequent rescue by those of my father's people still resident in this part of South Wales were now dashed, for it was obvious that I was already within the outlands of the Norman stronghold. It had been a forlorn hope at best, a hope bred of desperation. For who, of my remaining kinsmen would know that it was the daughter of their Prince, Rhys ap Tewdwr, who rode towards Penbroc so firmly contained within the custody of Walter, High Sheriff of Gloucester? I doubted also if I should still be recognized in my homeland, as for seven long years, I had been a hostage of the Norman kings. My mind only dimly recalled my father's court and memories of my immediate family grew less as each year went by.

I had been a mere child of eleven when my father had died by the hand of a renegade Norman band, outside Brecheiniog. I had met him infrequently throughout my childhood, but almost as if he knew that he should not live much longer he had sent for me only a few days before his death. On this occasion our meeting took place in front of the bards, in the many timbered hall of his mountain eyrie. The chief bard, I remember, had sung of my growing beauty and I recall how this compliment had strangely moved and pleased the venerable old man; an octagenarian who carried his four-score years as lightly as most men carry forty. He had taken my face gently into his hands and viewing my features gravely he had pronounced that I should one day be famous throughout the land, both for my beauty and for the fame and prestige of my sons. I quickly swallowed back a sob, for my father's kingdom now lay scorched and deserted. There were few of his own people left there now to sing over his lands.

On this particular journey we had passed through many a once fertile valley which had in my childhood fed and supported numerous families. Today, all one could see for miles were burnt out farmsteads and un-tilled fields. The conquerors had, with their harsh inflexible policy of eviction and burning, driven the survivors high into the fastness of the mountains. There was something else also, that my father had told me at our last meeting. "You," the old chieftain had said, before he bade me goodbye for the last time, "you, my daughter, are a survivor. Aye, perhaps even more of a survivor than my sons." It was the slim hope to which I had clung, after Earl Hugh had left me sobbing in despair on the grass at Gloucester Castle, but a week ago.

But now I was nearly at my journey's end, almost at the walls of my prison. I became aware that Walter, the Sheriff of Gloucester, had pulled his horse forward, to ride at my side. He was a strange, silent man, the perfect servant, but his manner towards me throughout our long journey had been both courteous and kind.

"The road grows long and tedious for you I fear, my lady," he said, averting his gaze tactfully to avoid direct confrontation with my obvious misery. "In another half mile, we shall begin to ascend the track into Arberth. It is an attractive valley and the castle offers much to comfort the traveller after a journey as tiring as you have been forced to endure, this past week."

"The journeying does not bother me sir, I assure you," I answered quickly. "I am young, and have ridden much and for far longer in the past, than this, our road from Gloucester."

"Then perhaps you will allow me to advise you a little of the nature of your future life at Penbroc and of the man who is to be your husband," he suggested, with a certain amount of diffidence.

"I care so little for this match sir, that it would please me if you would not discuss it," I managed at last.

"Very well," he said patiently. "But there is a story about the castle which I think you might be interested to hear, nevertheless." As I did not object, he began to relate a strange and exciting story, which eventually overcame my desire to remain alone with my misery. "The year 1096 was a turbulent one for South Wales," he began. "The castle which you saw last night, near Carmarthen, fell into disrepair when William fitz-Baldwin died. Because of its loss, three chieftains of mid-Wales managed to sweep back down through your father's old kingdom, eventually coming to the very gates of Penbroc Castle itself. Penbroc, a slender looking fortress in those days, did not appear to be a particularly formidable proposition. Its garrison was not large and as Lord Arnulf himself was away in Shrewsbury, the Welsh considered that it was not likely to last out for any length of time. They drove away all the cattle and the inhabitants of the small town and burning everything up to the castle gates, encamped a short distance away, to await the expected surrender of the fortress. A few of the knights who made up the garrison, fearing such a host, attempted to make off in a small boat down the river, which runs beneath the castle walls."

Becoming absorbed by his tale, despite myself, I was driven to express my utter contempt for these men. "Their commander thought so too," he said, "for he promptly captured them and having brought them back within the castle bounds, he stripped them of their arms and titles; later, investing their own young squires with these, to discipline the traitors. His courage so inspired the rest of the garrison, that they swore to fight it out, at all costs. This they did, until food became so short that the commander ordered the last four hogs in the castle to be cut up and thrown over the walls onto the heads of his enemies. This derisive gesture, he hoped, would convince the besiegers that he had so much food within the castle, that to starve him into submission was impossible." I was fascinated.

"This man had the instincts of a gambler," I cried. "Even though these men at his gates were undoubtedly my uncles, I cannot but hope that his ruse succeeded." Walter of Gloucester smiled one of his rare, but rather pleasing smiles.

"That is extraordinarily generous of you my lady, for these were indeed your uncles at his gates and you are quite right in your assessment of the man. The commander of Penbroc at that time, was however, not only a gambler but also a born survivor."

"A survivor!" I grasped the word with interest, my attention completely arrested at last.

"Your uncles were not sure that with winter approaching they could bear to sit outside Penbroc Castle indefinitely," the Sheriff continued, "but they were not entirely convinced either. However, our commander could ill afford to wait, not even for a week or so. He had thrown his last four hogs over the walls, remember? He and his garrison were starving. An even more subtle scheme came to him and he sent a messenger by night, who dropped a letter he had written to Lord Arnulf, right outside the door of the Bishop's summer Palace at Lamphey. Bishop Wilfred was still in residence there and he was a known nationalist sympathizer. Our astute commander had stated very emphatically in this letter, that Lord Arnulf was not to bother to send him assistance, or to try to raise the siege as he lacked for nothing and could hold out for a further three months at least and probably for the whole winter."

"Was my Uncle Cadwgan one of the besiegers?" I asked. Sheriff Walter nodded with grave amusement.

"He was."

"Then he would have lifted the siege at once," I declared. "For he dislikes trouble intensely and prefers to spend his winters at home in Powys or Ceredigion."

"And so he did. The siege was lifted, the Welsh chieftains went home with their spoil and Penbroc Castle gained such a reputation for impregnability and its commander Gerald of Windsor such a reputation for resourcefulness and courage, that the castle has never been attacked since."

"Oh," I said flatly, looking straight ahead, between my horse's ears. I had been tricked.

"I am sorry," my companion said in sober tones, "but I felt that you had to know something about the man you were to marry. You have consistently refused to talk about him. I have had much to do with him in respect of the Shire Courts at Penbroc and his reputation and ability are of the highest – "

"Many men are good soldiers, sir," I replied coldly. "They may also be able administrators. That does not necessarily make them attractive or desirable husbands."

"But Gerald of Windsor is – "

"I do not wish, sir," I cut in defensively, "to speak further of the Constable of Penbroc." Walter, Sheriff of Gloucester made me a polite bow from the saddle.

"As you wish, my lady," he replied, without emotion. "You will excuse me," he stated, as he moved towards the front of the column of armed men. As he left my side I became aware that we approached the outskirts of a long village that straggled up towards a distant castle mound. We had arrived at Arberth.

Like most castles this little outpost situated in its mellow tree-lined valley, began life as soon as the day had broken. Before the sun had shaken itself fully awake the next morning, all was bustle and activity around the small courtyard. Doggedly, I lay still upon my couch, refusing to be hurried. That this was a black day for me, I could not doubt. There were no mitigating circumstances, I felt, in being married to a man that I had never seen before. A man who, I was certain, wanted me as little as I wanted him. I picked at the bread, meat and wine which my maid, Branwen, had offered for my breakfast. "I am not hungry," I said at last, pushing it away. She removed the salver and then, rummaging in my clothes chest, held out a brand new kirtle of fine blue wool with loose sleeves and trimmed at neck and cuff with gold braid. A delicate white cambric undergarment completed what was indeed a striking and becoming town. "Put it away," I directed. "I do not intend to wear such fine work to impress the Constable of Penbroc." Branwen demurred.

"My lady, the Sheriff of Gloucester ordered me to set out your most elegant raiment – "

"Do you think that I care to obey the orders of the Sheriff of Gloucester over such matters," I snapped. "You have been in border castles yourself, you must know the type of men we are likely to find at Penbroc. Unruly, unkempt and uncouth. Put the kirtle away, Branwen, I shall wear the green mantle in which I have ridden from Gloucester. You may find me a clean saffron undergarment and a fresh kerchief." Branwen braided my hair quickly with her slim deft fingers. She was the daughter of one of my father's followers, now also dead. This was the only concession which had been made to me during my years as a hostage and that only when I had reached the age of fifteen and Prince Henry had begun to notice me favourably. The services of a Welsh maid had enabled me to retain the Welsh tongue, something which had been a great comfort to me in my lonelier moments. Branwen was fiercely loyal. She had been raised in a small fertile valley near Carmarthen, a valley through which we had ridden a few days ago. It was the place where the burned out shells of the indigenous Welsh cottages had been most evident. Witnessing her deep distress at the sight had been almost more than I could bear.

When we reached the courtyard after a summons from our escort that our horses were ready, I was aware of a quick appraisal from Walter of Gloucester. He said nothing, however, although it was apparent that he noticed that I had not obeyed his instructions to don my most becoming gown. As I was lifted onto my palfrey a group of horsemen clattered into the courtyard. They were led by a mere youth, younger than myself. Walter the High Sheriff of Gloucester actually frowned. "Ah, de Ville," he greeted the youth. "Where is your master?" The young man flushed and made a quick obeisance in my direction.

"The Constable of Penbroc begs your pardon sir and sends profound apologies for his absence, but he was unable to journey thus early to Arberth, owing to a suspicious Irish vessel that anchored in the river mouth overnight, the which he wishes to investigate." The Sheriff's displeasure was hardly veiled and his reply was crisp.

"It is to the Princess Nesta you should tender your master's apologies, de Ville. In that case, let us commence our journey without further delay, for the Prior of Monkton expects us around noon." The young man, de Ville, urged his horse to my side and stammered apologies of an infinite length until I felt genuinely sorry for him. It was, after all, the grossly bad-mannered snub which his master had tendered to me, which had caused his embarrassment. As we moved away from the castle gate I glanced to my right and a stab of pain smote me, as over the shoulder of a wooded mound I glimpsed through haze, the blue peaks of the Prescelli mountains. Mountains, on whose ridges I had often ridden and played as a child, on many a faultless summer day. The memories they recalled were too painful for such a day of sorrows. De Ville eventually moved forward to converse in low tones with Walter the Sheriff and I was left with my own bitter thoughts and a rapidly growing resentment towards this Norman upstart to whom I was to be forcibly married, on the King's command this very afternoon. By the time we reached the environs of Penbroc town a few hours later, I was totally consumed by an overpowering anger which smouldered, barely concealed beneath the surface.

However slender Penbroc Castle had seemed four years ago when my uncles had sat outside its walls, it had lately become a very powerful and formidable looking fortress. No wonder it had the reputation of complete impregnability. I was amazed by the smart fresh paint much in evidence on its towers and the neat rows of houses which lined the main street of the little town. There was a general air of assurance and well-being, which must have been achieved over the last four years since the great siege. For had my uncles not burned Penbroc to the castle gates and stolen or driven off every other movable object? After we had been admitted through the large gates in the town walls, I was aware of a mild curiosity which prevailed amongst the relatively busy citizens of the town. They must have seen Walter the Sheriff of Gloucester before, but not only were there many armed men of Gloucester with us today, but also a detachment provided by the Earl of Chester. This curiosity in the town of Penbroc, polite though it was, only added fuel to my temper, already in a highly inflammable state.

We rode across a small stream that led onto the steeply sloping track that wound up to the castle gates. One of the Penbroc men at arms sounded a silver trumpet and the drawbridge began to lower to allow us entry. As we waited below the formidable pallisades which formed the castle's outer defences, I looked up. The solid wooden scarp rose steeply from the deep ditch by which we had reined in our horses. High above our heads I could see the helmets of the armed guards, as they patrolled the heavily reinforced battlements. From the highest white tower within the castle compound, a red and gold standard curled lazily in the faint breeze, which blew in from the sea.

I was tense and had great difficulty in controlling my shaking limbs, as de Ville formally led our party towards a carved oaken door. The Sheriff of Gloucester took my hand; his touch was reassuring. "Do you wish for a few minutes with your maid," he asked, "before we go in? We are to meet your future husband here, in the Western Hall." As I wished to conclude the ordeal as speedily as possible, I signified that I was ready to proceed at once. Although the interior of the hall was dim, I was immediately aware of the great number of people gathered within its four walls. I was also amazed by the incredible cleanliness of the place and the spruce neatness of its inhabitants.

Standing a little apart from the group by the top table, I could see a tall man of early middle age, with slightly

greying hair. I was certain that he must be the Constable as
he was approximately the same age as the King. In silence
and with as much dignity as I could muster, I stood before
this group, while Walter of Gloucester made the formal
introduction. The tall man moved forward and taking this
as my cue, I made to give him my curtsey, but instead of
greeting me, he began to recite a prepared but concise
introduction of Gerald of Windsor. Realizing my mistake, I
managed to retreat a pace or two by the time he had
finished speaking and stepped aside. A cool easy voice said,
"Thank you, Serjeant at Arms," and before I could fathom
out exactly how it had happened, a young man of no more
than six and twenty stood before me. His hair, cropped in
the usual Norman fashion, was fair and curled slightly at
the temples. His very perceptive grey eyes held a distinctly
distant expression and he was clad in the whitest, best
pressed tunic I had ever seen gracing the frame of a mere
captain of the guard. He inclined his moderate height
towards me in a bow, even cooler than his expression.
"Princess Nesta," he murmured, in tones into which no
warmth had been instilled. "Welcome to Penbroc."

He took my hand as a duty and gave it the indifferent kiss
of a courtier. My confusion must have been evident to my
temporary guardian, Walter of Gloucester, who in
conciliatory phrases, commented that he was sure that I
had expected the gallant commander of the 1096 siege to be
a somewhat older man. Out of the corner of my eye, I saw
the Constable of Penbroc flush angrily at this remark. I
asked to be introduced to the other officers of the castle and
this was duly accomplished. As in a dream I listened to the
recitation of names and ranks, but only Stephen de Ville,
whom I had already met, stayed in my mind. He was the
Constable's chief lieutenant and he could hardly have been
more than seventeen years old. They took command and

came to maturity early, the knights of this border stronghold.

The fact that my future husband was a precocious young adventurer rather than the battle-weary middle-aged soldier I had expected, did nothing to mitigate my anger. I felt more than ever that I had been tricked and there was a discerning coldness behind those unwavering grey eyes that frankly unnerved me. Adopting the only defence available, I too became more disdainful. As soon as possible I gave Sheriff Walter to understand that I should need a full hour in which to complete my toilette, before the marriage ceremony took place. This, I gathered, was to be consecrated in the Great Hall, as soon as the Prior of Monkton was ready for us. I made it plain, in the hearing of my prospective husband, that the ceremony would take place only when I was ready and not before.

Sheriff Walter, looking faintly uneasy, assured me that a convenient place to which I could retire with my maid would be provided as soon as I and my betrothed had had the opportunity of a few minutes conversation on our own together. For we must, must we not, become acquainted before our marriage?

Branwen, sensing my discomfiture because I had not changed my dress, while the inmates of Penbroc Castle had apparently arrayed themselves in their finest in order to humiliate us, spoke up directly to the Constable himself. "Sir," she accused, "where is the chamber that my mistress shall occupy privately? You would surely not expect a Princess of Wales to change her raiment and sleep out here in the hall, amongst the common soldiery?" Although her voice was barely raised and there was much noisy conversation taking place in the confined space of the hall, the Constable again reacted instantly. A swift ebb and flow of colour indicated the extent of his irritation.

"It shall be attended to immediately," he pronounced, with a finality that prevented even Branwen, who was afraid of no one, from opening her mouth again. A few minutes later Sheriff Walter had cleared the Western Hall completely, withdrawing himself also, with a misplaced tact which I did not welcome.

Standing irresolute by the quietly smouldering log fire, I was left face to face with the one man whom I had no especial wish to greet. Silence dwelt heavily upon the smokey air between us, until at last as if making a supreme effort, he spoke. "I trust my lady, that you will find Penbroc to your liking?" he volunteered, his tone implying that he was certain that I should not. It was enough to put the spark firmly amongst the kindling. My anger flared.

"I think there is no need of pretence," I answered crisply. "Both you and I know, sir, that I shall not find Penbroc to my liking. I should be a hypocrite indeed if I pretended to care for those who have plundered and despoiled my father's kingdom. Particularly the man who has evicted the people of Deheubarth and burned their houses over their heads."

"And where may I ask, did you see this burning and eviction, or is this merely hearsay, bandied about the court at Winchester, amongst the Welsh exiles? Old sores heal slowly, but even so, the excesses of '96 and '97 are best forgotten."

I turned on him passionately. "I do not deal in second-hand reports sir," I snapped. "This I have seen with my own eyes, on my journey this past week, a mere eight miles from Carmarthen. I speak of the Gwendraeth Valley, where fields lie burned and unhusbanded, where the charred remains of the houses have been thrown into the river. Aye, and many bodies too. And the rest of the people, driven like cattle into the hills."

He stirred restlessly, as if even he, had a conscience of

sorts. "Ah," he sighed, "the Gwendraeth. So that is what you have seen."

"Enough sir, to turn me from this mockery that the King and Walter of Gloucester dare to term a marriage." I looked up for long enough to see a shadow pass over his face.

"I think my lady, that our feelings coincide upon this proposed union. Neither of us wish for it, but it has been forced upon us. We have no choice in the matter, for what are either of us, but the pawns of kings?" The assurance of his bearing and his cool acceptance of the situation in some strange way inflamed my frayed nerves and further exacerbated my temper. It would have been so much easier to channel my wrath if he had been as old and ugly as I had expected. Now, I wished to wound, for I needed a fight, to relieve my angry soul of its burden.

"For you of course it is pure advantage, is it not? Yet you speak but grudgingly of your gain, the union with the royal House of Tewdwr," I cried, my voice rising. He turned directly towards me.

"Regrettably ma'am, the reason why you have no bargaining power when it comes to dictating terms is the fault of none other than His Majesty the King." His meaning was painfully clear. The discarded mistress of a king had little value on the open market.

"And so," I cried, "I am cast to the farthest corner of his kingdom, to be forced into an unequal union with an ill-favoured Norman adventurer!" No sooner were the words out, than I regretted them, for I actually saw him flinch. There was an awful silence while he apparently fought for some measure of control over his white-hot anger.

"I think that you should understand," he rasped, "that in spite of the many advantages promised me by the King's messenger, I find the prospect of this marriage quite as distasteful as you yourself apparently do. In a world that is

full of obliging ladies, I have no need of its constraints."
Before I could conjure up a suitably blistering reply he had
stalked away from me, down the echoing hall.

As he left, I felt the scalding tears rise, but fought them
off urgently, for I knew that I should not long be left on my
own. Very soon, Branwen and the Sheriff of Gloucester
came in search of me. The Sheriff gave me a penetrating
glance, from which I gathered that he had met my
betrothed on his way across the courtyard. He wisely
refrained from questioning me however, instead he directed
Branwen to take me into the chamber which led off the
main hall, in order to make my toilette. An iron resolve to
fight this man to whom I was to be united against my will
gave purpose to my weary limbs. When two retainers
carried in my chest of clothes, I knew exactly what I had to
do. "The blue kirtle with the gold braid and the white
cambric camisole," I directed Branwen. "Lay them across
the couch!" Hot water was left at the door and with it, I
refreshed myself completely, for the morning ride had been
hot and dusty. With steady, regular strokes, my maid
brushed out my long hair and then re-braided it skilfully.

"It adopts the hue of the raven's wing, in this light," she
announced with satisfaction. "The colour of Deheubarth."

Half an hour later, when my temporary guardian
knocked tentatively at the door, I was ready. Walter, the
High Sheriff of Gloucester was not an old man, perhaps he
had reached his fortieth year, I could not be sure. But from
the way which he drew in his breath as I appeared at the
chamber door, I knew that I had succeeded in what I had,
with great deliberation, set out to do. His eyes, usually
careful and unexpressive, left me satisfied. "You look
extraordinarily beautiful, my child," the Sheriff confided
quietly, as he led me, unresisting now, for I knew I could no
longer fight the King's will, to my marriage in the Great
Hall. As we progressed down the aisle made by the waiting

soldiers towards an altar which the Prior of Monkton had made upon the high table, a strange hush fell over the assembled throng.

The Constable of Penbroc stood stiffly to attention when I had taken my place beside him. From his tone, he appeared as coolly indifferent to the responses as I, but when the time came for him to place the ring upon my finger, he fumbled slightly and it almost fell from his grasp. "Clasp hands," the Prior directed, in a piercing whisper, when the band of gold (ironically also provided by the King) had found its destined resting place. Apparently the Constable of Penbroc did not hear him, for he failed to comply with this request. The Prior repeated his order, in an even more sibilant whisper. For a long moment my new husband paused, as if smitten with a wish to retreat and then at last, his hand closed over mine and the priest visibly relaxed. "Those whom God hath joined together, let no man put asunder," he muttered rapidly. As he intoned the blessing, I could have sworn that a slight tremor passed through the hand that clasped mine. Whether it was a ripple of anger, or discontent, I could not tell and perhaps never would.

The marriage ceremony was followed by an elaborate dinner, the meal usually taken at Penbroc soon after noon. Long trestle tables were set up along the sides of the hall by footmen, under the watchful eye of the castle butler. It was a spectacular feast, featuring dressed pheasant and swan, with roast wild boar and gigantic venison pasties. Many side dishes of small birds and whole fish were pushed onto the groaning board to jostle for room, with table centres of fresh fruit which overflowed from ornate silver salvers. I could eat but little, picking at small quantities of each dish as it was presented.

As soon as the meal was over the two men who had so

ably carried out the King's commands, the Prior of Monkton and the Sheriff of Gloucester got up to leave. "Much as I would like to stay and drink wine with you, to the music of Bleddyn's splendid harp, my flock calls," stated the Prior, a jovial, paunchy priest. He took my hand and looked me directly in the eye. "You make a handsome pair, my lady," he stated, his meaning scarcely veiled. It was almost a directive, that I should produce an heir for the Constable of Penbroc as soon as was decently possible, or else be deemed to have failed in my duty.

I removed my hand after a respectful interval and turned to the Sheriff of Gloucester. In my heart, I wished to throw myself at the feet of this grave kind man and beg him to take me away with him. Instead, I stood before him, mute. At last, unable to keep back the flood tide completely, one wretched tear emerged. I bowed my head and saw it fall upon the richly decorated sleeve of the blue kirtle, as he raised my hand to his lips. "Life is seldom what it seems, my child," he observed quietly. "It is quite possible for one to make a hell out of heaven, or a heaven out of hell. And I do not think," he concluded with his rare smile, "that Penbroc is either of those two extremes. Thank you, for making my task both pleasant and a great deal easier than I expected. I shall see you again when I next travel this way and I look forward to that occasion."

The stewards then cleared away the dishes used for the main courses and I was left sitting at the centre of the top table with my gaoler. Wine was poured and in my dire need I hurriedly swallowed all that was set in front of me at the first serving. The small drinking horn set in silver contained far more than I had imagined, and the wine, which was a good French burgundy, went immediately to my head. It was as much as I could do to remain upright, but by dint of clutching the board in front of me, I managed to maintain a relatively dignified pose. My husband called for the bard and as one in a dream, I became aware of the most beautiful harp music, the like of which I had not heard since leaving my father's court. In the centre of the Great Hall, a harper sat hunched over his instrument, his eyes were half closed and from each string as he delicately plucked it, came sounds as from an angel host. Stephen de Ville, who sat on my left, noticed my interest.

"Bleddyn is one of your own countrymen," he said courteously. "He plays like a man possessed, does he not? Perhaps, because he is blind, sound has become more important to him and that is why he manages to produce such exquisite notes." Stephen leaned over to refill my horn with wine. "He plays these Welsh airs in your honour," he confided ingenuously. "My master bade him so, particularly."

The Constable of Penbroc sat at table silently. Whether he listened to the music or no, I could not be sure. His chin rested on one hand and he stared moodily into the distance, the fingers of his free hand twirling his silvered drinking horn continuously upon the polished board before him. I noticed that he drank from it but seldom. Eventually, during a break in the music he got to his feet. "I beg your pardon," he said obliquely, "but pressing duties call me for a few hours. Perhaps Stephen will show you the main parts of the castle, while I am gone." Stephen readily agreed to take me on a conducted tour and he was duly thanked by his master, who immediately disappeared. I did not see him again until we all gathered for supper in the Western Hall, in the early evening.

During our wanderings that afternoon Stephen found me a wooden bench with a superb view of the river and I sat there for some time, watching the villeins coming and going to and from the corn mill on the north side of the castle. When Stephen had to go, to carry out some routine duties, he brought Branwen to sit with me and there we remained in the sun, until summoned by the supper bell. Stephen had informed me that we had only used the Great Hall today for both wedding ceremony and feast, on Lord Arnulf's orders. Otherwise it was usually only opened on special days, or when Lord Arnulf himself was in residence, which was seldom. "The Western Hall is our home," the youth had announced happily. He patently enjoyed his life at the castle and unashamedly worshipped the Constable. A fact that I noted with considerable cynicism.

Supper was far simpler than dinner, and was over in under the hour. When it had finished, Stephen tactfully removed himself on the pretext that he had to attend to something in the stables and one by one, the other higher ranking officers asked to be excused and went about their duties, either real or imaginary. I became increasingly restless as, with nowhere in particular to go, I was forced to remain there in silence, with a man who had not spoken to me directly throughout the whole meal. At last, he too made a move. "Your maid was enquiring about a chamber for your personal use," he said without expression. He indicated the door of the room behind the dais, on which we sat. It was the one which I had used as a retiring room to change my clothes, before our marriage. "That is the only private chamber available to us," he stated, "and it is the most roomy and comfortable in the castle, other than Lord Arnulf's personal apartment, which we may not use. I have informed your maid and by now she will have got the porters to move all your chests into it." He stood up and I could feel the sudden build up of tension in the air. "As you have shown such obvious distaste for this marriage, I am unlikely to attempt to share it with you," he observed, in impassive tones. Before I could move, or make reply, he had bidden me an abrupt, "Goodnight," and left the hall.

Although my couch was comfortable and my new chamber spacious and tastefully arranged, I slept but

fitfully on that first night at Penbroc. My husband's curt
decision had initially overwhelmed me with a sense of relief,
but as the night wore on, all the vexations and humiliations
of the day came trooping through my mind to plague and
torment me. There were many things which I now wished
unsaid, both from his lips and mine. Somehow I had to plan
the days ahead that I might be fruitfully employed. If this
were not so, I feared that the boredom and tedium of this
alien place might make me lose all reason, or will to live.

On the chest beside the door that led into the oriel which
connected my room with the main hall, a bowl of fragrant
seeds had been placed. The scent of lavender filled the
many recesses of the timbered room and left an indelible
imprint of that night upon my mind. Branwen, who had
placed her pallette in the oriel to be aware of my every need,
came to me soon after dawn, with a light breakfast and hot
water. "The noise in this place," she grumbled. "It is worse
than Winchester. I hardly slept at all." She accepted my
non-marital state without comment, but with a barely
hidden satisfaction. With her abrasive temperament, it was
already obvious that she would have little or nothing in
common with the autocratic Constable of Penbroc.
Branwen, with her fiercely possessive loyalty, was
convinced that I needed none other to protect me than she
herself.

The late August weather remained settled fair, so I took
my embroidery frame as far as the seat which overlooked
the river. The miller was already working industriously,
with all the usual altercations with his customers that
characterized millers all over the countryside. I saw him
chase at least two villeins from his door, brandishing his
wooden spade like a cudgel. No doubt either he, or they,
had accused one another of pilfering grain. The water mill
and its occupants provided a mild entertainment for which,
at that precise moment, I was extremely grateful. Of my

husband, or Stephen, there was no sign. Below the castle, on the townward side, a tilt was being used for practice and on the hill yonder, beyond the small stretch of water called Monkton Pill, I could see archers perfecting their skills, against gaily painted targets. The castle was a hive of activity, as was the small town beyond its pallisades. Around the courtyard, carpenters hammered, armourers freshened chain mail by rolling it in barrels of sand and the cooks and pot boys, with their open-air kitchens, argued incessantly.

I had been sitting for over an hour on my own when I heard the tapping of a blind man's stick, and the uninhibited prattle of a small child. Looking up, I could see the blind Welsh harper being led towards me by an engaging urchin of about four years old. The man, who was not nearly as old as I had previously believed, halted within a few feet of me and bowed most graciously. "My friend Philippe, and I," he said, with a scarcely concealed twinkle, "have come to make the acquaintance of the Princess Nesta. That is, if you ma'am, have no objection to giving us an audience."

There was no trace of sarcasm in his gentle voice, and he spoke to me in the musical tones of our own tongue. I replied that the Princess would be delighted to receive them, and would they please be seated, as it was a warm day, and standing about could be most fatiguing. The child was vaguely familiar, for I realized that the day before, as I had progressed with my escort towards the altar, I had noticed him peeping out at me from beneath the skirts of his nurse. It had never occurred to me then that he was any other than child of the Serjeant at Arms, or one of the other officers of the castle. Now I was not sure. There was something about the way his fair hair curled and the grey of his questioning eyes. "I saw you yesterday," the child remarked innocently. "You wore a fine blue mantle worked with gold and the Prior of Monkton married you in the Great Hall, to my papa." The shock of his frank statement made me momentarily dumb. At last, I dared ask if he had been present in the Great Hall with his mama. "Oh no," he stated firmly. "I was with Jeannette, my nurse. My mama went away last winter. Brother Gregory says she went to live with Jesus and that she will be very happy."

I was hard pressed to contain my relief, though I could not reason why. The bard then spoke. "His mother, Adrienne, died last November, the poor child scarce remembers her." He placed an affectionate arm around the small boy's slight shoulders. "But I, Bleddyn the bard, could not exist without my friend Philippe," he stated, as though making a proclamation to mankind. "My stick is well enough and on it I am able to hobble at snail's pace from here to there, but Philippe is my eyes, my very being."

"Bleddyn is my best friend," Philippe explained simply. "He teaches me many things." In a completely relaxed way he came closer to lean upon my knees with his small elbows, eventually putting a curious hand up to touch my plaited hair. "Jeannette says that you are very beautiful," he stated, examining my face intently. "What is beautiful?"

"Why, all Princesses are beautiful," Bleddyn insisted. "They are born that way. It just means that they are very pleasing to look upon."

"Oh," Philippe murmured with a rather puzzled frown. At that moment, the miller began his third altercation of the morning, a far more serious one apparently, for this villein he chased right along the river bank opposite us.

"Thank you," I murmured softly to the seated bard, who listened with interest to the battle over the water.

"You must not mind the lad," he said protectively, "his innocence makes him over frank at times."

"I do not mind him in the least," I replied emphatically. "I find him a charming little boy."

"Then that is good," Bleddyn replied, "for the child is enormously attracted to you."

That morning was to be the start of a lasting and unusual friendship for although Philippe had begun a minimal amount of formal education under the tuition of a pale youth from the Priory, called Brother Gregory, he had many hours left to brighten up my days. As well as his Latin texts, he learned music from the patient harper and riding from the Serjeant at Arms. On fine days, the small boy and the bard, made a habit of joining me upon my seat overlooking the river, where between listening to Bleddyn's music and long magical tales, the three of us would make wagers about the miller. Sometimes he would actually pick men up and throw them into the shallow stream that ran off from his water wheel. I was surprised that he did not repeatedly find himself at the Shire or hundred Courts on a charge of being disorderly. But Philippe assured me that 'papa' turned a blind eye to most of the miller's brawls and unless he actually did anyone bodily harm, he generally got away with it. "Papa feels that he is very much provoked," Philippe solemnly declared. "And he says that a miller's lot is not a happy one, for most men argue that he steals their corn."

I very soon came to care a great deal for the Constable's illegitimate son, 'by the French woman', as he was described, in all but his father's hearing. For it was clear that Philippe adored his father and that his father returned his love tenfold. When they were together, for rare moments, nobody else seemed to matter. I seldom saw my husband, whose industry and efficiency was undeniable. The whole castle and its inmates were a living testimony to his leadership and he worked long hard hours. We were forced, however, to meet in public at the top table for dinner, or at the evening meal, and sometimes for both. There were days when he visited other parts of Lord

Arnulf's estates, but he usually returned at nightfall. It was more often than not an outlying Court Session that kept him away, in one of the cantrefs or hundreds. Bleddyn did remark one day, that it was a pity that the Constable's duties seemed to have doubled since my arrival, and that he appeared to be working far more than was good for any man. After a few weeks I began to get used to my rather lonely, pointless existence at Penbroc. Everything that could be done to make life comfortable and pleasant had been done by my husband's servants and I was treated with deference and respect. I soon began to realize, that at the times when I was not noticeably present, the Constable adopted an easy, far more relaxed attitude, although no one was ever foolish enough to cross him, or ever refused to carry out his commands. It became patently obvious to me however, after few weeks at Penbroc, that he had gained the considerable loyalty which he enjoyed, out of respect and not fear. As time went on, I became sure that somewhere, there must be one or more of the obliging ladies of whom he had spoken after my outburst before our wedding ceremony. I began surreptitiously to look about me for evidence, but could find none. There could be no doubt that the women who came into contact with my husband during his daily round, found him attractive, but I saw no outward signs of encouragement on his side.

I had been at Penbroc for a full month before I came into collision with his absolute overlordship. Branwen had just finished my hair one morning, when the most horrifying scream rent the air, so loud that it sent my blood running cold. "What can it be?" Branwen cried, her hand going protectively over her heart. "Some poor soul in the hands of the tormentor, surely," and she crossed herself with resignation. I stood quite still, feeling sick as I always did, when I was expected to approve, even passively, of any cruelty; even that administered in the name of law and order. The scream came again, long drawn out and agonized. By the time the third unearthly shriek had rent the air, I was already approaching its source, in the centre of a small crowd in the courtyard.

"Hold," I cried in ringing tones, as I reached the fringes of this closed circle. The group parted, pulling back to allow me through, to the place where I could see my husband standing. What I expected to find I do not know, perhaps a new and sophisticated kind of torture. What actually met my eyes was so ordinary that I pulled myself up with a jerk. A youth of about sixteen years old, was tied to a whipping post. He was stripped to the waist. As I viewed him thus, uncertainly, he continued to moan and whimper, even though nothing seemed to be happening to him. A large man stood over him with a whip, which he had ceased to wield as I had pushed through the surrounding throng. I held out my hand imperiously for the offending weapon. "Give that to me," I ordered. The soldier complied nervously. I examined the whip meticulously. To my utmost surprise it was of its type, quite inoffensive. There were no bars, sharp pieces of metal or even ordinary knots, on the leather thongs.

A ragged old woman, her face disfigured by a terrible contusion, which ended in a jagged cut, came towards me. She threw herself piteously at my feet. "Blessed lady," she cried in supplicating tones, "do not let them harm my poor boy, my only son. I beg of you." I put a protective hand on her shoulder and turned angrily towards the man who had held the whip.

"Of what is this youth accused?" I asked clearly.

My husband, who had stood apparently speechless at my first intrusion, now stepped forward. He ignored me completely. "Go home, good mother," he advised the old woman in vexed, but not unkindly tones. "You can do no good for the lad here. Go back to your cottage quietly and rest." To my surprise the woman scrambled to her feet still weeping, but now with resignation she turned, and crept away from the group around her son.

"Of what is this youth accused?" I insisted once again.

"Master Jordan, you were the foreman of the jury," my husband said in icy tones. "Pray read the sentence again which you latterly passed on this youth," he nodded towards the cringing boy tied to the post, "so that all present may hear."

A middle-aged man, obviously a merchant from the town judging by his non-military dress, unrolled a small piece of parchment from which he read in wooden tones: "That the said Thomas, son of the late Daniel of this town, as due and just punishment for the unnecessary ill he has caused his mother, Bertha, by striking her with the aforementioned wooden trencher about the face and head, shall be taken out, and given twelve strokes of the leather in ordinary, in full view of the members of this jury, the Constable of Penbroc, and his Serjeant at Arms." The man's voice droned to a halt and he viewed me uneasily. I had by now begun to feel a little unsure of myself, but I tilted my chin and asked resolutely if there had been any witnesses to the crime mentioned on the parchment. After tracing the ink with a shaky forefinger, the merchant began to read again. "Witnesses," he began and then faltered. "Ah Ruben of the red cottage," he muttered. "Giles the shoemaker and his apprentice Jonas. The widow of Barnabus the Fletcher and –" he looked apologetically at my husband, "the Constable of Penbroc who was riding by and heard the woman's cries."

"Thank you Jordan," my husband pronounced crisply. There was a moment of excruciating silence, during which I realised that I had attempted to pervert the course of justice in a perfectly legitimate case.

I handed the whip back to the soldier. "But why," I

asked, in a small voice, "does he scream in such a disturbing way?"

"I don't know, my lady," the soldier replied uncomfortably, looking straight ahead. "He've only had three strokes so far and it haven't even marked him."

"I'll tell you why the youth screams in such an unnatural fashion," my husband rasped in disgust. "He does so because he is a coward, as well as a bully. This is not the first time that this young thug has abused his mother. I have had many complaints of a similar nature before, from old Bertha's neighbours. But I will not tolerate such brutal violence in the town of Penbroc and this prisoner will receive his full sentence." He looked down at the boy with derisive eyes. "Why, I have known men receive ten times the punishment, and never open their mouths. And to think, that I have agreed to take this worthless bully as a recruit for the castle guard – ." The lad ceased his whining and looked up at the Constable in amazement. "Do you wish to become a soldier?" my husband enquired sternly. The youth nodded his head slowly. "Then grit your teeth and take what comes in a soldierly spirit," he was advised. "I have grave doubts of your worth, but am taking you into my ranks to prevent you from beating your mother to death. The discipline will either make you or break you and the money which you earn will keep your mother from starvation." He stepped back.

"Sir?" enquired the soldier.

"One minute, Ralf," came the cool reply. "Lieutenant de Ville," my husband said evenly. "Will you please escort the Princess Nesta to the door of her chamber." Stephen, appearing less than comfortable, approached and after a deep bow, offered me his arm.

It was not until we had entered the door of the Western Hall, that I heard the Serjeant at Arms shout an order, but there was no further indication that the sentence was being completed. I was unable to do more than mumble my thanks for Stephen's escort, before entering my chamber and throwing myself upon my couch. There I wept bitter tears of shame and humiliation. Branwen, in a state of anxious concern, hovered over me, offering comfort with a spate of Welsh endearments which she crooned to the accompaniment of various pithy remarks about the castle officials.

"But Branwen, it was I who was at fault, not they," I sobbed.

"Nonsense," she insisted, with totally misplaced loyalty. "One can never trust the French!"

A faint knock came at the door and I immediately buried my head in the pillows. "I can see no one," I sniffed. "No one!"

A small voice, full of concern, asked, "Mama, la Princesse, she is not ill?"

"Philippe," I called. The child ran to my side and I caught him to me impulsively. He crushed me in a gigantic hug.

"But princesses never weep," he insisted. "Bleddyn has told me so, many times." I sniffed again, and mopped my eyes with a damp kerchief.

"Bleddyn is right," I declared, springing to my feet at last. I offered my hand. "Come! Let us walk out to see how many men our miller has thrown into his stream today." By dinner time, I had outwardly regained my composure, but the episode had shaken me considerably. My interference in the execution of a sentence passed by a jury of the Shire Court, was serious enough, but I had actually questioned the authority of a commander in chief, in his own castle courtyard, and in front of his own men, not to mention the burgesses of the town.

I crept into the Western Hall at the sound of the supper bell and waited as unobtrusively as I could for my husband to appear. At best, I could expect little more than a thoroughly unpleasant evening. At length I heard the Constable approaching, with Philippe trotting happily at his heels. They were deep in conversation. It was the unaccustomed sound of his laughter which made me swing round to face him, as he entered the hall. My husband never laughed in my presence. "But he cannot continue to do such a thing," he protested humorously, to his son. "Indeed, my child, if it is as you say, he will block his millrace completely with incapacitated villeins, and then you will have no trencher on which to eat your supper. I shall have to speak to Rollo the miller and persuade him to dispose of his angry customers in some other tidier way."

When he reached my side, his greeting was unexpectedly courteous, and he assisted me to my seat with a further disarming gesture, which only served to increase my unease. As the meal progressed his manner began to remind me forcibly of Philippe when he was at his most charming. I had been aware for some time that the only part of his complex character that I had officially been shown so far had been the efficient, cool, over-polite remnant that he reserved for those that he was unwilling to take the bother to impress. Sometimes, when he had been unaware of my presence, he had exhibited a far warmer, more relaxed disposition, even with the meanest of the servants. This was undoubtedly how he obtained the unswerving obedience and loyalty of his men, and all who served him. Now, for reasons best known to himself, he had turned the full force of his considerable personality onto me, despite my gross interference into his concerns.

At length, in spite of myself, I became more relaxed than I had been since my arrival, and I actually began to enjoy an evening, which at its outset, I had been convinced would be a disaster. "I feel," I murmured eventually, "that I owe you some sort of an apology for my behaviour in the courtyard this morning. I had made a grave error and I am sorry for it."

"If we had been indulging in the type of brutality which you feared, you would have been quite within your rights to have objected on humanitarian grounds," he replied soberly. "We live in a barbaric age and soldiers are often forced to be ruthless in order to survive. But I also believe that strength should never be used for the purpose of inflicting unnecessary cruelty on others. Justice and humanity command a more enduring type of loyalty." I asked quietly if he really meant to take the offending youth into the ranks of guardsmen at the castle. "I'm afraid that I have to, both to protect the lad's mother, and to give him a chance in life." His tone was inclined to be cynical and for the first time I became aware that there must be certain aspects of his job of which he was not particularly proud. I was just about to savour my wine, when he uttered a reprimand so severe that it immediately shattered my new found ease. "The next time you fear a grave miscarriage of justice," he remarked, with unmistakeable authority, "I would appreciate a quiet word in private, rather than a repetition of the awkward situation in which we found ourselves today."

Although the rebuke was justified and I had initially been expecting worse, I felt angry that he had not delivered his rap over the knuckles earlier in the evening. I finished my meal in silence and then begged to be excused, because of a tiresome headache, due no doubt, to the undeniable hint of thunder in the air. With an inexplicable frown, he nodded his assent.

The most violent thunder storm did indeed rend the silence of the night, bringing torrential showers in its wake. I rose the following morning to find the surrounding countryside smelling sweet and freshly washed. There was a clear blue

sky and a slight breeze coming off the estuary. But
apparently the storm had left a trail of damage throughout
the heavily ripe corn lands, a few of which still remained to
be harvested. As I crossed the busy courtyard I met an
uncharacteristically downcast Philippe. It was not fair, he
declared petulantly, that he should have to attend lessons
with Brother Gregory while papa rode around the
demesne to assess the damage to the corn fields. I walked
on as far as the battlements. From my vantage point on the
rampart walk I could see one of the grooms leading the
Constable's beautiful black filly around the perimeter to
quieten her. A number of rustics, astride stringy cobs, sat
patiently until the castle officials were ready to leave with
them, to inspect their damaged crops. At last, I saw my
husband mount his horse and the ill-assorted group rode
slowly away from the castle. Subconsciously, it was an
opportunity for which I had been waiting, and I crossed to
the castle mound as soon as the horsemen had reached the
other side of the stream. Curiosity as to the true character
of the apparently distant man who was now legally my
husband, had been mounting steadily over the last few
weeks. For some time I had been aware that he must have
his quarters somewhere in the White Tower, which topped
the motte and served as watchtower for the castle and its
dependant town.

A footbridge gave onto the motte and I climbed this
rapidly, taking the sentinel in the lower doorway
completely by surprise. He sprang rigidly to attention,
flushing painfully. He could not have been many years into
his teens and I did not anticipate much difficulty in gaining
entry. "They tell me," I observed in innocent tones, "that
the view from the top of this tower cannot be equalled
anywhere else in the whole of Penbroc."

"But my lady," the lad stammered. "The Serjeant at
Arms will not allow anyone access beyond – " I slid past his

pike and smiled at him sweetly.

"I am quite sure that my husband, the Constable, will explain my presence satisfactorily to your Serjeant. You need have no fear." I put my foot firmly upon the wooden spiral that led aloft. "My husband's private room is on the first floor, I believe?"

"The second ma'am," the boy swallowed nervously. "Take care on the stair, my lady. It is dark in places." I thanked him suitably and grasping the newel as I turned each bend of the steep staircase, I shortly gained my objective. I was immediately struck by the spartan aspect of the room. It was the barrack room of a soldier, scrupulously tidy, but uncomfortably bare. A few hand arms hung on the low slung timber cross beam which supported the roof. Apart from this, there was merely a pallette bed and little else. It was so unlike the comfortable, tapestry-hung chamber which he had allotted me on my arrival, that I experienced a sudden, remorseful pang. Did he have to live as if life was a penance? My eyes were suddenly drawn to a brass crucifix which hung above a wooden bracket, opposite an arrow slit. The arrow slit cast upon the crucifix a ray of early morning sunlight, which illuminated it eerily. On the bracket, a candle end in a holder lay beside a finely worked piece of cambric. I stepped over to it and taking the cambric up in my hands, examined it carefully. It was a woman's kerchief. The way in which the kerchief had been placed beneath the crucifix, imparted to the whole arrangement, the air of a shrine.

A movement in the doorway made me swing round nervously. There, with an inscrutable expression in his eyes, stood my husband. My colour came and went, as I frantically attempted to find words to explain my presence.

"My horse cast a shoe while we were still in Penbroc town," he remarked in casual tones. "She is too valuable to ride until she goes lame. I turned back and the others rode on. I can overtake them fairly quickly, once the smith has attended to her." His unperturbed manner, under the circumstances, did him great credit. He came across and took the kerchief out of my shaking fingers. "It belonged to Adrienne, the mother of little Philippe," he stated simply, replacing the flimsy fabric back in its rightful place, beneath the crucifix. "She was killed in an ambush, at the river ford in Llawhaden, last autumn."

"Then if you keep it here thus, you must have loved her," I prompted softly. My husband turned towards the arrow slit and scanned the river which ran below.

"Yes, I loved her," he replied in a voice which suggested that he was disinclined to discuss the matter further. I stood with my head bowed, thoughts crowding through my mind, tumbling over each other as they at last began to sort themselves out. This explained much, his fierce blood tie with Philippe, and the look of pain when he had firmly stated that our marriage was something about which we could do nothing. He remained still, gazing at the river with an intensity that troubled me, until he at last, visibly, threw off his sorrow. "The view from the catwalk on top of the tower is superb, as I am sure that Stephen must have told you," he remarked pleasantly. "If you can bear heights, it is worth the climb." I assured him quietly that heights held no horrors for me.

At the summit, we perched on the narrow walled walk which ran around the conical tower. It was a splendid point from which to admire the panoramic view which lay before us. The town ran alongside the river, its houses stretched out in a neat parallel line. Even the larger manor fields appeared to be a patchwork in miniature, the many coloured stripes of different crops, blending in perfect harmony with patches of woodland and scrubby sprawling commons. "The sea is beyond the headland yonder." He pointed to westward. "But it just escapes notice, because of the Monkton parklands." A seagull appeared at shoulder level and steadying himself on a passing current of air, subjected us to an inquisitive scrutiny. Then, on a whim, he banked suddenly, and made off in the direction of the sea.

"What delicious freedom," I murmured with a sigh. "He can fly wherever he wills." My husband did not reply until we had descended as far as his private room, where he turned to me seriously.

"I feel that you have been cooped up in this castle far too long," he said. "Today it is my intention to visit Carew, a demesne that rightly belongs to you, for it came to us in your marriage portion. Would you care to ride out with me, to see it?" His generosity was more than I deserved, for I was acutely aware that I had been trespassing and quite expected to receive another of his crushing rebukes.

The quiet palfrey on which I had arrived at Penbroc was soon saddled and after I had been lifted onto its back by the head groom, I began my first full day's expedition away from the castle. As we left the courtyard, two armed horsemen fell in quietly behind us, remaining at a discreet distance as they followed us through the small town. When we reached the open road, the heady feeling of fresh air and freedom got the better of me. "I think your farmers may well be tired of waiting," I said, giving my horse a sly kick. The palfrey was fresh from the stables, and she immediately broke into a canter and then, as the spirit of the situation suddenly appealed to her, a modest gallop. The swift rush and movement of air, the exhilaration of being in the saddle once again after so long, lifted my spirits beyond all recognition. I kept the horse at full stretch until she slowed through sheer fatigue. The Constable soon realized that I was in no danger and let me have my head. We drew up at last, under a clump of trees to await our escort, who followed us along the turfy track at a quiet hack. I felt as if I had blown myself free of cobwebs at last.

"I'm sorry," I laughed, breathlessly attempting to rearrange my escaping hair, "but I just could not resist the temptation."

"Well, it is obvious that the first thing that we have to do is find you a better mount," he declared. "That animal is no more than a packhorse. Anyone who rides as well as you, deserves a horse with more mettle." He glanced down at his own superb filly. "I think that I know where to find a suitable animal. Llinos here, had a very handsome half brother, I believe."

I raised my brows. "Llinos, the linnet?" I was surprised that the young mare should have a Welsh name. He treated me to a humorous scrutiny and then laughed with delight.

"No, I did not steal her from one of your uncles," he assured me. I replied instantly that such a thing had never crossed my mind. "I rather think it did," he said, "for such a thought was written clearly all over your face. However, it is possible that one of your cousins may have bred her, for one does not always ask who breeds the best horses in Dyfed."

At Milton Manor we caught up with Stephen and the slow moving procession of farmers arriving at the demesne of Carew in time to eat the light midday meal which the servants had carried for us. It was a mellow, sheltered piece of countryside, full of autumn tints and rich hedgerows, hanging with berries. While we ate, we allowed the horses to crop the grass on a smooth plateau beside the tidal estuary. Across a wooden footbridge I could see a cornmill nestling into the elbow of the valley; it was small and quaint. "Oh," I cried. "How Philippe would love that little mill; what a pity he is not with us." His father looked at me sharply.

"I am usually accused of spoiling the child, not depriving him," he remarked dryly. "I did gather, however, that Philippe didn't exactly relish his Latin texts this morning. I almost had a mutiny on my hands."

"But he is only four and a half," I replied defensively, "and Brother Gregory is an excessively boring young man. Philippe learns far more of real worth from Bleddyn." He did not pursue the matter, but I was again aware of a close, penetrating glance, as he rose to his feet.

When we arrived back at the castle, a mere hour before the supper bell, I realized that I had actually had a most enjoyable day, something I had not previously considered possible at Penbroc. My husband had visibly relaxed and as the day wore on he became far less distant and forbidding. It was at times like these, when his humour and personality appeared so very reminiscent of that of his charming little son, that my prejudices were forgotten and he became an interesting and absorbing companion. The advice of Hugh the Fat, Earl of Chester, came back vividly to mind at the end of that particular day. "Find the most attractive man at Penbroc and take him. There is no need for tears." It was quite clear that Earl Hugh had never been to Penbroc or he would have appreciated the irony of his words. For it had become apparent to me over the last twenty-four hours that the most attractive man at the castle by far, was undoubtedly my husband. And my husband appeared to be a man who so mourned the memory of his dead mistress that he neither wished nor cared for any other woman.

Over the next few weeks I was allowed to accompany my husband and Stephen on many an interesting tour of the estates. An active gelding had replaced the jaded palfrey and I began to get adequate exercise from my excursions around the manor lands on horseback. These tours were often brightened by the presence of Philippe, riding with stiff back and leading rein and Bleddyn, who owned an awful old nag which knew how to follow the lead horse and so never became lost. I began to appreciate at last the enormous burden of responsibility which my husband carried. I also endeavoured to spend more time with Philippe. Together, we set up a hopscotch frame, scratched into the fine gravel of the rampart walk.

We were absorbed with our game, one fine afternoon, when my husband suddenly appeared. Philippe, not at all sure how our unruly behaviour would be received, remained perched upon one leg, his tile in his hand, eyeing his father with an anxious frown. "Does our noise disturb you papa?" he asked.

"Yes, your noise did disturb me," his father replied, with the disarming smile they both shared. "I could hear you both from the stables. But if by 'disturbing me', you mean, does your noise make me angry, then the answer is no. Show me what you do!" With a considerable flourish, Philippe went through his energetic ritual once more. My husband shook his head, when he had finished. "But that isn't how we played the game at Windsor. You both make it far too easy. Let me show you." He looked at me. "May I alter the squares?" He scrubbed out a number of lines and then drew a complicated figure, almost twice the length. "Lend me your tile." Philippe, utterly fascinated, passed him his piece of crock. With an agility that did not surprise me, he had completed the course even faster than we had, on our shorter frame. Philippe was tremendously impressed. "And my elder brother William could complete it faster than any of us," my husband concluded, "so you had better practise hard."

Philippe made a few experimental throws. He agreed that it was much more difficult now. A discreet, but disapproving cough broke our concentration. My husband looked up with a flash of irritation. "Well! What is it, Serjeant at Arms?" he snapped.

"The patrol sir, from the north. It has just come in."

"Very well, I suppose that I must see them." I fancied

that he looked tired. "Now remember," he told us, "when you are able to master the Windsor method you really will be able to play the game." Then he had gone, as quickly as he had arrived.

"Poor papa," Philippe said. "He doesn't have much time to play. No wonder his brother William could always beat him." But Philippe himself was playing and this I felt to be a tremendous improvement. I also began to attempt to interest him in manuscripts. At Winchester an old prioress had taught me a great deal about illumination and I had commenced while there to make my own Book of Hours. Over the last few days I had searched out my tinctures and parchments.

"If you come to my chamber after supper," I promised Philippe, "we can work on the Book of Hours. Branwen managed to wheedle an almost new candle out of the butler, only this morning, so we shall have light." I made my excuses early that evening and went to my chamber, where I laid out my parchment squares and two pens. The lines were scored by the time Philippe knocked at the door. "Now you mustn't be impatient," I warned. As parchment is so valuable, we must work very carefully." I began to sketch out a Celtic O and in a short while we were completely absorbed. How long we worked I do not know, but one by one the familiar noises began to cease, although I could still hear talking and a certain amount of shouting, from the hall. "Now, when we have finished this serpent's eye," I told him, "you must be good and go to bed. It must be quite late by now – see, our candle has burned a long way down."

We were just making the final markings down our serpent's back, when an agitated knocking sounded on the door. My husband stood there. He looked ill. Without a word, he stepped past Branwen. "Oh papa," the weary Philippe enthused, "do come to see our serpent."

"Philippe!" his father cried in shaken tones. "Why child, we have searched the whole castle for you. Jeannette is frantic." Philippe lifted horror struck eyes to mine. I began to frame an apology, but my husband had swept the boy up into his arms, before I could speak. "Oh my son," he declared, low voiced. "I thought that we had lost you." The arm he held around the child actually shook.

"I'm sorry," I said quietly. "We had no idea of the time. I had no intention of upsetting you so much. I suppose that Philippe and I had assumed that everyone knew where he was."

"It's all right," he replied quickly. "We must have panicked when we couldn't find him with our first search." He carried the child to the door and called Stephen. But Philippe ran back into the room and gave me a quick hug.

"They must not be angry with you," he said, in his quaint, adult fashion. "It was my fault too. Thank you so much for teaching me to paint serpents." He momentarily tightened his grip around me. "Next to my papa I love you best," he whispered, in easily audible tones. He went to his father and solemnly clung to him for a minute, and then he allowed Jeannette and Stephen to carry him to bed. I became painfully aware, that my husband was standing absolutely rigid in the doorway.

"To say that I am sorry to have caused you so much anxiety seems grossly inadequate," I murmured. "We had no idea of the time, really I suppose, because we were so completely absorbed by the work we were doing."

He pulled himself together, and looked me straight in the eye. "The child adores you," he said simply, "and naturally, had we known where he was – " I again repeated my apologies and asked what time it was. He thought for a minute. "About midnight now, I think."

"Midnight!" I was shocked. "No wonder you gave way to panic."

He smiled, in a far less strained manner. "I had not been aware until then that I had such a vulnerability," he owned. "It is a great weakness in a soldier."

"I don't feel that you have a right to chastise yourself because you love your only child," I said seriously.

"May I see what you were doing all those hours?" he asked. I presented him with the stretched parchment. He sat on the settle, by the small charcoal brazier which I was allowed on cooler evenings, and examined our work carefully. "It is very delicate," he said at length, "I had no idea that ladies could do things like this."

"A prioress called Florence taught me the art, while I was at Winchester," I explained.

"I have been wanting to thank you for some time, for your generosity to my son," he declared rather formally.

"There is no need to thank me," I said, "he is a very lovable little boy."

"But there is a need," he replied, "far more than you think. When his mother was killed Philippe became quite withdrawn. Now, largely thanks to you, he has become a normal, healthy little boy. He seems to have needed a woman's understanding and love, plus a fair ration of hopscotch."

I looked away. "But I have needed him, as much as he has needed me," I explained. " – to fill the gap left by the loss of my own child."

He moved restlessly. "I was very much against the King's wishes over that matter," he vowed soberly, and I urged them to allow you to bring your baby here, but the King was adamant. I am very sorry that I could do no more to help you."

"That was one of the things for which I did not blame you," I admitted honestly.

He got to his feet and took my hand. "It is late and I must let you rest," he declared. "I have not, in any case, inspected the guard yet." He bent over my hand to kiss it. "Goodnight Princess," he murmured and departed swiftly.

A kind of precedent had been established as a result of my involuntary kidnapping of Philippe. From that evening on, my husband drifted quite naturally into the habit of coming into my chamber after supper, to talk for an hour or so. We spoke of everything except our own predicament and each new conversation helped in some strange way to break down the barriers created by the unfortunate circumstances of our marriage. Often he would tell me quite intricate details about one or other of the manors, or the demesne of Carew.

In our hearts, I believe we both realized that this situation could not go on for ever. Each night, he would courteously bid me goodnight and leave me to inspect his guard. Whether I merely wished it, or whether I actually sensed it, I do not know. But I realized that sooner or later, he would one night inspect the guard before he came to me, and then he would stay. I remained certain that I could never wholeheartedly love this man, to whom the King had forcibly married me, but I had, if I was honest, to admit that I found him increasingly attractive.

In town and countryside alike both the indigenous Welsh and Norman French, appeared to admire and respect my husband, not only for his proven military genius, but also for his strong decisive government. His great personal ability and reputation for fairness and justice were beyond reproach, and in this, he had also gained my unfailing admiration and regard. In many ways, the joint love which we both held for Philippe had helped our relationship, for this had shewn me the other, softer side of his nature, which would otherwise have remained concealed.

At all times, however, I continued with great skill and subterfuge, to cover those warmer feelings which I was loath to be the first to express. Bleddyn, who kept us entertained on cool wet days when the autumn mists blew in from the sea, was aware in some measure of my dilemma. There was something in the Celtic temperament which made us conscious of these unspoken things. As a result, he sang in the romantic, chivalric vein of knights and their ladies and deeds of heroism until I brought him up short one morning, with the sharp reminder, that his tales were largely exaggerated and untrue. Life, for most, I stated, was a mixture of misery and debauchery, with a fair measure of cruelty thrown in.

One of his audience immediately called for the tale of Madog and Ithel. For they were, were they not, he urged, realistic enough and so recently guilty of their crimes that the Princess Nesta would appreciate the topicality of the tale. Bleddyn hesitated, but only momentarily and then, driving every syllable home, he told me of the massacre and rape of the Gwendraeth. The beautiful valley, despoiled, so I had believed, by the hands of my own husband. "Madog and Ithel," Bleddyn emphasized, were brothers, but of an evil blood, so evil, that like Cain and Abel, they set out almost from birth to destroy one another. From the first, from his intonation, I knew how the story would end – "And so Madog, taking his sword, smote off the head of his brother, Ithel, and then burning the crops and dwelling houses of his brother's people, he cast them into the sweetly flowing Gwendraeth. And those who did not perish, those few fled, with all they could save of their flocks and their herds, into the mountains of Ystrad Tywi. And the mountains and valleys wept."

"Is this true, Bleddyn?" I asked, but I knew in my heart that with such tales he only dealt in truths. The bard bowed his head and I felt relieved that his eyes as they rested upon mine, had no sight.

That evening, my husband brought a jug of wine and two drinking horns, and we drank the wine companionably, by the warm firelight. Philippe came for half an hour to play Back Gammon. After Jeannette had collected him, I began to tell my husband of Bleddyn's story. I ended my recitation with a profound apology, which he lightly but firmly, cast aside. "It was worth the whipping that you administered," he averred, with a wry smile, "for you are at your most beautiful when acting as counsellor for the prosecution." I felt myself flush painfully, for although the compliment was graciously intended, I felt ill able to handle it at that precise moment.

"I think," he said slowly, getting to his feet, "that it would be better if I left you. I will call Branwen. She is I believe, still in the hall?" I muttered something polite, but he remained, standing there with an uncharacteristic irresolution. I murmured that he did not have to go yet, if he wished to stay. "I think I must," he replied, in low tones. "For if I stay now, I shall almost certainly say, or do something, that will distress you." At this statement, I looked up at him in rather naive surprise. As soon as I had seen the look in his eyes, I immediately dropped my gaze and moved away a few paces. My pulse raced, completely out of control.

"If you wish to stay – in that way, you may," I told him quietly. "You have every right, you are, after all, my husband."

"I am not," he informed me in strained tones, "in the habit of taking ladies against their will, whatever the Prior of Monkton may have had to say upon the subject." I agreed that the Prior had made such remarks to me also, and that he had hinted most pointedly, that every union should be blessed with children. My husband replied that he considered the Prior's views on that particular subject to be of little account. "I should not in any case, expect the Princess Nesta to start a dynasty with 'an ill-favoured Norman adventurer'," he added warily.

I quickly assured him that I had made such ill-chosen comments when I was quite beyond myself with pique and fatigue. I begged him to forgive them and if possible forget them. "It must be obvious to you, from the unspoken compliments that you continually receive from many women, that you are not in the least 'ill-favoured'," I ventured.

"From many women, perhaps, but by no means all," he returned, with dogged obstinacy. Formally, I informed him in a small voice, that I had realized my error as soon as the words had been uttered. Indeed, I had only made such remarks, because he was so much the reverse of the old and ugly man I had originally expected.

"Do you wish to start a dynasty?" I asked, in barely audible tones.

"I should like nothing better," he replied seriously, "than that my sons should inherit the blood of the kings of South Wales. I do not ask for your love," he continued with great dignity, "but only that we should live together in a spirit of peace and concord. That we should enter into a Pax in fact which will enable us both to make the best of our situation." He took my hands and looked down at me, with a fair degree of amusement. "I am relieved that you no longer consider me to be a mere ill-favoured adventurer," he said, with a trace of self mockery. "You see, the King's messenger had nothing but praise for you, which made things rather more difficult in my case. He informed me that the King was sending me the most beautiful woman in the whole of Wales. At the time I was sceptical. But from the moment that you stepped into the Western Hall and began to attack me on all fronts, I realized that the King had indeed sent me a unique and most attractive gift. There is still however, an unanswered question, is there not?"

He drew me into his arms and kissed me with surprising gentleness. A gentleness which was swiftly replaced by the unmistakeable combustion of a forest fire. Breathless, I at last buried my head deep into the folds of his tunic.

"You wished to ask me a question," I muttered, greatly daring.

"There is no need to ask it, I already know," he answered with confidence. "I had to be sure that you wanted me, as much as I want you. I have my answer." I lifted my head and as I did so, he kissed me again. I could feel myself tremble and even in his firm clasp there was a hint of the strange tremor which had run through his fingers, on the day of our marriage ceremony in the Great Hall. He released me at last, with obvious regret. "I have to go now, for a short while, to make sure that the guard is secure and the curfew observed," he said quietly. "I had better send Branwen to you, or she will be justifiably offended if she does not prepare you to retire, on your wedding night." He paused at the door, with a slight air of apology. "Will you, when you send her away, suggest that she sleeps from now on, with the other women in the hall?" At the implication of his words, I felt my colour surge suddenly upwards. "You are very beautiful, Princess," he added softly, as he shut the heavy oak door behind him.

PART II

A slight sound at dawn roused me momentarily from my sleep. It was the quiet closing of the chamber door and my husband's firmly retreating footsteps, as he left me to begin a new day around the castle precincts. I drifted comfortably back into the contented sleep from which I had been temporarily diverted, not waking again until Branwen arrived a few hours later with my breakfast on a salver.

My husband, Gerald of Windsor, had proved to be an accomplished and considerate lover, a fact over which I had not ceased to marvel during my many wakeful moments throughout the night. I had been seduced by Prince Henry at the immature age of fifteen, during a forest ride. By sixteen I had conceived and by seventeen, borne him a son. Because he was the brother of the King and a man of thirty years old, I had in my innocence, believed him to be the perfect lover. I had mistakenly assumed that his proficiency in satisfying his own basic needs, was all that one could expect. I had become accustomed to the unsophisticated concept, that my own desires would never be consulted. I now found that it was essential to my husband that they should be.

He had come back to me on the previous evening far sooner than I had expected. I was robed for the night, but Branwen was still busily brushing out my long hair. Thanking her cordially for her services and taking the hairbrush firmly from her reluctant hands, he had promptly evicted her. Sensing my acute nervous tension after he had barred the door, he had come quietly back to my side and seating himself comfortably upon the bench beside me, he had begun with gentle strokes to brush my hair. As he brushed, he had spoken in comforting tones of common everyday things. His tenderness and sensitivity for that first rather difficult hour had ensured a compatability later, which I had not thought could possibly exist. But what had caused me even further wonder, had been the depth of his passion once he had achieved this ultimate rapport. I remembered also that sometime later, when warmly encircled by his arms, I had wept without apparent reason, into his shoulder.

Branwen broke into my reverie with a disparaging sniff and asked if I was now ready to rise. Agreeing that I was, I washed and dressed in my most becoming kirtle and then donning my warmest cloak went outside for a swift turn about the courtyard.

A party of armed men, about eight in number, were just preparing for the road. They were a routine patrol which rode the boundaries of Lord Arnulf's estates, watching for any unusual movements in the neighbouring commotes. My husband saw them safely away and then walked over to join me on the gravel pathway. There was an element of undeniable humour in his voice, as he declared: "I trust, my lady, that you will find Penbroc to your liking?"

They were the first words that he had spoken to me, on my arrival at the castle, after Walter of Gloucester had left us so ostentatiously alone together. I looked up at him, unable to repress a smile. "I find Penbroc very much to my liking, today sir, I thank you," I replied demurely. He laughed delightedly and pulling my arm through his, turned to walk with me around the castle boundary.

"I hardly dared ask," he admitted, "for the last time I

uttered those words, you virtually took me to pieces, limb from limb. "Are you truly happy at last, Princess?" he asked wistfully, halting his stride and gazing at me with an intensity that I found baffling.

"Far happier than I ever expected to be again," I murmured seriously.

He nodded. "I know, I feel the same. Two months ago I was angry and resentful that you were to come to Penbroc at all. And now – " He shrugged. "It is a new awakening, that neither of us expected."

We reached the wooden bench, my favourite resting place, opposite the mill. Bleddyn was seated there, with a small crowd of birds around his feet. I noted that he dropped them the odd crumb, for which they quarrelled noisily. "Come," he cried, "listen to this wonderful music."

"But Bleddyn," I corrected, "most of them are starlings and they are chattering morosely to one another, the air is full of their snide asides."

"Ah, but there is far more to hear than just the starlings," he declared. "Over yonder a heron grumbles by the mill race and there also, the water whispers musically over the paddles of the miller's wheel. To the east, the oyster catchers fly down river, screaming their displeasure, because they have been disturbed. Here, beneath the pallisade a sleepy queen bee moans that the cold winter winds will soon be here and she has as yet, no warm winter quarters ... and the curlew bubbles from Monkton Hill, but the best song by far, the strain that outplays the rest, is the music that I hear in your two voices, as you walk together in the last of the October sunshine. Soon the winter will be upon us, but neither of you will feel the cold, because you have at last found one another and that is as it shall be written." I felt my husband's grip tighten suddenly upon my arm.

"We are very happy, my wife and I," he said soberly.

There was an element in my husband's demeanour that puzzled me. "The air is cool," I excused us. "We must keep walking to keep warm."

As we passed the bench, to my great surprise, my husband gripped the bard's shoulder, as if in a gesture of comfort, man to man. When we had proceeded out of earshot I mentioned that I was sometimes puzzled by Bleddyn's perception, but half understood it, being Welsh myself. "I think that he has 'the Sight'," I said.

We came to an abutment, a small piece of the pallisade that jutted out and made an angle, which hid us from the rest of the courtyard. I turned to him, in the shelter of this angle. "Gerald. What is it?" I begged. "Has Bleddyn made you angry?"

He caught me to him fiercely and I thought that even man that he was, he was about to weep. He buried his face in my hair. "Not angry," he said in strange cadences, "just terribly sad. I have everything, and he has nothing. He came of a noble line, but when he arrived at Penbroc he was a broken man."

I looked at his bowed head above mine, in complete bewilderment. "How so?" I asked, in puzzled tones. Suddenly, he pulled himself together and smiled down at me in his usual confident way.

"Bleddyn must tell you his own story," he said firmly, "and I do not doubt, that one day he will." He rapidly changed the subject. "I have to go to one of the cantrefs this morning, but if you care for it we can ride together this afternoon, wherever you will." He kissed me without haste, eventually releasing me with a sigh. "I would have given much to have stayed with you this morning," he said, "but my job is such that if I neglect it for any reason, many lives could be forfeit."

By the time we celebrated Christmas at Penbroc, I knew that I carried our first child. Gerald, my husband, was warmly enthusiastic over the news. It was almost as if we had performed some miracle, that had never been undertaken before. I reminded him that it was not my first child, or his, and that he must not, on any account, make Philippe feel discarded. In fact, from the beginning, we both went out of our way to interest 'our son', in the idea of the newcomer. Philippe, who was unable at this stage to think in abstracts, had no fears and as I became less active and unable to ride out for any distance in comfort, he welcomed the unborn child that kept me longer by his side. There were no scares or border conflicts in our area that winter, and wrapped in the luxurious blue velvet mantle lined with ermine that my husband had had specially made to shelter me from the cold, I spent a relaxed and very contented winter.

As early summer came and our child grew heavier within me, I began to wonder, whether my husband would take another woman at this time, as the King had always done. But he showed no signs of needing another, for he continued to share my bed. It was thus, lying there holding me comfortably within the circle of his arms, that he planned the inheritance of our first-born. He told me during this time, much about his boyhood at Windsor and from these reminiscences, I came to understand the basis of his wisdom and humanity. He adored his father, now an old man, who had been castellan for the Conqueror at Windsor, almost from the time that the new fortress had been established there, in 1080. The elder de Windsor had also held the position of lord warden of the forests of Berkshire, but owing to infirmity, his eldest son William, now bore these heavy responsibilities as well as that of the royal stronghold.

There was still a trace of the boyish hero worship of a younger brother for an elder, evident in my husband's voice as he spoke of the present castellan of Windsor.

"Then if we have a son he shall be called William," I promised, "and if you think it apt, he shall inherit the demesne of Carew."

He turned to view me seriously. "You would give your blessing to that?" he asked.

I nodded. "But only if Philippe is well provided for. I will not have him deposed. After all, he was one of the first friends I ever had at Penbroc."

Although I was not supposed to know, I became aware of the mounting tension between Branwen and my husband, as I came nearer my time. They had a number of hotly contested arguments, about who should tend me at my confinement. One day I overheard Branwen asserting obstinately that even though the midwife of whom he spoke, from Penbroc town, might be a good enough woman, she was not good enough for the Princess Nesta. "I delivered her first child and I shall deliver her second," she declared, in a tone of such finality, that most people would have given her best, but not my husband.

"We shall see," he promised ominously. "I will not have her life put at risk. I am to be sent for immediately, you understand, wherever I am, when she commences her labour." I lay back on my pillows, amused by their bickering. I was young, very strong and so well cared for that I had no fears about the outcome of my pregnancy. Fortunately perhaps, for both Branwen and me, I started to contract almost as soon as my husband had left the castle, at about nine o'clock one morning. It was quite unlike the birth of my first child, for everything this time began to happen with amazing rapidity.

"Lie down," Branwen ordered and I did so, without more ado, gripped in a turmoil of emotions and sensations.

She began to sponge my brow. "The Constable, your husband," she suggested. "He wished to be called, my lady – "

"No!" I answered, gasping for breath. "Oh Branwen, I cannot let him see me like this. All I need is a good nurse. Stay with me, I pray you." After tossing and turning for some time, unable to escape from the tremendous force which seemed determined to rend me, a moan like that of a small puppy in distress was at last drawn out of me. Branwen released my hand suddenly and began to delve with frantic haste into a nearby chest. "Don't leave me," I pleaded.

"The clean linen," she explained. "That which I put aside to wrap the child in when it is born."

"Too soon," I rasped, seeing her face clearly but as if from afar. "Too soon!"

She examined me, "Oh no," she cried, "not too soon. Now," she directed, "as I count." As she counted in Welsh, I strained with every ounce of strength I possessed. The whole world appeared to divide, and stand still. "Splendid!" Branwen cried enthusiastically. "It has jet black hair, the colour of Deheubarth." Rapidly, she did some adjustment that made me wince and then she began to count again, in rousing tones. At the count of three my child was delivered from me. I lay back exhausted. There was a loud indrawing of breath and an even louder cry and then Branwen began to mutter endearments in her soft Welsh.

I looked back over my shoulder, to where she busily tended the small creature. "Your son is well, my lady," she told me joyfully. "See now, I have tied the lifeline which held him to you with such strong silk, that he may easily retain his new found independence. Rest now, while I wrap him."

Somehow, the further essentials were accomplished and Branwen satisfied at last of my safety, left me in peace while she called for hot water, with which she carefully washed my son. "Don't wrap him in swathing bands yet," I begged. "I wish his father to see him as he is, with all his fine sturdy limbs on view."

"His father," Branwen muttered thoughtfully. As soon as she had made the baby comfortable, she went to the door and called for a messenger. I heard her giving directions that someone was to ride at once for the Constable, who was at the southern end of the estate, to give him the news that his son was born and that both the child and the Princess Nesta were safe and well.

With hot water and many clean towels, Branwen deftly removed from my body, all signs of my labour and then, attiring me in clean white camisole and my most attractive kirtle, she stood back to view her handiwork. I leant back, with a long sigh of contentment.

"You are so good to me Branwen," I told her gratefully, "and so skilled with delivering children." Branwen flushed with gratification.

"It is to be hoped that the Constable, your husband, is of a like mind," she replied crisply.

"He will be," I promised her, lying back blissfully comfortable at last, with my eyes closed.

"He wanted to get a midwife from Penbroc town to tend you," she said, watching my face carefully.

"I know," I murmured, without visibly opening my eyes. "I heard you both arguing over it endlessly. I was determined not to have her, but to have you."

At that moment my new son, deciding that he was in need of a meal, began to roar in loud demanding tones. Branwen picked him out of the wooden crib and soothed him as best she could.

"May I hold him," I coaxed. "I really am quite recovered. It was all so ridiculously easy, now that I can look back on it."

Branwen gave me a serious scrutiny, as she carefully handed me the loudly protesting heir. "Perhaps it was short," she agreed, "but it was not as easy as all that. However, you are a true daughter of the Prince Rhys and can bear much with fortitude." I smiled at the extravagant compliment.

"But one thing I cannot bear with easily, is screaming babies," I told my son, holding him close and examining him with pride. As if the child understood, he ceased his noise and bother, and screwing up his gnome's face in a prodigious yawn, lapsed again into sleep. I was holding him thus, in my arms, when his father stalked into the chamber. He came straight to the bed and examined me anxiously.

"I told them to send for me the moment you began," he flung accusingly, at Branwen. I held out my free hand to him.

"I am afraid that your son was so impatient, that he would not wait until you arrived," I said easily. "It was all over so quickly." He grasped my hand tightly, not once taking his eyes from my face.

"And you?" he insisted. His hand was shaking.

"I feel wonderful," I answered truthfully. "Far more comfortable than I did this morning. Nothing could have been more simple or straightforward."

"Then why, if it was so easy, do you have those black rings below your eyes?" he argued doubtfully. Branwen came forward boldly.

"She has them because no child ever enters this world, without causing its mother a certain amount of anguish, but my mistress is right, there was no danger at any time, either to her, or to your son. Thanks be to God."

I held the baby towards him. "Branwen deserves our wholehearted thanks," I prompted, "but would you not like to meet your son?"

His face softened as I showed him the healthy well-formed body and thick black hair, of our 'first-born'. To my surprise, he lifted the small bundle gently and stood looking

down at the minute face nestled against his surcoat, with
the mixed emotions of tenderness, humour and pride,
which I had often seen him exhibit when he played with
Philippe. "William fitz-Gerald," he murmured. "The first
of a noble line. It is a good name." He viewed me seriously
over the baby's head. "Has Philippe seen his brother?"

I said that I thought that after dinner, he himself might
introduce his two sons. "Yes," he agreed, "that will be
most appropriate." He solemnly carried the child over to
Branwen. "Perhaps, you will lay him down in his crib for
me," he suggested politely. Branwen accepted the rather
crumpled bundle from him and straightened it out with
efficient fingers, before placing it in the wooden cradle.
"You must train a girl as nurse at once," he stated quietly.
"It is too much for you to do on your own. We owe you our
thanks," he declared courteously. "I greatly appreciate
your skill and goodwill in this matter and realize now, that
in my anxiety before the birth, I perhaps did not do your
experience justice." It was a gracious apology, and
Branwen was, I could see, suitably mollified. She dropped
him a royal curtsey.

"I have a girl in mind sir, and I will speak to her at
once."

"Very well," he agreed, "and I will get a message sent
down to the carpenter's wife, who had her own child last
week. She will feed the baby, as soon as he needs it."

I sat up in bed, suddenly. "But I intend to feed him
myself," I said clearly, so that there would be no mis-
understanding. I am not sure who my words shocked the
most, my maid, or my husband.

"I could not allow you to do any such thing," he
protested. "It just isn't acceptable and this woman from the
town is decent and I will see to it that she is clean." My
rebellious air, did not escape him. He came to sit on the

edge of my bed. "Nest," he said in disarming tones, "it could weaken you and then you could become ill."

"It doesn't make the carpenter's wife ill," I insisted, "and she is expected to feed two babies. If I fed the King's son," I argued rather unfairly, "surely I can feed yours." Branwen looked at me sharply. "Oh yes, I did," I informed her. "I sneaked in to him regularly when no one was looking. Only his nurse knew." I lifted beseeching eyes to my husband, with immediate effect. "If I promise to give up if I feel ill, or he isn't thriving, please will you let me? It is one of the most rewarding things in the world and I find it easy." He stretched out both his hands to take mine which he kissed gently.

"What can I say? How can I deny you anything today, particularly this. But," and he attempted to look suitably stern, "if your condition deteriorates in the slightest, then William has to have his meals with the carpenter's wife. Do you understand?" I nodded, full of quiet contentment. He stood up. "Thank you for my son," he said simply and then with a swift kiss, he was gone.

Philippe examined the new member of the family minutely that afternoon. He was not terribly impressed. "He will have to grow a lot before he can do anything very much," he stated, wriggling up onto the bed beside me and curling into the crook of my arm. "Mama la Princesse," he said, his eyes sparkling. "Bleddyn has made the most beautiful song in the baby's honour, and already they begin to sing the chorus all over the castle, even in the kitchens. But better still, he has made a short one, specially for me." In a sing-song tone, he proudly recited:

> Ask Philippe
> If you want a peep,
> At the new born Prince of Wales

I laughed without restraint at this piece of delightful doggerel.

"When are you going to get up?" Philippe asked. "You did promise that as soon as my brother was born we could go out for a ride together again."

"Have patience my child," I urged.

For a few hours, I believed that nothing could destroy our happiness, until late that evening when a travel-stained messenger arrived from the north, with a brief note in his satchel for my husband. Lord Arnulf would arrive at Penbroc in two days time, it stated. He was at this moment en route from Shrewsbury. The Constable and staff were requested to prepare their lord's apartments without delay.

No sooner had Arnulf Lord of Penbroc set foot in his own castle courtyard than a wariness and nervous tension became apparent, which was quite foreign to that usually cheerful place. I became aware of this change only gradually, as I remained confined to my chamber after the birth of my son. In order to give more comfort to my lying-in period, my husband decided to use his private chamber in the White Tower. This arrangement became an extremely convenient one for Lord Arnulf, who was thus able to approach his chief officer at any hour of the day or night with administrative problems, which at this time, appeared to be endless. On the rare occasions when I caught sight of him, I was deeply shocked by my husband's gaunt appearance. For fresh signs of strain were only too evident, both in his eyes and the taut lines which had become etched around his mouth.

The castle, always alive with noisy activity, now reached fever pitch. It was only after I began to walk outside again, that I could see that which I had most feared, that the castle was undergoing a massive re-fortification. Looking over these new fortifications, towards the town, I could see that similar work was also being carried out there, on the civic defences. In the valley and along the busy river banks, flocks and herds were being driven into paddocks and water meadows, hard by the castle boundaries. It could only mean one thing. I eventually cornered Branwen and demanded to know everything that she may have seen, or heard, since the arrival of his lordship.

"One of Lord Arnulf's bodyguards, the ugly blonde one, talks wildly when he has drunk any quantity of our local ale," she explained. "After his evening meal, on the second day that he was here, Bleddyn heard him say that Lord Arnulf and his brother, Earl Robert of Shrewsbury, plan treachery against the King. Earl Robert has raised a strong castle at Bridgnorth, without the King's permission, and that is treason. They expect help, both from the Duke of Normandy, the King's brother, and King Muircertach of Ireland." She looked at me with a strange light in her eyes. "They say that three of your uncles, including Cadwgan, have sworn to aid Earl Robert of Shrewsbury. Perhaps in this way, our people may once again obtain their freedom."

I turned away, sick with apprehension. "And to think that I have just brought another child into this turbulent world!" I cried. "No one, no one I tell you, will ever succeed in overthrowing this monarch in such a way. King Henry will, by a mixture of sheer force, guile and persuasion, crush any who try to oppose him and heaven help those who survive. I must talk to my husband as soon as possible."

Branwen hesitated. "My lady, your husband the Constable has changed mightily in the twelve days since Lord Arnulf returned to Penbroc and informed him of what he and his brother intend to do. None dare ask him anything now, for fear of his sharp replies." I appreciated her warning. My husband had become unapproachable and she did not wish me to be rebuffed, but I also understood the look which I had seen on his face. It was the expression of a man, who having received certain orders from his lord of which he did not approve, felt constrained as a soldier to carry them out. I was convinced that I could in some way persuade him to see the folly of the course on which he and Lord Arnulf were set.

Two days later, my husband happened to pass by that section of the courtyard which contained my seat over-looking the mill. To my relief, he immediately came to sit by my side. "You look wonderful," he observed wistfully, and then he took my hand, holding it tightly. "If only there were not so many damned men at arms about," he said, viewing them with considerable displeasure. "I have wanted to see you for days, but when the lord of the demesne first returns after a long absence, there is so much to be attended to. And one must do repairs while the weather remains fine," he added, but his voice was not terribly convincing. "How are you?" he asked quickly, before I could reply. "And our first-born, little William? I hear that he thrives."

"I am in excellent health, I thank you," I answered, "and have completely recovered now from the arrival of your son. It is also true, that William grows visibly every day. It is his father who most concerns me at present, however. I fear that if he goes on working at such a pace he will become very ill." He moved, uncomfortably.

"Yes. I'm sorry," he said soberly. "It cannot have been very easy for you, to have been left thus, immediately after the birth of our first child. I hope that we shall have completed most of the work in a few days time. Then perhaps we can ease up slightly."

"It is true that your long hours do trouble me," I admitted, "but what you are doing troubles me even more." I gripped his hand urgently. "Gerald, do you realize what you are about? It can never succeed. The King is utterly ruthless and he will use any means, no matter how devious, to crush the house of Montgomery, if they come out against him in open rebellion. Believe me, I know him only too well. If he succeeded in gaining the throne of England by such adroit manoeuvring, do you think that he will allow two petty marcher lords to defy him? He will wipe them from the face of the earth and in doing so, remove many others innocent of intent, such as we ourselves. Go to Lord Arnulf. Use your considerable gifts to divert him from this course, which can only lead to disaster." Slowly and deliberately, he removed his hand from mine and got to his feet. There was an iciness in his voice, that chilled me painfully.

"I have sworn fealty to my Lord Arnulf," he declared, "and thus can never question his decisions. I am a soldier under orders. In the same way that I expect instant obedience from the men who serve me, my lord expects, and will obtain, instant obedience from me, while I am subject to his commands. He is our lord, yours, as well as mine, and we are merely the tools whereby he lives. I bid you, take your questioning no further." Before I could utter any defence he had observed the courtesies that two strangers would employ, and moved away from my side.

I did not catch sight of him again for another three days, and when he did come, it was to tell me that he was to sail for Ireland on the next high tide. His manner with me was cautious, and a trifle distant. I could tell that he was determined at all costs not to have a scene. Burying my emotions, I asked in even tones, how long he expected to be away.

"About two weeks in all," he replied, in a voice that exactly matched mine. "Lord Arnulf is petitioning the Irish King, Muircertach O'Brien, for the hand of his elder daughter. I have to go with others, as emissary to the Irish Court on his behalf."

"I see," I said, running out of stilted comments.

"Nest," he murmured, catching hold of me for a brief moment. "Everything will be all right. I promise you."

"Will it?" I asked, near to tears.

"Yes, you will see. If I return with a favourable answer, then we can relax over the winter. Muircertach will hardly send his daughter to Lord Arnulf until springtime." We did not meet again before he boarded the small galley that was to take him to Ireland and I became convinced that I should never see him again.

I was afraid at first that Lord Arnulf might prove difficult to handle. His dark, sensuous eyes, turned speculatively in my direction when I took my place at the supper table that night and I was treated to a number of fulsome compliments. As I failed to respond to these overtures, he shortly turned his attentions to a winsome youth who sat on his right hand, who, I soon realized with great relief, to be far more to his liking. I marvelled that I had ever considered this effeminate fop as a husband, however fleetingly.

It was almost a month later that the small galley returned from Ireland, laden with gifts from the Irish King and messages of goodwill. King Muircertach was apparently delighted with the proposal from a powerful Norman lord, for the hand of his daughter. He had given his consent gladly, offering ships and armed men, to aid his prospective son-in-law in the forthcoming campaign.

No sooner had my husband returned, than Lord Arnulf, obviously gratified by the messages of goodwill and the priceless gifts from Ireland wished to send him away again. It was, so it seemed, imperative that as many knights as could be persuaded to join the cause must be gathered together as soon as possible. "You will go first to Manor Pyr," he directed his Constable, "and then straight from there, to Arberth and Haverford." I stood quietly on the fringes of the group gathered around Lord Arnulf in the

Great Hall, my anger becoming uncontainable at this news. So far, I had not even been allowed to greet my husband since his return, many hours previously and now he was to be sent away again immediately, to round up endless knights. I could bear no more and tight-lipped, I begged leave to retire, as I felt somewhat indisposed. His lordship looked surprised and not a little annoyed, but impatiently, he nodded his assent.

Before I could turn away however, my husband moved rapidly to my side and raising me in his arms, as if I was about to collapse, he muttered curtly, "Sir, I must attend my wife." Lord Arnulf, irritated by this further complication, at last granted us both grudging permission to leave the Great Hall.

As soon as my husband had escorted me as far as the courtyard, I wriggled free and taking to my heels, ran as fast as my shaking limbs would take me, in the direction of my chamber. Once there, I threw open the door and as quickly, kicked it shut, dropping the bar across on the inside. An imperious knocking came on the door. "Nest, let me in, I must speak with you," my husband ordered firmly.

"I wished to speak with you, a full six weeks ago, when I bore your son," I yelled, "and have, every day since, but to no avail. Go back to your master and do his bidding, there is no longer a place for you here." I put my hands over my ears and ignored his rapping and his numerous pleas for reason, on my behalf. At last he went away and going over to the baby's crib, I took the infant up in my arms and wept over him until I felt my heart would break. There was, I was certain, no point in my enduring this existence longer. I would take my child and seek refuge with one of my uncles, Maredudd perhaps, or even Iorwerth. Sadly, I resolved to creep away from the castle as soon as it became dark. Stephen would find me a horse, and I knew the country-side like a well-loved book.

My resolve was broken into by footsteps in the Oriel. It was Branwen. I lifted the bar with my free hand and twisting it from the metal brackets, dropped it upon the floor. Too late, I realized my error, for I heard my husband's voice thanking my maid, and her retreating footsteps. I turned around angrily. "I suppose," I cried in scathing accents, "that I should have expected as much." He came into the room and closed the door.

"I have," he declared, "persuaded Lord Arnulf that you are ill and need my attendance for two or three days. He has agreed to send Stephen to Manor Pyr and Arberth." I clutched my son, as if for protection.

"I do not need your attendance," I announced coldly. "I decided, soon after you departed for Ireland, that if I must live on my own, I would do so on my own terms and not those dictated by Lord Arnulf. I shall ask my uncle Maredudd for his protection." He did not appear to be the least impressed with my speech.

"Nest," he said evenly. "You cannot leave me. I need you."

"I am sorry if that is so. From your prolonged absence, I would hardly have believed it. But I do not need you," I declared. He moved even closer.

"I think you do, your reactions this evening have proved that fact to me, quite conclusively." Holding his arms out for the infant, he took him from me and deposited him rather summarily into his cot. "Your son shows greater equilibrium under stress than your husband," he observed cheerfully. "See, the child sleeps through all our brawling." He stretched his arms out, invitingly, towards me. I fled into them and clung to him convulsively.

What my husband had told Lord Arnulf that evening when he had returned to the hall, I do not know, but it must have been evident that his lordship had pushed the Constable too far, and he had obviously been made aware of it. Lord Arnulf also knew that he could not manage his affairs without the full co-operation of his competent chief officer, and in the following six months, he did, although grudgingly, allow us the minimum amount of time together. Many soldiers of fortune flocked to Penbroc during this particular autumn. Men who were willing to trade their fighting skills for hard cash.

During a calm spell of early fine weather at the end of the winter months King Muircertach sent a messenger to Penbroc. If Lord Arnulf would come to meet her, the Irish King stated, his daughter was ready to leave her father, to become his wife. Anxiously, I begged Bleddyn to tell me if he could, whether or no the house of fitz-Gerald would survive the pending holocaust. He replied to my query in a way which I failed at first to understand. "One day," he promised, "your husband, Gerald of Windsor, will be supreme in Dyfed." With these few strange words I had to be content.

When at last the daughter of Muircertach O'Brien came to Penbroc only two ships of indifferent size came with her. For Magnus, King of Norway and Man, had suddenly appeared off the Irish Coast and his menacing presence had prevented the Irish King from sending his fleet with his daughter. Almost on the day that she arrived we received word that King Henry had already marched on Arundel, the most southerly of the Montgomery strongholds, taking it completely by surprise. By offering him a better bribe, the King also alienated my uncle Iorwerth from the two earls, whose border lands in Shropshire and North Wales he then began to sack and pillage. As this adverse news came in, I longed to discuss it with my husband, but dared not, for he became far more distant and preoccupied, and almost as much of a stranger as he had been six months before, when Lord Arnulf had first arrived at Penbroc.

When the promised help from King Muircertach of

Ireland did not materialize, an ominous, expectant hush descended upon the castle. Men at arms began to bicker, and my husband began to deal with the offenders in an arbitrary short-tempered fashion, quite unlike his usual magnanimous brand of justice. At last, one day in high summer, a small troop of the King's men rode into Penbroc, bearing a message for its lord. Lord Arnulf received it in silence in the courtyard, then immediately summoned my husband. They were closeted together for a long time. Eventually my husband came to seek me. He wished to speak with me, he indicated, at once and in private.

"Earl Robert of Shrewsbury, beset on all sides, has gone to the King, who at present lays siege to his castle at Bridgnorth, to ask his permission to leave the kingdom," he declared in sombre tones. Seeing my confusion, he outlined in grave phrases, exactly what this meant. "Earl Robert has thrown himself upon the King's mercy," he stated. I did not give much for his chances of survival and said so. "On the contrary," he replied, "the King has shown amazing forbearance in this matter and he has agreed to allow Earl Robert to retire to his Norman estates, so long as he leaves England immediately. He will never be allowed to return. This," he said, viewing me with the utmost seriousness, "now leaves Penbroc completely isolated. We have no strength from which we can treat with the King. He says, that our lord must either go to him, 'with his head in his lap', or follow his brother and leave the kingdom."

"What will he do?" I cried helplessly.

"I have advised him to leave the country without delay," he said quietly. "We have no hope of holding this castle, strong as it is, against the King's might, now that all promised help has failed." He moved over to the low table and stated abruptly. "Lord Arnulf wishes me to accompany him to Normandy." Some residue of my old defiance rose to meet the challenge.

"And will you accompany your lord to Normandy?" I asked.

He shook his head. "I think not, for you would hate it."

"I?" I answered, unsure of his meaning.

"Yes, you, Princess. I cannot ask you to uproot yourself so entirely from your native land. We must take our chance here."

"You say 'we'," I replied hesitantly, "but under such circumstances you do not have to remain shackled to either wife or children."

"I choose to stay," he answered tersely. "However, we dare not loiter at Penbroc. The King will soon send more soldiers, under a new officer, to re-garrison the castle. Our only chance of survival is to sink into obscurity on our own demesne at Carew. Will you come with me, and bring our children?" As I nodded, he stepped over to me and caught me to him in a swift embrace, moved momentarily beyond words. "I think that I know of a suitable place for us," he said at last, "and I shall arrange at once for our discreet removal. Gather together all of your personal possessions and those of the children. Everything must be ready for us to leave, as soon as I deem it necessary."

On the next available high tide, Lord Arnulf bade adieu to Penbroc, leaving only one man who positively mourned his banishment. The Prior of Monkton, head of the religious house endowed by the lord of Penbroc some four years before, was openly apprehensive about his new status under the King's jurisdiction. His lord paid little heed to his fears, caring nothing apparently, for anyone's future save his own. Those who wished to follow him to Normandy, were at liberty to do so, those that decided to stay behind, might shift as best they could. But someone must remain to hand the castle over formally to the King's chief officer, and the new garrison.

Stephen, who had decided to go to Normandy, generously offered to do this last duty. He begged my husband and me to lose no time over our departure. It was, he stressed, a bloodless victory for the King and so no reprisals would be taken; of this he was certain. But something I overheard made me fear for my husband's safety. It was possible that he might be arrested and held as a warrant for Lord Arnulf's good behaviour. I thanked Stephen gratefully and attempted to speed our leave-taking. My husband, however, seemed unable to drag himself away. He had thought it necessary to send Branwen and Bleddyn, with the bulk of our possessions, few though they were, to Carew the day before. The children and I should have gone then also, but I refused to leave until he was ready to come with us.

As it was, the lookout on the White Tower had seen the King's soldiers enter the far end of the town before we actually left the castle precincts. We were dressed as civilians in plain homespun and my husband on Stephen's suggestion, had allowed his beard to grow unshaven over the last two days. We took one horse only, a broken down cob. Llinos and my handsome chestnut gelding were perhaps one of the hardest sacrifices we had to make. We pulled the hoods of our outer garments well over our heads and mingled with the crowd that stood along the roadside.

The King's new chief officer, a knight called Saer, looked mightily pleased with himself that day, as he rode the length of Penbroc town, to take up residence in one of the most formidable strongholds in Britain. Saer rode at the head of a strong body of horsemen, followed by a winding column of foot soldiers, which stretched as far as the eye could see.

We stood in silence, my husband grasping the bridle of the broken down nag, with Philippe's small fist gripped tightly in his other hand. I held our youngest son, now almost a year old, slung upon my hip within a shawl, in the fashion of the country woman. As the new garrison reached the castle gates, orders were shouted and the drawbridge slowly descended for them to enter. I saw my husband raise his head and immediately witnessed the red pennant being lowered from the White Tower. With difficulty I swallowed back a sob, and glancing up at that moment, caught sight of the face of the man who stood beside me. Beneath the eyelids of the gallant commander of the 1096 siege of Penbroc two tears balanced precariously, ready to fall. "Perhaps we should begin our journey now," I suggested quietly. With a supreme effort, he gathered himself together. In unemotional tones, he said that we must just wait a few minutes more, to make certain that Stephen was quite safe.

It was not long before the small band, the remnant of Lord Arnulf's impressive army, marched down the winding track from the castle. At the edge of Monkton Pill they embarked in several small boats for the galley which lay waiting in the estuary to take them to Normandy. All my compassion was reserved that day for the silent figure who escorted me with impeccable dignity, away from the scene of his former triumphs towards the mill house at Carew. Jean the miller, had a long wooden storehouse there, which stood in the fold of the hill, behind his mill. He offered it gladly when approached by my husband. A new storehouse could soon be built before the worst of the winter set in he suggested, and we were welcome if the building would suffice. He and his generous spouse were fiercely loyal and unlikely to talk around the demesne.

Branwen and Bleddyn had worked hard for the two days prior to our arrival to make the draughty building into something like home, and over the next few weeks we did our utmost to adapt ourselves to our new life. With a characteristic stoicism my husband immediately turned his considerable energies firstly to improving our living quarters, and then, the business by which we should survive. Bleddyn who had hidden his harp and lute in the rafters on his arrival, now spent his time with a wooden frame strapped to his back, carrying in lengths of timber for my husband and Jean, who did all of the new building work between them.

Strangely, we were not bothered immediately by anyone from the castle at Penbroc, although Carew, now a demesne without a legal owner, should by rights have been annexed at once by Saer, the knight who now held Penbroc for the King. Jean and Bleddyn heard rumours from time to time that this new occupant of our previous home spent many a day on the hunting field. On wet days it was said that he rested, playing cards and dice and listening to his fine band of musicians. My husband had begun to do a fair amount of hunting himself, and he and Jean, when not running the mill, slipped away regularly with their bows, the results of their expeditions bringing a welcome supply of fresh meat to our cauldron.

The first winter which we spent at Carew was an exceptionally mild one and in spite of my anxiety over the possibility of a warrant being out for my husband's arrest, I began to enjoy the unexpected bonuses of this new life. I found the closer family unit far more to my liking. I expected to bear another child as a matter of course, but when springtime arrived and I was still not pregnant, I began to wonder what could possibly have gone amiss. Gerald and I never discussed the matter between ourselves, but Branwen did comment, and she bluntly conveyed the fact to me that it was my anxiety as to the

King's intentions which prevented me from giving the master another son.

One bright, early summer morning, I went with my husband to deliver two sacks of grain to an out-lying farm, and on our return journey, he led the old cob home with the children and me on its back, as we had done on the day that we had first arrived at Carew. Perhaps because we had had such a peaceful winter our natural caution was momentarily lulled, but without a second thought, we mounted to the high road on the way home. We were in a carefree family mood and the children had been urging their father to coax the cob into a trot for some time, until in good natured humour he did so, running with great agility by the side of the lumbering but willing beast. Philippe, astride the animal in front of my saddle, was beside himself with glee, urging Rouge to even greater efforts with whoops and cries. At a respectable trot we quickly rounded a bend to cross the ford at Milton Manor, when we found ourselves progressing at speed towards a sizeable group of horsemen.

My husband pulled the animal up sharply, but it was too late. "Hey, you there," a voice called in authoritative tones, as we attempted to do a right about turn. "You there, fellow! I wish to speak with you." We turned once again, to face the group. The man who had hailed us was dressed in sober clothes, such as clerks and minor ecclesiastics wore. As he beckoned us to come closer I noticed one who seemed to be the leader of the group. When my eyes rested upon this man, I could hardly suppress my alarm, for it was none other than Walter, High Sheriff of Gloucester. Although I immediately bowed my head I was certain that he had recognized me. I drew my youngest child closer to my bosom and waited fearfully. "Where are you from?" the clerk enquired.

"From the mill, over there sir."

"Over there? And where my good man, is over there?" remarked our inquisitor impatiently. My husband bit his lip.

"The village of Carew, sir," he replied unwillingly.

"Ah Carew," the clerk mused. "It is a demesne, is it not?" My husband nodded. "Well, speak up man," he was prodded.

"Yes sir," he admitted, with icy politeness. I saw Walter of Gloucester move forward slightly.

"Perhaps you can tell us who owns the demesne of Carew?" he prompted. My husband averted his gaze from the speaker.

"No sir," he replied slowly. "I'm afraid I cannot. I only work with Jean, sir, at his mill in the valley."

The clerk interrupted somewhat rudely. "It is no use asking these peasants, sir. They have no knowledge of anything much beyond their own narrow field." Walter of Gloucester considered my husband's averted profile with an interest that I found ominous. Gerald's disguise was insufficient, I feared, to mislead those shrewd eyes.

"Perhaps the man who once owned the demesne of Carew is now in Normandy," the King's Chief Justice of Gloucester suggested.

"That could be so, sir," my husband agreed, without moving a muscle.

"Yes, I am convinced of it," the Sheriff decided. "Master clerk, there is no need for us to go further. Pray erase the entry from your record books. I will personally notify the King of this matter."

"But sir," the clerk protested, "Saer, the Officer at Penbroc should surely administer the estate meanwhile. The King may take some time to decide on the ownership of this demesne, and good government is not effected by allowing loose ends in the administration."

"You may rest assured that I shall see to the matter personally," Walter of Gloucester advised him, in a voice which suggested that the matter was now out of the hands of 'Master Clerk'. "I like loose ends as little as you apparently do," he told the group of horsemen in general. He turned his horse's head in the direction of Penbroc. "Thank you my friends, for your co-operation," he remarked to us pleasantly. "You have a fine family there, Master Miller, an exceptionally happy family. Apart from one aspect, your joviality, you make a group very reminiscent of the Holy Family. A picturesque little tableau to be sure, similar to that of the flight into Egypt by the Holy Mother and her child, led by St Joseph, but without the usual pathos." I held my breath as he made this analogy. The flight into Egypt to escape from the wrath of a king. Could it be that the King's Chief Justice on circuit in Dyfed intended to overlook our presence in his sovereign's land? My husband muttered his thanks in a suitably humble vein, and the party of horsemen moved away.

When they were well out of earshot Gerald turned and gripped my hand. "Thank you, Princess," he murmured. "You have so gained the affection of the Sheriff of Gloucester that he will never betray us."

"But he recognized me," I cried in distress. "I know he did, as soon as he set eyes on me."

"He recognized us both," he replied, in surprisingly cheerful tones. "But he does not intend to hand us over to Master Clerk and his like."

"How can you be sure," I answered in anguish. "Oh Gerald, I am so afraid that he will inform the King, who will send at once to arrest you."

He smiled confidently. "Good wife, do not grieve, for you are according to the King's Chief Justice so reminiscent of the Holy Mother."

"But why?" I asked. "Why should Walter of Gloucester

be so good to us? We are nothing to him."

"Perhaps you are something to him," my husband
suggested, a twinkle lighting his eyes. "At best, he probably
identifies you with the daughter he never had, at worst – "
He looked up at me and laughed openly.

"At worst?" I prompted.

"Who knows," he replied, with an enigmatic shrug.
Scarcely a week later a dozen horsemen arrived at our door.
They asked to speak "to the bearded young man who helps
Jean the miller". In an acute state of alarm, I sent Branwen
into the mill to fetch my husband. He appeared, covered in
a fine white film of dust. His manner was cautious. "You
have corn to be ground?" he said, in businesslike tones.

The serjeant shook his head. "My master, Saer, the chief
officer of Penbroc, requested us to bring you in, to meet him
at midday."

"Good wife," Gerald said, in a comforting voice. "A
clean smock for your husband, if you please." He turned to
the serjeant. "Can you wait, while I don clothes more
suitable to meet your master?" The soldier replied that the
miller could wash if he wished. I went with my husband to
our chamber and silently produced a clean short tunic from
a chest. He had a swift sluice in a wooden bucket, emerging
from behind the towel which I had handed him, with most
of the signs of his toil removed. "Nest," he said softly when
he had finished, "don't look so distraught. These men have
not come to arrest me, of that I am certain." He kissed me
with a surprising tenderness. "I shall be home by night-fall,
you may depend upon it." I watched, full of foreboding, as
my husband climbed into the saddle of the spare horse
which the serjeant produced from within his ranks. He rode
away with them more as an equal than a prisoner and with
this I was forced to be content.

It was dusk when my husband rode back into the valley
on the same strong horse on which he had left that

morning. He would tell us nothing, although we were all agog for news, but much of his old assurance had returned. All he would allow was that Saer of Penbroc wished us no harm and that he had his word that we should be left in peace. On the following day, a Wednesday, he rode off early in the morning and we did not see him again, until the sun had almost set over the tidal estuary. Soon, he was spending three days a week away from the mill. He did not however, return to us empty handed, for many a fine haunch of venison and game pasty began to find its way to our table and Jean's, to eke out our careful housekeeping.

Bit by bit, we learned that my husband had been persuaded by the bungling Saer, who had become more and more muddled over the running of the affairs of Penbroc, to aid him as an adviser. Jean and Bleddyn continued to work the mill however, with great industry and dedication, "for who can tell," they said wisely, "how long this may last?" In all, it lasted for another twelve months, during which time I often caught a more sober expression evident, upon my husband's face. Bleddyn gathered from the many itinerant pedlars who passed our road end to and from Penbroc town, that things in that burgh were not always well.

Quite unexpectedly one day, the visits to both the castle and Penbroc town ceased, and the good strong saddle horse was no more to be seen grazing our paddock overnight. I at last asked him why he now ground corn with Jean on every day of the week. "Would you rather that I did not?" was the reply. "Perhaps you now suffer from a surfeit of my company?" I ignored the latter remark.

"Why?" I asked pointedly. "Something has happened, hasn't it?"

"Yes, last Monday morning a group of burghers of Penbroc met me as I entered the main gate of the town. Their spokesman informed me that they had only recently

realized who I was. On the previous night, things had come
to a head. A rogue pirate galley from Ireland had sailed into
the haven at high tide and its crew ravaged half a dozen town
houses, carrying off much in the way of goods and four
young girls, one of only twelve years old. Five men of the
town were killed and a number of others injured. The castle
garrison ignored the entreaties of the citizens to turn out to
their aid, leaving them to fight it out with the pirate ship as
best they could. The burghers have sent a petition to the
King, via Walter of Gloucester, asking for the removal of his
officer Saer, on the grounds of incompetence. The
spokesman made it clear that they had no wish to implicate
me and they advised me to stay away until the dispute was
settled." I sank down on to the nearest bench, my limbs
shaking.

"But Saer could implicate you, by a mere handful of ill-
chosen words," I cried, "and none could safely defend
you."

"You worry far too much," he declared evenly. "It will
be quite all right. You will see." We eventually heard by
our usual route, that the King's messenger had come to the
castellan and he had ridden off with a group of his own men,
leaving but a few dozen foot soldiers, to hold the fortress.
Every day I expected a warrant for my husband's arrest.
Some few mornings later, a considerable number of horsemen rode into the lane and approached the mill.
Instinctively, I realized that they were a company of the
King's men. The officer on the lead horse swung to the
ground and came towards me.

"I have a message for Gerald de Windsor, from His
Majesty the King," he informed me in clipped accents. I
wished to scream to Gerald to run, to escape before they
could take him, but no sound came from my constricted
throat. The officer saw him standing by the mill door.

"Gerald de Windsor?" he barked. My husband walked towards him.

"I am he," he announced clearly. The officer sprang to attention smartly, saluting him with respect. He held out a scroll of parchment on which I could see the great royal seal.

"A message for you sir, from His Majesty," the soldier announced briskly. My husband broke the wax seal and his eyes rapidly scanned the page. "Thank you, lieutenant," he said at last, with great dignity. "I shall be happy to obey the King's commands. Are you able to convey a verbal message to His Majesty?"

"Oh yes sir, word of mouth sir," the man replied, without a flicker.

"Then you will tell King Henry, that I, Gerald de Windsor, loyal knight in the King's service, am happy to accept the position of Constable of Penbroc, under the King's command, for as long as he shall deem me fit to hold such an office." The man saluted him again and sprang onto his horse. "You may inform King Henry also, that in view of the present unsettled situation in the town of Penbroc, and the small garrison left to defend the castle, I am taking up my duties at once." The man wheeled his horse.

"Yes, sir, I understand, sir. The King is to send reinforcements within the next seven days, by way of Arberth. Good day to you, sir." The officer called to his troop to fall in and he rode out of Carew, as abruptly as he had entered it. I stood in the mill yard, clutching a gate post, with tears of relief running unashamedly down my cheeks. My husband's eyes were very bright.

"Nest," he announced accusingly. "You are crying," I nodded and sniffed. He rapidly put a supporting arm around my shoulders. Jean and his wife hung back a little,

on the fringes of the excited fitz-Geralds. My husband left
my side to stride over to them. "But for you, my good
friends," he declared, "we should have fared poorly over
the latter years. My wife and I can never hope to honour
fully the great debt we owe you."

In a few hours we had hired a cart and piling our
belongings up to its rim we set out for the castle. It was in a
sorry state of repair, for we had been almost three years
absent, and Saer had never thought in terms of care or
renovation. As we stood in the Great Hall, attempting to
assess the damage, Philippe rushed in and caught hold of
our hands, dragging us out into the courtyard. "What is it
Philippe?" I asked in alarm.

With his eyes shining, he hauled us up to the rampart
walk, overlooking the town. "Mama," he cried ecstatically.
"Look! Look there, and there, and towards Monkton. The
good folk of the town light bonfires. And hark!" he put up
an imperious finger. From the main street I could hear
singing, good humoured shouting and much happy
stamping of feet. He lifted his radiant face to mine. "The
good burghers of Penbroc light fires, and there is singing
and dancing in the street because papa is their Constable
once again, and they wish to show him how much they
admire and respect him. And they also call your name.
Hear them?" From below, I caught the faint echo, fanned
towards us on the clement evening breeze, "Princess Nesta,
Princess Nesta". It was a strange, heart searching cry.
"They call and cheer you, as well as papa," the boy assured
me, "because you are a Princess of Wales and they cannot
help but love you." I looked at the man by my side, who
stood attentively, watching the scene below.

"They give me much to live up to," was the only
comment he would allow his contented soul to utter.

One by one, people who had served us in some capacity
or other before our banishment came back to the castle, to

ask my husband to reinstate them in their previous posts. Many had been in hiding with friends and relatives in Penbroc town and its surrounding manor lands. With so many willing hands and the generous co-operation of the townspeople, the castle was cleaned and refurbished in a remarkably short time.

One of the first things that my husband did in his judicial capacity was to call an enquiry into the tragic raid on the town by the piratical Irish galley. As a result of this council the town walls were strengthened and manned day and night, and a lookout tower raised on Monkton Hill, to give advance warning of any vessel approaching either town or castle, by way of the estuary. We had been back in residence only a few weeks, when I knew with certainty that I carried another child for my husband. He was both delighted and amused by the news. "So," he declared with humour, "the Princess Nesta, who scorned to bear a child for the miller of Carew, has no compunction over immediately producing another heir for the Constable of Penbroc – a very discriminating lady."

"I cannot think why," I replied demurely, "for the Princess was uncommonly fond of the miller of Carew."

He drew me towards him. "Then," he sighed, "it must have been nature's way of ensuring that we had no further mouths to feed, at that rather difficult time."

Our second son, Maurice, who was born almost as easily as his elder brother had been, arrived at Penbroc in the spring of 1106. This, the second son of our dynasty, was if anything more handsome than our first-born William, for he had the fair good looks of both Philippe and his father.

When Maurice was but three months old, we received an unexpected visit from Walter, the King's Chief Justice of Gloucester. After he had been released from his duties and had but to wait for his supper, he sought me out as I sat in the warm spring sunshine. After a formal greeting, he came to sit companionably by my side. "Your husband the Constable has such boundless energy," he grumbled mildly, "that I have been hard put to it to keep up with him today. His enthusiasm still never fails to amaze me."

I looked up and smiled. "You had already ridden from Arberth," I pointed out, "a long enough ride for most people in one day, and Gerald is thirty-two years old next month, so you must forgive him for being restless while he may."

"I forgive him freely," the Sheriff observed pleasantly, "for seldom have I met a man who exhibited such competence and excellence in the King's service. He comes from an outstanding family; I knew his father well." He paused and a delicate silence hung between us for a few seconds. "Tell me," he said at last, in quiet tones. "Have you been happier at Penbroc, my lady, than you intended?" I answered him truthfully.

"A great deal happier than I ever imagined possible, I thank you sir."

"Then I am content," he answered soberly. "I did not relish my role as gaoler, when I was forced by royal writ to bring you to this place. But I knew the worth of the man to whom you had been sent, whereas the King did not."

"You have been extraordinarily good to us," I murmured, with a rush of gratitude. "For you did recognize me that day, did you not, at Milton ford?"

"Instantly," he agreed, getting to his feet with a smile. "Yours, Princess, is not a face one could easily forget."

Within a few days of the departure of the Sheriff of Gloucester we had another unexpected visitor. Stephen had literally ridden right across Britain to get to us, after he had reached landfall at Hastings, from Normandy. His four years on the battlefields of France had aged him almost beyond recognition. He begged for his old post of lieutenant, and it was gladly given. As he settled down, the harsh lines, gradually smoothed away from his jaw, and he began to relax. He was an able second in command, and the experience he had obtained in the many battles, of which he was so loath to speak, was invaluable to Penbroc, for even though we currently enjoyed a comparative peace, we could never entirely cease our vigilance.

Early in the year of 1108, when I awaited the birth of the third of my husband's children, many strangers came to the cantref of Rhos, to the north side of the Penbroc Haven, where they settled upon the upper banks of the river Cleddau. Branwen waxed indignant over the way in which the French King, Henry, had crudely 'planted' these settlers on our doorstep. "Who are they these 'Flemings'," she cried righteously, "whose land was supposed to be robbed from them by the sea?" I could not find it in me to like these drab newcomers, but they were a gifted industrious race who brought many new skills to Dyfed.

As the town and manors of Penbroc grew and flourished, so my husband began to delegate certain functions to promising young men whom he trained for both military and administrative posts under his command. On one of his visits, Walter of Gloucester had persuaded my husband to appoint a young clerk from his own retinue to act as Clerk in Chief at Penbroc. The weight of work, with Shire Courts as well as those in the cantrefs, was too great for the Constable to continue to carry alone with only the aid of a few local scribes, the Sheriff rightly pointed out. The new clerk, a sober, learned young man of abstemious habits, called Hait, soon became the perfect secretary. He was efficient and unobtrusive, and we rapidly became accustomed to the sight of his studious, polite form, bent over his books as he sat behind the wooden screen in the Great Hall, making meticulous entries in his numerous ledgers.

It was mainly due to Stephen, and my husband's new

secretary Hait, that we at last began to snatch a few hours and sometimes even whole days of leisure, in which we could indulge in the occasional luxury of being together with our children, away from the pressing problems of the castle and its environs. For some time my husband had spoken of building a summer residence for us. At first we considered placing it on our own demesne of Carew, but he knew that try as I would, I could never quite suppress a longing for the mountains and glens where I played as a child – those rocky haunts beneath the blue shadow of the Prescelli Mountains, in my father's old kingdom of Deheubarth. After the birth of our daughter, who put a spell on him far greater than that of his much loved sons, my husband took me to ride across the north of Dyfed, where he had acquired a modest estate some years before, as part of my dowry from the King. On this estate was a small wooded village called Cenarth Bychan.

It was a magical spot and we first viewed it from a grassy crag, overlooking a wooded gorge through which the Teifi river whispered mysteriously, as it wound its way towards the sea. As we sat there in the late September sunshine, a huge grey heron rose from the tops of the trees on the farther side of the valley. With slow irregular wingbeats, it lifted its aristocratic body high into the air and with the aid of a warm breeze, sailed effortlessly past above our heads. I sighed, and my husband drew me close, within the circle of his arm. "You like it, Princess?" he asked.

"Ah, yes, I like it more than I can say," I replied, filling my heart with the scents and sounds of that wonderful place. "It reminds me of my childhood. It has a hiraeth, a sadness and yet a beauty that I find hard to resist." I turned to face him. "Could we really have a home here? Is it safe and above all, is it sensible?"

"Your uncle Cadwgan of late seems to be reconciled to our presence, as long as we stay within reasonable boundaries," he said at length. "Yes, I think we can erect a stronghold here. A small residential castle, all our own, where we can bring our children and our belongings and spend a little time together as a family. A place where I could come sometimes for a rest, to enjoy the company of my wife and children." I tilted my head backwards to scrutinize his face the better.

"And it is good hunting country and the fish are fat in the river yonder," I suggested softly.

Only Bleddyn disapproved of the scheme. "That old fox Cadwgan could never quite be trusted," he pointed out, "fitz-Richard may have put up a ring of lookout posts," he declared, "but they are little more than that, and the Prescelli Mountains, a good friend but a bad enemy, lie between Cenarth Bychan and Penbroc." As Bleddyn became more distrustful of the scheme, so the rest of us became more wildly enthusiastic. If my husband had any reservations he hid them admirably in the face of my absolute delight. Before winter had set in, a group of carpenters and two Flemish engineers had set about levelling the site and felling enough trees outside the gorge for the building to begin. By May 1109 our dream of a castle retreat at Cenarth Bychan had become a reality.

At first we meant merely to occupy it at scattered intervals during the warmer summer months, but the place wove such an enchantment into our souls that we craved to be there whenever we had a spare moment. It was one and a half days ride from Penbroc and we began to use a conveniently placed motte as a 'lodge', for our overnight stopping place to and from our new home. Stephen encouraged us to take a rest over the winter festival, at the end of that year. It was thus that we decided to spend the Mass of the infant Christ in our stronghold in the north. To our surprise Bleddyn, believing religiously that no one ever made war during the colder months of the year and certainly not Cadwgan, whose efficiency waned as his years progressed, agreed to accompany us. When we arrived the castle was mellow and surprisingly warm in the winter twilight that spanned the gorge. The logs sparkled between the stone kerbing in our modest baronial hall and the greenery, carried in to dress the walls by the servants who had preceded us from Penbroc, glowed in the added torchlight.

When we woke on the second morning of our stay a thin powdering of snow covered the pine trees on the far side of the gorge. Our sons were delighted. The two eldest went outside to track the wild deer, whose spores stood out clearly, across the clean snow. My uncle Cadwgan, also seemed to be in festive humour. We learned from a travelling musician, who ate at our table, en route to Castell Cadwgan, many miles north in Ceredigion, that the ageing Welsh chieftain had called a great meeting of his kinsmen over the Christian festival. There was to be a grand feast, with music and dancing. "They come from far and wide," the harper enthused. "Why it is even rumoured that Cadwgan's eldest son, Owain, Prince of Powys is determined to be at his father's feast tomorrow night, and his lands lie far to the north, almost to Eryri."

Some days later Philippe sought me out privately and informed me with serious eyes that he feared that Bleddyn was very ill. "He sweats without ceasing," the lad explained, "and he certainly has a high fever."

"Does papa know?" I asked, preparing to follow him to the bedside of the sick bard.

"Papa is already with him."

When I reached the alcove where Bleddyn lay, or should have lain, he was not upon his couch. He had flung himself to his knees, at my husband's feet, and in shaken tones, he muttered rapid, broken phrases of supplication.

At my approach, my husband swiftly drew the man to his

feet. "Philippe," he said in stern tones. "I did not ask you to fetch your mother."

I pushed through quickly to Bleddyn's side and placed my hand on his brow. "My friend, my friend, what ails you?" I asked in rapid Welsh.

"It is nothing to worry you with, nothing at all," my husband broke in, before the man could speak on his own behalf. "Bleddyn thinks he has had some peculiar vision. It was more like a bad dream."

The bard straightened up suddenly. "It was no dream, my lady, that I swear," he declared in shaken tones. "I beg you, take to horse without delay, and do not stop until you reach Penbroc gates!"

My husband put a hand on the bard's shoulder and shook him roughly. "That is enough!" he ordered. "Tomorrow, you shall travel with Ralf and half the garrison, back to Penbroc. My wife and family will follow you the next day, under my escort, when we have closed the castle here, to our satisfaction."

Bleddyn turned his pleading sightless eyes in my direction. "My lady," he begged. "Go at once."

I moved beseechingly towards my husband. "Gerald," I urged, "Do not be angry with Bleddyn, surely you can see that he is ill?"

"Bleddyn, you will say no more," my husband directed the musician firmly. "He is not ill," he advised me quietly, "just in rather an acute state of shock. I plan to send him back to Stephen tomorrow morning, but meanwhile I will not have him upsetting you in this way." His manner was at its most formidable and the bard sank onto his couch and turned his face to the wall. "Thank you," my husband declared with meaning. "I will have a draught sent to you, as soon as it can be prepared. Now try to sleep, for you leave here at dawn."

PART III

Bleddyn, and half the garrison of Cenarth Bychan, rode away in the direction of Penbroc as soon as day had broken. Bleddyn had recovered enough to ride, although he seemed downcast and pale. Those of us who were left began to pack our belongings in a leisurely manner. The weather was crisp, but remarkably sunny for a winter's day. After much coaxing from Philippe and particularly William, who at eight years old had become a hardy horseman, my husband was persuaded to take the men folk, who were bored with such pedestrian activity, for one last hunting expedition. The snow had brought a pack of wolves down from the mountains, in search of an easier food supply. The boys were intrigued as they seldom had the opportunity these days of sighting wolves anywhere near Penbroc; the Flemings had systematically cleared them from the surrounding countryside.

We had hardly resumed our task after bidding adieu to the huntsmen when a guard from the gatehouse came to inform me that three young men were outside, seeking admittance. "They have ridden this morning from Ceredigion, my lady," he said cautiously. "One, a dark young man, swears that he is a kinsman of the Princess Nesta."

"A kinsman," I declared, rather amused. "Indeed, I have so many in this part of Wales, that it would be difficult to discover someone who was not! Do they seem peaceful in their intentions?"

Extraordinarily so," the guard replied. "For Welshmen, they exhibit very few weapons and do not seem bent on war." I considered for a moment.

"And did this visitor give his name?" I enquired with interest.

"I was to tell you that Owain Cadwgan, Prince of Powys, was at your gate, and wished to seek the acquaintance of the Princess Nesta, his second cousin."

"The eldest son of my uncle Cadwgan." The bards had written and sung much of this particular young man. "You may let him in, with his two young friends," I said at once. "I will receive him in the hall." For a few minutes I retreated into my chamber to re-arrange my hair beneath its kerchief. Owain Cadwgan, Prince of Powys, was a tall black-avised young man, with a commanding presence. He viewed me with a close, almost embarrassing interest, as I entered the hall and held out my hand to him with a smile. "So we are cousins," I announced, with a twinkle that I was unable to repress. "Did you ever know any of us of the blood royal who were not?" There was an answering gleam in his eye.

"I had it from the chief bard, only last evening," he declared, throwing back his head, in order to scrutinize me the better. He then intoned: "For Cadwgan ap Bleddyn my father, was he not a first cousin of Gwladus, daughter of Rhiwallon? And was that Gwladus not mother of Nest," he bowed in my direction, "the pride of all who behold her, the veritable 'Helen of Wales'? And were Bleddyn and Rhiwallon, our grandfathers, not brothers? Sons of Cynfyn, by Angharad, daughter of King Maredudd." His quaint grasp of the genealogical intricacies of our pedigree was so truly Welsh that I laughed happily.

"Then if your father's chief bard says it is so, then it must be so," I allowed. "It is many years since I have been treated to such a long recitation of my pedigree." He raised his dark brows, quizzically declaring that he could begin on the other side of the family also, if I so wished; that of the Prince Rhys ap Tewdwr, my father. "There is no need," I pleaded, "I believe you implicitly. Pray be seated and I will send for some wine. My husband and sons are unfortunately out, on one last hunting expedition, for we must return to Penbroc tomorrow."

"Tomorrow!" he seemed surprised. "The travelling harper, he who ate at your table a few days ago and who sang at my father's feast of your exceptional beauty, said, I am almost certain, that you were to stay at this place for two weeks." He had a bold eye, this cousin and his overt scrutiny reminded me much of the premier Earls of England, during my adolescence at the court of William Rufus. Those who had not openly followed the whims of the Red King would have been troublesome to me at that time, had I not been carefully guarded by the King's brother Henry, whom all men feared.

"There is little enough time for us to spend in recreation I fear," I told him, "for my husband's duties at Penbroc take up most of his time."

"Oh, the French garrison town," he replied carelessly. "Yes, no doubt. Do you hear aught of your two brothers, Gruffudd and Hywel?" he enquired suddenly. The loss of my two brothers was something about which, I did not care to think, but at last I informed him quietly that Gruffudd was in exile in Ireland, at the court of the High King, where he had been brought up, and that Hywel was still prisoner in one of King Henry's border fortresses. I rose to my feet, to signify that it was time for him to leave. He took my hand again, and held it in a warm, familiar grasp. "It has long been my aim," he declared, "that the two houses of ap Bleddyn and ap Rhys ap Tewdwr might one day hunt side by side. Perhaps your brothers may not always be either imprisoned or in exile."

His meaning was obscure but I immediately wondered if he intended to make an attempt to free my brother Hywel from his long servitude in King Henry's prison and whether this was a hint to me of his intent. Taking my other hand in his also, he then bent his head low over mine. I felt a rush of emotion and a pang of something akin to fear. My rising panic was unfounded however, for my cousin calmly advised me that although the bards had sung at length about the magic of my form, they would never fully capture the splendid reality. Then he released me. It was with considerable relief that I watched my visitor and his two companions ride away from Cenarth Bychan that day. I had found an overpowering element present in his personality that in some subtle way, had unsettled me.

I was also seriously shaken by the dangerous implications posed by my cousin's visit and for the first time since we had ventured north I found myself longing for the greater security offered by the towering might of Penbroc. The visit was mentioned casually over supper, and I was disturbed to see the shadow which passed momentarily across my husband's face. It could not be very easy for him, I reflected, to know that his wife was closely connected by blood with the men he had fought so tenaciously in the siege of 1096. We retired early to our beds for the forthcoming journey was long and arduous during the winter months.

The hall at Cenarth Bychan was on the same pattern as that of our temporary home at Carew. A long building, with a chamber at each end, one for my husband and me, the other for Branwen and the children. I slipped easily into a deep sleep once the bars had been dropped across the doors. What eventually woke me, I could not precisely say, but as soon as I had been jerked out of my initial slumber, I became instantly aware of impending peril. The first thing I recognized was the acrid smell of burning wood. I could clearly see the sinister flickering of many creeping flames, glowing through the cracks between the walls and eaves of our chamber. They surged and leapt against the pitch black dark of the December night. There was an immense amount of noise, made I believed at first by our own people, rousing themselves to fight the flames and then, with a sick premonition, I caught above the terrifying din the war cry of Cadwgan.

My husband threw a tunic over his head and reached for his sword which he kept beside his pillow. With trembling fingers I drew my fur-lined mantle about me. There were now, the unmistakeable shrieks and cries of men cut down, which sounded clear above the rest of the infernal noise of shouted oaths and the clashing of weapons. At once, a mighty hammering came upon the door of the hall, and a great and terrible cry. "Princess Nesta, Princess Nesta, fear not, but throw out the Norman cur, that we may kill him and re-unite you with your own people." The man, whose death they howled for so savagely, stood erect, his eyes upon mine, his sword held in his hand. In the eerie flickering light, he waited, challenging me for my decision. At last, he moved slowly towards the door of our chamber, stirred by that awful knocking and the men outside, who bayed like hounds for his blood.

"No!" I cried desperately. "No, wait, you cannot fight them thus, they will cut you down like a dog." I ran to him and caught his free arm, urgently. "You cannot fight your way out. It is Owain Cadwgan."

"I know," he replied, low-voiced. "We are surrounded. Far better if I die fighting on my own threshold than in here, cowering like a frightened child."

"You must not go out, for your enemies are all around you," I cried, exerting an abnormal strength to restrain him. "There is another way, our only chance and I beg you, I implore you to take it. Come!" I dragged him to the head of our bed and wrenched the curtains aside that concealed the door that led to the garderobe. It was built onto the end of the building, and emptied over the very edge of the gorge. He pulled back as I attempted to lift the wooden seat.

"I refuse to run and leave you and our children here, undefended," he declared in shaken accents.

"If you stay, you will surely die," I moaned in strangled tones. "He will not kill me and I swear to you that I will save our children. You have to trust me, and get away while there is still time." I pushed him towards the stinking void, which was the only route that could save his life.

"Go!" I ordered, "and when you have climbed to the bottom of the gorge, hoot like the owl that flew in the mill yard at Carew, that I may know that you have descended safely." With a desperate groan, he eased himself into the narrow channel. For a moment, I stood with the lid of the privy in my hand and then, when I knew that he had begun to climb down the sloping cliff, I replaced it and gave my hands and arms a quick rinse in the stone basin that stood by the door to our chamber. While the howling invaders continued to rage outside the building, I quickly threw off my soiled robe and donned another, which hung there on a wooden peg. A phial of rosewater stood on a shelf and I scattered it over myself and my clothes to mask the smell of the latrine, while I waited impatiently for the signal.

After what seemed an eternity, I heard the faint, but unmistakeable hoot of a barn owl from the valley bottom. I returned the way I had come, carefully closing the garderobe door and pulling the curtains across, to obscure it from view from the chamber. A battering ram was now being employed to smash open the main door of the hall. By the lower chamber, Branwen stood white faced, with my four trembling children. "Mama," Philippe wept piteously, "they call for papa to go out to them, so that they may kill him!"

I put my hand on his shoulder. "Papa is safe," I whispered. "Now do everything I say without question and if I begin to pray use your head and mark carefully every word I utter." I removed a small dagger from the boy's shaking fingers. "No, Philippe, it is safer thus," I directed. I secreted the dagger in my girdle as I walked towards the door. "Owain, son of Cadwgan," I called in ringing tones. "Why do you shout in vain? He whom you seek is not here. He has escaped." There was a roar of anger and then the stout door, made by the Flemish master builder, gave, and they entered over its shattered remains. My cousin Owain stood there, a torch held aloft in his right hand.

"Search the place, the cur is crouched in some corner. There is no way out," he snarled to his companions. He remained facing me, while they did so. His nostrils were flared and a wild light shone in his eyes, like that of an animal about to make a kill. Rigidly I held his gaze, steeling myself as his men pulled my home apart, searching for the man they most reviled. As they hacked each coffer to pieces, cutting curtains and tapestries alike from the walls, I held myself as upright as a birch tree, refusing to flinch at each vile oath they uttered over my husband's name. Inside my breast a small glimmer of hope still burned, and kept me from swooning. It was the knowledge that somewhere, out there, he still lived. When I realized that their anger had almost reached boiling point, as they devastated the building and yet still found him not, I called the children to my side. We huddled together in the centre of the hall, a still small group, waiting until their patience should be exhausted.

Suddenly my cousin moved, jerking Philippe from my side and twisting his arm cruelly behind his back, until the lad screamed in pain. "Now cousin," he snapped, "you will tell me where the Norman dog, who dares to call himself your husband, lies hidden. My men have turned the place inside out. There is only one refuge left – ." He looked up, towards the shadowy roof tree. As he glanced upwards, I snatched the dagger from my girdle and with both hands on its hilt, held it poised over my heart.

"If you wish to take me, while I still live my children must be guaranteed safe conduct at all times," I cried in defiant tones. His eyes immediately returned to mine and in their turbulent depths I read what I already knew. He had come to Cenarth Bychan this night out of desire for me. My husband's death was of secondary importance to him. "I carry the blood of Rhys," I declared. "Like the she-wolf, I am not afraid to die, cousin, if my children's lives are in jeopardy." He hesitated. "Let the boy come back to my side," I directed. With a rough thrust, he threw Philippe from him and the lad fell to the ground at my feet. "I require your oath, Owain, son of Cadwgan," I stated formally. "An oath, that my children shall never suffer harm, while in your custody. If you want me, you must give it or I will die now by my own hand, before you can ever take me." Philippe, who understood it all, cried out in anguish, and at his cry, I began to intone a prayer in Latin. The boy at my feet lay still at last, obediently listening. "My son," I intoned, "your father is safe, thanks be to God. This man is dangerous, do not provoke him, or we may all die at his hand. Put your trust in me, that we may all live, and God willing, one day be restored to your father."

"Cease your prayers," my captor snarled ungraciously. "I will swear that your children shall live quite safely within my custody, if you will put away that dagger. You know well enough cousin, why I am here?" I nodded, and almost fainting with relief, I lowered the weapon to a safer position. "Get these children and their nurse out of here," he told his followers roughly. "But take good care with them. Put two guards over the door, and see that I am not disturbed until I wish it. Gather the spoil and make ready to travel to my father's place as soon as I give the word. We shall burn this building last of all. Now, get out!"

I was painfully aware that my children were still within earshot when he tore off the mantle which covered my nakedness. Then lifting me hastily in his arms he swiftly bore me towards the shattered bed in my own chamber that his men had so recently despoiled. A terrible smell of blood, sweat and wood smoke clung to his beard and the clothes which he hurriedly cast aside. Fighting down a swift feeling of revulsion and a perilous tendency towards nausea I knew with unerring intuition exactly what I had to do. Every minute he loitered by my side was another minute of life for the man moving silently towards safety, in the under-growth of the woodland yonder – and an added assurance of safe conduct for my children. Without resistance, and with as much simulation of pleasure as I could contrive, I allowed him to take what he demanded of me. In a few nightmarish minutes, it was all over and he lay, temporarily tamed, by my side, in the ruins of what had until an hour ago been my marital bed. After a while, when I knew with certainty that he slept, I crawled into the far corner of the room, and heaved my heart up amongst the trampled rushes.

He lay for a short while, deeply asleep. In case he should wake, I crept back to his side when I had recovered myself sufficiently. He woke up as suddenly as he had fallen asleep and lay there in the darkness beside me for a few minutes, with his eyes wide open, before he made any movement. I waited fearfully. When he did move, I was made instantly aware of his purpose. Once again, I was forced to relive the nightmare. Willing myself to give no sign that I was anything other than fully complaisant I managed to endure this further violation by my cousin. My senses told me firmly that I must, for by now, my husband could well be nearing the helpful shelter of one of the border outposts. Mercifully, he gained his satisfaction speedily and no sooner had he done so, than he left the couch, demanding that I should hurry, as we must leave before first light. Shakily I crawled out from amongst the bed covers, shivering violently.

"Here," he declared abruptly, handing me my night robe with the ermine lining. "Take this fur-lined wrap, the night is cold." I donned it and followed him silently through the vandalized Hall, to the courtyard. In a few minutes the building we had just left, had been set alight from end to end. Many of our household possessions and a hoard of valuables had found their way onto the backs of pack horses. Amongst the smouldering ruins I could see the sprawled and contorted bodies of our guards.

"But these men," I protested, attempting to restrain him as we made to ride away, "some of them may be merely wounded and require help."

"My men take good care never to leave any wounded," he replied callously. "They are all dead. Ride on!" he ordered. Amongst the armed men I could see Branwen riding pillion, with my little daughter clasped tightly in her arms. The child was wrapped in a blanket against the freezing night air. Slightly ahead of her rode my three sons, closely hemmed in by guards. Philippe held his youngest brother, Maurice, who was not yet four years old, protectively upon the saddle pommel in front of him. I shrank away from the dumb misery pictured upon the faces of the two elder boys. My cousin made certain that my horse never strayed more than a foot or so from the side of his tall roan. I was wracked by convulsive shivering as we progressed, largely as a reaction from the horrors of the night, but also because of the keen frosty winds that blew down the northbound track which we pursued. My ermine mantle failed to provide adequate protection to my abused body from this added onslaught. The icy north-easterly cut at our faces viciously as it swept and gusted along the exposed coastal plain, which led towards the mountains and Castell Cadwgan. In the cold of that bitter dawn I could gladly have slipped from my horse, and succumbed by the wayside.

My uncle Cadwgan had gone to Powys as soon as his feast was over to attempt to reconcile some of the more turbulent dissenters in that kingdom, for the tyrannical rule of his son, my cousin Owain, had sparked off the seeds of revolt there. My cousin was more than content to loiter with me at his paternal home while these diplomatic moves were taking place, and for the first few days I was the focus of his undivided attention. He continually informed me with a lewd directness when he was the worse for wine, that the bards only knew half the story. "To the Princess Nesta," he would state, holding aloft an overflowing horn to make a toast. "She who knows better than any other woman how best to fulfil a man's longing." His excessive demands always required instant satisfaction and he would subject me to the most personal intimacies at any time, only removing to the partial privacy of a curtained alcove off the hall at my emphatic insistence.

I had long ceased to expect anything but acute misery from these constant excesses. I became numb, drained of all positive emotion. In vain did I hope and pray that my cousin would rapidly tire of me, but as the weeks went by his infatuation seemed only to grow stronger, until I sensed that I exercised a subtle power over him, which I had not anticipated. I waited, until such time as I could use this influence to my own and my children's advantage. The children, whom I saw seldom, were constantly in my mind.

Early on, I had warned Branwen to keep them well away from the uncertain and unstable temper of their unwilling host. Painstakingly, she kept them fed and clothed, and as well occupied as was possible, under the circumstances. But it was Philippe who concerned me most, for he suffered in withdrawn silence, mutely aiding Branwen with the younger children as best he could. One day I laid a hand on his shoulder, and fiercely whispered. "Do not judge me so, my son. I do what I do, because I have no choice." He did not answer, but turned away, and my anguish at this apparent rejection almost broke my heart – he was so much like his father.

One of the most significant facts about my relationship with my cousin was that at no time did he ever strike me. I recognized that there was some element in my personality which prevented him from doing me physical injury. This was all the more remarkable because his reputation with women was notoriously violent. Although he could not bring himself to injure me physically however, he had no compunction over exercising his own peculiar brand of mental cruelty; and one of the ways he tried to hurt me particularly was through my brothers. As he lay in bed beside me, on the first morning after we had reached Castell Cadwgan, he had brutally revealed to me that my brother Hywel, who was still in the King's custody, would never produce heirs for the Kingdom of Deheubarth. "King Henry saw to that, with characteristic thoroughness, when you were both taken after your father's death in ninety-three," he said. "Your other brother, Gruffudd, should he venture here from Ireland, would assuredly suffer the same fate if he ever fell into the hands of the King."

I covered my face with shaking fingers. "Hywel!" I sobbed into my pillow. "My poor Hywel. I had no idea of this. I have not set eyes on him for over sixteen years."

Hywel, I always remembered, as by far the gentler of my two brothers.

"Did the Norman who called himself your husband give such small importance to this fact that he had never advised you of it?" my cousin sneered. "It seems also, that the man who held Penbroc from my father, is not the chivalrous knight whom the bards continually extol," he proclaimed with a jeering laugh. "I had counted on that fact last night – that his sense of honour would not allow him to leave you and your children undefended. Had I but killed him, I could have married you in the lawful church of our land and thus, we could have produced a legitimate line of kings, to secure the re-conquest of Wales from the usurping Norman." So although desire had been the original driving force, he had also thought to make political capital out of my abduction.

"But the Norman, my husband, has escaped," I suggested tentatively. "Our heirs, yours and mine, can never now be lawfully able to succeed. I am at best, a mere concubine ..."

My cousin's black brows had met in a thoughtful frown. "I am not sure," he had replied. "The laws of Hywel Dda, our ancestor, reach far and wide, even to within Church law. There may be some way, although the Norman cur still lives. My father's lawyers shall look into the matter for me."

One morning, many weeks later, my cousin abruptly bade me mount my horse and accompany him. Half a dozen armed men rode with us and soon we turned inland, traversing a sheltered valley. At the far end of this peaceful backwater lay a modest priory, the single cell of a solitary priest, who as we approached extended to us a cautious greeting. I could see that this holy man was not entirely at ease, encircled as he was by a group of soldiers, bristling with weapons. "Your name is Caradoc?" my cousin enquired. The monk inclined his head gravely. "And you are a priest?"

"I am sir," the cleric agreed. "And how may I serve you?"

"You may serve me and this lady here," my cousin informed him. "By marrying us at your altar yonder, in all the correct rites of the Celtic Church." I gasped audibly, and at my demur, the monk turned to scrutinize me carefully.

"The lady is not entirely happy?" he suggested respectfully.

"Sir, I am already married," I cried impetuously, "and have many children. I am not at liberty to marry my cousin."

"Nest, be silent!" my cousin ordered angrily. "It is perfectly lawful, your marriage to the Norman was made under duress, and performed by a priest of the Roman Church. You are a Princess of Wales. Our Church, the Celtic Church, does not acknowledge such a marriage as being valid. It is, so my father's advisers assure me, null and void." He swung from his horse and insisted on lifting me down from mine. "Now, Sir Priest," he directed, his manner taking on an element of threat. "I bid you lead us to your altar and let this marriage ceremony commence. My men here will be witness." The priest ignored the veiled threat and spoke directly to me.

"You are the Princess Nesta, daughter of Rhys ap Tewdwr?" I nodded and mutely held my outstretched hand towards him, exposing the band of gold that my husband had placed there. "Sir," he declared bravely to my cousin, "As God is my witness, I may not marry you to this lady. I have heard of your abduction of the Princess Nesta from her husband's hall and I cannot condone this blasphemy, this mockery of the sacrament of marriage." The man stood his ground thereafter, in dignified silence. In a towering rage, my cousin snatched my hand and twisting the ring from it viciously he threw it into the nearest gorse bush.

"The lady is free, my father's men have assured me. Now marry us!" he thundered.

The monk shook his head. "Then your father's advisers have misinformed you, possibly because they knew what you wanted them to say. But I tell you now, that by all the laws which govern me and above all in the eyes of God, this lady is married already and unable to be your wife." Scarcely had he finished speaking than my cousin stepped towards him and felled him with a savage blow. The priest sank to his knees and then rolled over upon his side, as though dead. Blood issued from his nose and mouth, and his already pale face took on a greyish tinge. With an exclamation, I rushed to his side and kneeling beside him I gently raised his head.

"Leave him!" my cousin declared abruptly. "There are many more holy men who will speak the ceremony. Certainly for a little gold they will oblige us."

Some reserve inside me snapped. "I will not leave him," I flared glaring at my cousin. "He is injured, almost to death." I jerked my head in the direction of one of the armed men. "Fetch me water, immediately," I ordered, in a voice which brooked no disobedience. The man moved in the direction of the small stream which ran beside the little priory. My cousin chafed angrily, while I bathed the priest's wounded jaw and splashed water upon his brow. His will had not been crossed in such a way for years, and I could see that he was taking time to decide upon his next move, which I was certain would not be in my favour. The priest opened his eyes and looked at me hazily. "Do you have the Latin, Father?" I enquired softly. He signified, just as quietly, that he did. By now, I was certain that he was fully conscious once more. "Latin is quite incomprehensible to my cousin," I whispered. "Will you please go through a form of service in Latin, but make sure that he does not realize that it is bogus." He looked confused. "It will be safer," I assured him, "for all of us. Please father."

His eyes registered assent. "Tell me child," he asked gently. "Art fond of the husband from whom you have been stolen?"

I bowed my head miserably. "Yes, Father."

"Then God have mercy on you, my child," he prayed. With my help the injured priest got to his feet. "I will marry you to your cousin, Owain, son of Cadwgan," he announced clearly. "But I shall say the service in Latin. I am a scholar, not a parish priest, and as I received a wholly classical education I learned the sacraments only in that language." My cousin walked back to us with a satisfied smile on his face.

"I thought you might feel that way, after you had time to consider the matter. I care not how you say it as long as you get on with it. It must be according to the rites of the Celtic Church mind, and none other."

The priest said, "So be it," and leading us to his church door added, "Only nuptial Mass may be taken at the altar. You will be married here, as is customary." My cousin agreed impatiently. His religious observances were sketchy enough and I knew him to be illiterate. As was usual we went through our ceremony, 'hand in hand at church door'. The priest was superb and although he must have been faint from loss of blood, as a result of the sledge hammer blow on the head, not once did he falter. He began by asking pardon of the Lord for this illegal union. My cousin moved not a muscle. His head was bowed in a reverential manner. It was obvious that he understood not a word, and his henchmen even less. With almost imperceptible alterations of wording and another strong plea from the priest, that there was every reason why we should "not be joined together in holy matrimony", we were ostensibly married.

The priest gave the blessing and we walked with him across the green to the horses. He was still unsteady after his injury and I begged him to go to his couch to rest. "Thank you my child," he said gravely, "but I must pray." His words were so significant that I could feel the unshed tears of many weeks, perilously near as I bade him goodbye. As we rode away, my cousin became far more expansive than I had ever known him and his good humour was in danger of bubbling over. He had got his own way and like a spoilt child was prepared to be pleasant for a short while afterwards. As I watched him, my courage grew within me. For the first time since my abduction I had, with the aid of that honourable, holy man, actually outwitted him over so great a matter that I could have sung for joy.

As we rode back through the village that lay to the south of Castell Cadwgan, we noted a small knot of people gathered around a man who sat on an upturned barrel in the market square. A terrible wailing came from their midst. "It is the Irish pedlar who plays the pipe with the bellows," one of our men at arms volunteered. "He comes through here regularly."

My cousin vaulted down from his horse and helped me to the ground. In his present sunny mood it was a harmless diversion. We stood in the crowd, listening to the Irish pedlar's scanty repertoire. I watched him quietly, wishing that I could escape from this square, and walk all the way back to Penbroc, but my children, left at my uncle's court, were sufficient hostages to make that an impossible thought. My cousin put me up onto my horse and I stretched down to take my bridle from the hands of a helpful bystander. He stood on the opposite side of the animal from my cousin, hidden from his view. A hand came over mine as I gathered up my reins and I immediately looked down to discover the impediment. At that moment, the man turned his head towards me, the hood of his tunic fell back slightly, and I found myself looking down upon the well-known features of Stephen. I closed my eyes and drew a deep breath; when I opened them again quickly, he put a finger swiftly to his lips, urging caution. We moved away and I had wit enough not to look back.

My previous small elation suddenly took flight, blossoming into a gigantic ray of hope. My husband must have sent Stephen here to shadow me, partly because of his experience in dodging hostile groups all over Normandy and because he was the best Welsh speaker amongst the Normans in the whole of the Penbroc garrison. But all such thoughts were rapidly dispersed when we reached the castle, for in the courtyard all was turmoil. My uncle Cadwgan had returned from Powys. I suppose that as a child, I must have met Cadwgan at my father's court, but as it was over twenty years or more ago, I could not recall it. The thing that struck me most was the great difference between Cadwgan and his eldest son. The old warrior had a curiously benign expression beneath the long dark locks liberally streaked with grey. And when his eyes fell upon me I could also note a slightly apologetic air. He was courteous over his greeting and then as if screwing himself up for something unpleasant, he murmured, "My son, I wish to speak with you alone."

His eldest son shrugged and growled: "Very well, if you must," in what was hardly a respectful manner. He then slouched after his father into the hall. They did not even attempt to close any doors, but it would have mattered little if they had, for every word must have been audible all over the castle. The gist of the row between father and son was my abduction.

"If you had to steal someone else's woman," the old man

roared, "did it have to be wife of the strongest Norman magnate in South Wales, the King's servant, the Constable of Penbroc, he who is supreme in Dyfed? This time you have gone too far," the old chieftain warned. "King Henry will not overlook either the violation of the lady, a previous concubine of his and his favourite if truth were told, or the injury to his steward and his steward's property." There were angry snarling replies from his son, who was apparently not impressed by any of his father's arguments.

Eventually my uncle Cadwgan came to speak to me, in a distressed if not apprehensive frame of mind. The King would, he was convinced, take strong action. He, Cadwgan, could well lose his principality over this. He admitted frankly that Owain had been more trouble to him in his short span than any of his other sons, and they were numerous. As he spoke, I caught a glimmer of the charm which had endeared Cadwgan to the considerable number of women who had borne him children. I liked him far more than his predatory eldest son, but realized that his continual wish to please everyone accounted for many of the excesses of his wayward heir. He was just not strong enough a sire to manage so vicious a cub, for the angry scenes did not appear to upset my cousin Owain in the least.

That night, realizing that I should perhaps never get my cousin in so pliable a frame of mind again, I lay beside him and deliberately set out to exert that power which I knew I held over him. The power not only of my body, but also of my personality. I made much of him, and reclining with his head nestled into my shoulder, I stroked his hair, as one would with a favourite child. He sighed with the utmost satisfaction. "No woman I have ever known, has been so perfect for me as you," he admitted.

"Then if you would have me true to you and wish to keep me with you for always, have my children escorted back to their father," I murmured softly. Entwining both arms around his neck I kissed him generously. "Let the children go back to Penbroc," I whispered. "What do you want with these little Normans? You don't even really like children and we can always make some more of our own." He leaned over me ardently.

"Will you? Will you give me an heir, Nest? A son who could one day rule the whole of Wales?"

"I already hold your heir," I said solemnly. "So if you are pleased with me, say you will let my children be escorted safely back to the Constable, their father."

In a rush of emotion, he gave his solemn oath that the children might go. "They may go tomorrow," he declared. "A dozen men may escort them to the main border post of fitz-Richard, the one nearest Penbroc. Their nurse may go also, a hatchet-faced woman whom I shall be relieved to see gone." When he had done with me and fallen into a deep contented sleep, I lay there, going over this remarkable day, step by step. Somehow, it seemed as though the priest in the valley must have had some hand in all this good fortune. We had successfully thwarted my cousin's attempt at bigamy and then miraculously, I had realized that Stephen was near at hand, ready to engineer my escape. I longed to slip down the hall to the place where the children and Branwen slept, to advise them of this wonderful turn of fortune. But I wisely stayed where I was, afraid that I might make a false move and rouse my cousin's ready anger, so that he would prevent the children's journey on the morrow.

Branwen however, was unwilling to leave me and so ultimately was Philippe, until I whispered that I had unexpected friends nearby and they must not fret for me. "Ask papa," I advised Philippe. "I can say no more now." I had kissed the smaller children and seen them mounted, when I realized that Philippe was still standing by his pony, unwilling to move. I went over to him and offered my hand. "Goodbye, Philippe," I said, rather formally.

"What shall I tell my papa?" asked the boy in uneven tones. I knew exactly what he meant. Compulsively, I caught him to me for a brief moment.

"Tell papa ..." I began and then could not continue. "Tell him that I will write him a message," I managed at last. Two weeks later, a cool formal note was handed in at Castell Cadwgan by a travelling musician. It stated briefly that the children of the Constable of Penbroc had arrived safely at their destination and were now in the custody of their father. Its tone was so cold and distant, that I was driven to tears of bitterness and despair.

Once my children had gone, my cousin Owain, feeling that I was bound to him sufficiently by the ties of both matrimony and pregnancy, began to relax his close watch over me. There were whole days when he and his father would go either hunting or hawking and at these times, accompanied by a pair of fearsome looking guards, I often rode as far as the shore. Then, when I had walked it from end to end, I would sometimes loiter in the village market place. I had not caught so much as a glimpse of Stephen since the day we had watched the Irish pedlar play his pipes. Perhaps my husband, having got his children back, no longer wanted their mother, who had brought so much disgrace upon his house? In such dark fits of depression I managed very clearly to lay all the blame for my abduction on my own shoulders. There was a small church in the village square and I began to go into it surreptitiously, to pray for God's succour in my fear and loneliness.

Four days after the letter had come from Penbroc my prayers were answered when I caught sight of a ragged villein, lounging idly against the door of the blacksmith's shop. As I scanned the solitary figure hopefully, he turned to face me with a slow, unobtrusive movement – It was

Stephen! I led my palfrey quietly into the square and threw the reins to one of my guards. "I wish to say Matins at the church yonder," I observed casually. "Take some ale with your fellow, while you wait." The small church was deserted when I entered and going across to the shrine of Our Lady of Sorrows, I lit my frugal taper from the rush dip which burned at her feet. Then, on my knees, I waited anxiously. Within a few minutes I became aware that someone stealthily approached; another taper began to gutter beside mine and another worshipper came to kneel a few feet away from me.

"My lady," he whispered, "we had better converse in Welsh, in case anyone should disturb us."

"Oh Stephen," I breathed. "Where did you go?"

"Back to Penbroc, my lady," he explained. "I was anxious when I saw Branwen and the children departing with such a strong body of armed men. I am surprised that he let them go." His voice held an element of incredulity, and something else that I could not quite place.

"It was not easy to persuade him," I replied slowly, "but when he knew that I carried his child he agreed to let them go back to their father."

"Oh, I see," he murmured, stiff with embarrassment.

"I don't think you do Stephen," I remarked sadly. "But I was determined to use any means whereby I could secure the freedom of my children, so that I might thereafter safely work out my own escape, without putting their lives in peril."

"But if you carry his child, how can you – " he began. I turned on him angrily.

"So you too believe that I contrived my own abduction," I cried bitterly. "Aye, I suppose that you and many others will believe that I wished to suffer both violation and indignity at the hands of my brutish cousin – and that I now rush to bear his child. Only God and Our Lady know what I have been forced to endure, and from Them only may I expect pardon."

"My lady, I beseech you – I did not mean," Stephen's faltering words came to a complete halt. I stood up and took his hands, holding them for a moment before I could reply.

"I really care for the opinion of one person only," I told him, "my husband, and when you disappeared I thought that he too had abandoned me."

"My lady," he assured me, "he has been like a man bereft these many long weeks. I believed that after the children were returned to him things would improve, but they have become steadily worse. His despair has deepened. He wished personally to come in search of you, but Bleddyn eventually persuaded him that he would immediately betray himself as his Welsh is so halting, and so he sent me back here, to seek you out." He looked at me uncertainly. "The King's steward at Shrewsbury has enlisted the support of four Welsh chieftains to sack and plunder the lands of Owain Cadwgan and his father, to avenge this wrong to your husband and the King. They have already entered the south of Ceredigion. We may have great difficulty in getting back through their hosts into Dyfed, as they will not be unduly discriminating. You have only two guards out there; we must try at once to give them the slip. I fear we have lingered long enough." At that moment, I heard voices and heavy footsteps approaching the door.

"That is my cousin Owain," I whispered fearfully. "He comes in search of me. Quick, you must hide!" In seconds, Stephen had melted into the dim interior of the aisled Church. I dropped once again to my knees. The door was roughly thrown open.

"Nest!" my cousin called sharply. "You must come at once. The King's steward has sent Llywarch and many others to drive us into the mountains. They approach rapidly. We must leave with my father at once, as soon as we have emptied and burned the castle.

"Burned it?" I cried, aghast.

"Yes, nothing must be left for them to live on when we have gone. Come now, quickly!" By the time we had ridden the few hundred yards to the castle the first string of pack-horses were ready to move off. Within the hour, the timber and thatch of the main buildings were blazing furiously and we had set out on our long and desperate ride to get ahead of the approaching Welsh hordes. By the time the light began to fade we came to a modest hunting lodge, situated at the confluence of the rivers Mynach and Rheidol. Almost at its door, a gigantic waterfall spilled over rocks, cascading noisily into the valley bottom. The answering roar of an equally voluble torrent made an echoing thunder a few dozen yards downstream.

Cadwgan and my cousin now began a lengthy argument about the safety of the lodge as an overnight halt. I sank down wearily and was relieved beyond belief when they at last ordered the servants to unload a few of the packhorses. A woman, whom I had seen in the kitchens of my uncle's castle, took charge of the arrangments for a meal. Noting my fatigue and weakness, she sat me on a low bench by the cold hearth and rapidly kindled a few sticks on the old embers. "Draw nearer to the blaze, my lady," she begged, with genuine solicitude. "It was too fast a flight for one in such a condition as you." My cousin scowled and called loudly for wine. It soon became obvious how he intended to soften the harshness of his flight. In a very short time the servants managed to produce a good hot meal, and after ravenously eating my fill, I quietly sought the comfort of a pile of sheepskins in a corner where I soon fell into a deep exhausted slumber.

At dawn, I was shaken awake and told by my uncle

Cadwgan that the servants wished to pack the sheepskins on which I lay. I crawled out from them at once, more dead than alive and went to heave up last night's supper outside the lodge on the grass. The woman who had been so kind on the previous evening came over to my side. "You are sick with the child, my lady?" she asked respectfully.

"It is worse than usual," I gasped. "But tend your cooking; I shall be recovered before long." She said nothing, but came back to me seconds later with some bread and mild wine.

"Take these if you can," she suggested, in kindly tones. "I know how it is; I have had five of my own. All grown up long since." I forced down the food realizing that it might be a long time before I was offered anything else. I knew only too well that I must somehow find strength enough to ride with them up into the mountains. Gradually, I began to feel a little better. Cadwgan had just satisfied himself that all the fires were out and all the goods upon pack-horses, when two men, whom he had sent out as advanced guards, burst into the valley, running as fast as their terrified legs would allow them.

"Well?" my cousin rasped. "Why do you run like frightened hares?"

The men fell at his feet. "My lord, not five miles hence, on the eastern slope of the valley bottom, lies a great host; they must have approached on our landward side, from the Wye valley."

"Then we are cut off from the mountains altogether," my cousin cursed.

His father nodded gloomily. "Aye, we shall have to ride towards the coast again, down the valley of the Rheidol and just hope that we are not cut off again by Llywarch, from the south." In two and a half hours we had reached the coast, and running parallel to it we struck north, skirting the large bog that lay between us and the ocean. Suddenly I knew that I could cling to my horse's neck no longer. My wrists and arms refused to hold me, and I swayed in the saddle. Seeing my dire distress, one of my uncle's guards caught me just as I felt the singing and surging in my head that signalled complete loss of consciousness.

When I woke it was dark. I seemed to be in some kind of hut, or perhaps a small cottage. As I looked about me I recognized the woman who had tended me so generously at the hunting lodge. As soon as I moved she came over to my side to offer a drink – it was warm mulled ale. She allowed me to consume it all before offering some broth upon a spoon. When a little of the warm food had penetrated my spent frame I weakly asked where I lay. "In a village on the banks of the Dyfi, my lady," she answered quietly. "This is my sister's cottage. When Cadwgan packed his goods to travel northwards I was glad, because I was coming home."

"My uncle Cadwgan and my cousin – " I raised myself on an elbow. "Where are they?" I asked, "and how did I get here?"

"You got here over the back of a horse, my lady," the woman replied indignantly. "I told them both, Cadwgan and that spoilt puppy of his, that it was no way to treat a lady, a Princess of Wales and the daughter of Rhys ap Tewdwr. But they were so afraid for their own skins, that to get this far they just draped you over a horse and rode onwards. In the end they decided that they could not take you, ill as you were, all that way."

"Take me where?" I demanded. "Where are my uncle and my cousin?"

"Cadwgan and his cub are out in the estuary, on an Irish galley, a merchant ship that called in two days ago to discharge merchandise. It sails tonight on the high tide for Ireland. Your cousin will sail in her to exile at the Irish court. They plan to put Cadwgan off in a boat onto the northern shore before they leave the river mouth. He means to travel overland, to stay in Powys. The King's wrath was too much for them." She pursed her lips in disgust.

So, my uncle Cadwgan and my cousin Owain had eventually abandoned me in a strange place, with a woman I hardly knew, almost one hundred miles from my home. With a strength born of desperation I sat up on the couch. A slight sound reached my ears from the open doorway.

As the man who stood there threw back the hood of his cloak and I recognized him, two tears of relief crept from beneath my eyelids and began to course slowly down my cheeks. "Oh, Stephen," I said unsteadily. "My uncle and my cousin have gone away to Ireland. Do you think that you could possibly escort me home?"

"I think so, my lady," he promised. "If you feel better in the morning."

Almost before his words were uttered, a strange woman flung herself in through the open doorway. "What shall we do, Oh sister? What shall we do?" she wailed dismally. "They who pursue Cadwgan come in a large host, with many horsemen."

Stephen lifted me gently into his arms. "Do you have a good safe place where you hide in times of danger?" he asked the two women.

"The cave on the shore!" they cried. Rapidly they scuttled across the roadway that ran before the house, and parting the bushes led us onto the river bank. The cave was little more than a fissure in the rocks that lined this side of the estuary, but it was well covered with gorse and scrub. Together the four of us crouched quietly against the damp rock, with the twigs of the wind-swept, winter-shorn bushes pulled right across to conceal the entrance. Stephen added a rapidly gathered armful of dead grass and brown furled bracken to fill in the obvious gaps and then with ears straining we waited anxiously. There was the sound of a large number of men and horses, as the oncoming host

tracked back and fore, searching the surrounding woodland. After much shouting and calling, several horsemen
burst through the scrub and rode along the gravelled shore,
hard by our refuge. We held our breath – Mercifully, they
moved away. Later, one called to another, that they had
found a cob, tied up by the cabin yonder. Stephen stifled an
exclamation of dismay.

At last, as the sound of hoofbeats receded in a southerly
direction, we saw a dull red glow glimmer and then grow
brighter, from the direction of the cottage. Bidding us stay,
Stephen crept out of our midst and silently moved away.
After a considerable time he re-appeared. "They fired the
roof," he whispered, "but I managed to quell the blaze
without much harm being done. You have lost some thatch
and there is one charred beam, that is all. But quiet now,
there may be stragglers." He had brought back some goat
skins from the cottage and we wrapped ourselves in them
for extra warmth. A few hours later we crawled stiffly out of
our hole and made our way back to the cottage.

The two sisters rapidly set the basic services of the
cottage to rights. Wrapped in a sheepskin, Stephen kept
watch, while we three women rested but although there
were no more alarms that night, we slept only fitfully. It
was not until we had eaten a frugal breakfast however, that
Stephen broke the news that his horse had been stolen by
the army searching for Cadwgan and that somehow, we
should have to make our journey south on foot. Before we
left the cottage, I slid Owain Cadwgan's elaborately twisted
gold wire 'wedding ring' from my finger and gave it to the
women who had succoured me so generously.

At first our journey progressed in relative quietness but
the searching hosts had left a trail of desolation and ashes in
their wake. There were many deserted, burned out hamlets,
and the people either seemed to have fled the area, or gone
into hiding. Stephen's plan was to gain the Sanctuary of

Padarn, which lay about twelve miles to the south, but we did not get within four miles of it by nightfall. In a burned out farmstead we discovered a partially gutted shed. Stephen sat up protectively, for a second night, between me and the menacing dark. We began the next short leg of our journey as soon as I felt able to walk and reached the Sanctuary of Padarn, as the brothers were about to eat their midday dinner. The monks were characteristically hospitable, placing us in separate wings of their guest house to rest and providing us with a meal and water with which we might wash.

The Prior promised to provide us with food and a donkey, that we might journey on in greater comfort on the morrow. Feeling secure, I slept for much of the afternoon, endeavouring to gain strength for the supreme effort I knew that we should need to make to regain the safety of Penbroc. Eventually, my sleep became more troubled. I felt, as I tossed and turned, that I was back once again at Cenarth Bychan. I could smell the fire about the buildings and the shouting of the attackers around the courtyard. Willing myself to come fully awake, to cut myself off from this awful nightmare, I made myself sit up on my narrow couch. As I shook the sleep from my eyelids, I realized with utter horror, that there was in fact, an attack being launched even upon that holy place – the Sanctuary of Padarn. I rushed out of the cell, into the open cloister. Knowing where Stephen lay, I threw open the door of his minute chamber and going to his bedside, shook him violently.

"Stephen, wake! Oh pray wake up!" I cried frantically. "I fear that Llan Padarn is under attack."

In a minute he had leapt to his feet and secured the short dagger which stayed by him as he slept. "Come!" he urged. "To the Inner Sanctuary."

We reached the chapel door as the large courtyard gates

were broken open. The Prior waved us through to the place
where the casket of relics lay, behind the metal grille. Two
wrought metal doors protected the small chamber. A
number of monks pushed after us into this holy of holies,
and I was jammed against the far wall. As the Prior called
for the protection of God and Padarn a number of hostile
armed men forced a way through the main doors of the
chapel and confronted him. "Stay!" he called, in
resounding tones. "No one shall violate the shrines of the
blessed Saints. Stay your hands and drop your weapons.
Pray with me, my brothers." Beneath the elbows of the
monks who jostled me in the Inner Sanctuary, I could see
the first soldier check, and halt his stride, uncertain of what
to do. Behind him however strode a giant with a red beard.

"A plague on your shrine, Holy Man," he declared, and
with a single blow from his flat sword, he cut the Prior
down where he stood. A great moan went up from the
assembled monks. I could feel myself sway, but was so
hemmed in, that I could not fall. As the red bearded
warrior stepped over his victim and advanced towards us,
there was a sudden parting of the ranks behind him and a
voice thundered.

"Hold, you devils, before I kill you all, you murderers of
monks!" There was an awesome hush and the red haired
assassin, paused, as if carved in stone, his arm raised, ready
to strike again. "When did the war band of Uchdryd ever
harry and kill innocent men of God?" the newcomer
demanded. "Seize that fellow." He pointed an avenging
sword at the cringing demon who had struck down the
Prior. Willing hands secured him. "Until I come to
judgement," the chief vowed, "I shall regret with abject
shame, the violation and massacre my men have caused in
this sacred place. My penance will be great." He indicated
the man who had killed the Prior. "This soldier shall be
duly punished, but outside these walls." In silence, the war

band of Uchdryd then withdrew, dragging the red bearded barbarian with them. As the monks crept, one by one from their Sanctuary, I sank to my knees beside the body of the dead priest.

"I killed him," I murmured, turning my face away from the crucifix that the Prior held clenched in his lifeless fingers. "It was I who caused the death of this innocent man." Stephen put a compassionate hand on my shoulder.

"Come away my lady, come to rest I pray you, while I help them bury their dead," he said sadly. When we left the Sanctuary some four days later, I followed Stephen slowly, for part of me had died also. I was later told that he had travelled southwards with me for five more days. After an eternity, we arrived at the border post twelve miles south-east of Cenarth Bychan. It was a wooden tower on a motte, surrounded by a single pallisade. When bidden, I lay down obediently on the heap of straw in the corner of the guard-room to rest. The officer in charge had a woman who lived with him. She tended me with a strange solicitude.

"Take the fastest horse here and ride for Penbroc," she directed Stephen. "You may do it in a day if you make haste. This lady, your master's wife, can be moved no further until you obtain a litter." I heard Stephen's muttered reply and then significant words which reached through to the last vestiges of my remaining consciousness. "She begins to bleed," she declared soberly.

Some time later, through the mists which surrounded me, I thought I heard my husband's voice. The words he spoke penetrated that deep darkness into which I had descended. At first, I thought he called my name and I tried to raise myself, to go to him. Then his voice came with such vehemence that it made me recoil. "I swear that I shall kill Owain Cadwgan with my own hands, before I die – so help me God," he declared – And then I heard Stephen's quiet remonstrance.

"Sir, you must not, I beg of you. Cannot you see that she stirs at your voice?" Then the mists swirled in on me once more, and there was nothing – .

For some long time I had been aware of muted voices and many people coming and going around me. Sometimes I thought that I had seen the face of my husband, grey and grave, looking down upon me from a long way off. That had been after the storm at sea, in which I had tossed in a frail craft for long hours, certain that the craft would sink and that I would drown. The people about me were noisy, when all I longed for was peace. One insisted that I drink, more and more, when all I needed was to sleep. I heard someone say that they were pleased, that there was hope. And then at last I fell asleep into a deep refreshing slumber that I had craved for so long and been denied. When I woke again, I could see that I was back in my own room, off the Western Hall at Penbroc. Branwen was there, she turned as I stirred. "Oh," I murmured weakly, "I thought it was you, Branwen. Why have you been making me drink the most horrible syrups when I did not want to?"

She came over to my side and put her hand on my brow. "Cool," she said and her voice was pleased. "You are cool at last. Thanks be to God."

"Branwen?" I asked, "What has happened. Why are you so pleased?"

"My heart is singing because you are better," my maid replied simply, raising me gently and offering me some concoction to drink from a small horn.

"It was this, that I hated so. Why do you offer it to me?" I asked peevishly.

"The surgeon made it up for you himself, and it has kept you alive for many weeks. Do not scorn it so, my lady," she chided.

"Have I then, been so ill?" I asked, lying back on my pillows.

"Well, you have never miscarried before," she replied cautiously. "It does weaken a woman, far more than a birth."

"Miscarried?" With a sudden, fierce rush of joy, I realized that my prayers had indeed been answered. "My cousin Owain's child?" I queried. "I no longer have to bear it?"

Branwen shook her head. "It has gone, but the loss of it nearly cost you – " she drew her lips together closely and began to fold some linen that did not require folding.

"You mean, that it nearly cost me my life," I said clearly. "But now I know that I am free of his child I shall recover miraculously," I promised, with a great surge of well-being lifting my heart. "Have you nothing more appetizing for me to consume than the surgeon's life-giving syrup?" I asked petulantly. "I am hungry."

I could not have pleased her more. Going to the door she called for a messenger. "Bring the venison liver broth," she directed, "and hurry, the Princess Nesta is famished." Although it sounded revolting the broth, of which I consumed half a dozen spoonfuls, was well flavoured. News travelled fast at Penbroc and it was not long before Philippe's face appeared around the door. He crept in cautiously. I opened my eyes and held out a hand towards him. He took it and I could see that he struggled to hold back the tears.

"It is good to see you, my son," I confided, in low tones. "So good to see old friends."

"Do you still wish to have me as a friend, mama?" he asked unsteadily.

"Yes," I said quietly. "I always did."

"I was not angry with you, at Castell Cadwgan," he

explained with a heightened colour. "It was life, which made me so angry, because it had trapped us all in such a terrible situation. But mostly, I was angry for your sake," he admitted. "For I was powerless to help you. When we returned here, Papa tried to explain everything to me. I think that he was afraid that I might not understand – But I did." He looked at me with beseeching eyes. "Papa is very hurt," he hesitated – "Will you talk to him for me?" he asked.

"Yes," I said, in choked accents. "I will talk to Papa as soon as I feel strong enough, I promise you." Branwen shooed him away after this, and I slept comfortably for a few hours. When I next awoke, the candles were lit, for it was dusk. "One of the most awful things about the journey back from the Dyfi," I announced dreamily, "was the extreme cold." I stretched luxuriously beneath the bedcovers. "Now, I am so warm, that I feel wickedly indulged." To my dismay, Branwen looked acutely embarrassed.

"My lady," she murmured. "The Constable, your husband – " The moment I had been dreading and yet longing for had arrived, without my even realizing it. My husband came slowly towards the bed.

"Nest," he said hoarsely, taking my hand in his and gripping it tightly. "It is as they have told me. In one single day, you have begun to make a remarkable recovery." Rapidly, I scanned his face. With a pang, I noted that deep furrows had become etched around his mouth and across his brow. He had lost a great deal of weight and many grey hairs were now visible. Our eyes met fleetingly, but the shutters had been lowered on his emotions so effectively, that I removed my gaze at once. I could sense the tension, even in his finger tips. It was obvious that neither of us was equal to a true analysis of our feelings at that precise moment. He remained a few minutes longer, then with a courteous, but somewhat reserved gesture, he left the chamber.

As the door closed I began to weep convulsively. Huge uncontrollable sobs wracked my poor weak frame and the tears slid down onto the sheet beneath my chin with alarming regularity. With an exclamation, Branwen came to my side. "There now," she crooned, sponging my face with a cool wet cloth. "It is difficult for the master, so fraught with anxiety has he been until today. He sat with you for days and nights on end when you were at the worst and I'll swear, that if he had lost you then, he would have killed himself. Don't weep so, my lady, for you are not fit to tax yourself thus. There now, take this and rest." She gave me something bitter to drink from a horn, and I rapidly returned to sleep.

As I began to eat again, so my strength grew proportionately and this, with Branwen's expert care and attention, speeded my recovery. The other children came to peer at me, nervously, at first and then, as they relaxed, they began to bring their games and problems to me, as they had always done. The youngest two crawled all over my bed, despite Branwen's protests and the family, on the surface at least, appeared to have swiftly returned, to a state of the utmost normality. But there was now a visible barrier between myself and my husband, that I did not initially have the strength to overcome. He would come to sit quietly by my side for short periods, but the reserve which I had noted at our first meeting became increasingly evident as my health improved. It seemed as though we, who had always had so much to say to one another, had now lost the art of conversation and the secret of companionship.

I became tortured by doubts, fearing that like others, he secretly believed that I had contrived my own abduction. And yet by proxy he continued to shower attentions upon me, and so I was constantly reminded of his presence. He

would send Philippe with armfuls of fresh spring flowers to
brighten my chamber, when I longed for him to bring them
to me himself. I remarked to Philippe rather sadly one day,
that I wondered why Papa could not bring his own flowers,
if he wished me to have them, but the boy looked so
troubled that in future I kept such observations strictly to
myself. Within a few weeks, I was able to walk about slowly
in the warm spring sunshine, and as soon as I showed
myself outside my chamber door I was dragged by my
enthusiastic children to see the wonderful surprise that
Papa had made for me. In my favourite angle of the courtyard, that had previously held my seat which overlooked
the mill, my husband had fashioned for me the most
beautiful little garden. One of the Flemings, a stone mason
of great skill, had paved and walled the small area, leaving
beds and shelves of rock for flowers. The picture was
tastefully finished with a wrought iron walking gate and a
seat with the finest possible view of the river. It was
sheltered and private and the whole, when I first saw it, was
already a riot of purple and yellow blossoms. The colourful
sweet smelling flowers and fragrant herbs generously filled
in the spaces left for them, between the stones.

"Papa planted them all by himself," the children cried
proudly. "Many were brought from the farthest ends of the
Manor, just for you. Isn't it lovely?" I nodded, quite overcome. "Then if you like it," they declared, "why do you
weep?" I sat down rather unsteadily on the carved seat.

"I suppose," I replied slowly, "it must be because I am
still not quite recovered from my long illness." Bleddyn
fortunately appeared at the little gate at that precise
moment, and craved admittance to paradise.

"A garden fit for a Princess," the bard declared. "A
fitting tribute from a grateful knight to his beloved lady."
The children eventually skipped off on important errands of
their own, and Bleddyn talked on in his soothing melodious

tones, of the various herbs and their magical properties. At last, because I just had to talk to someone, I remarked that I could not understand why a knight should shower his lady with gifts, when he so obviously believed that she had brought shame and dishonour upon his house. "You mean, Princess, that you do not understand why a knight should fashion so beautiful a thing, so mute a tribute of his regard as this garden, for a lady whom he so persistently avoids?"

"Yes," I answered softly. "You, Bleddyn, who understand everything, can you tell me why that should be so?"

"He may feel that he cannot bear the terrible shame of a man who knows only too well, that he abandoned his wife and children to a murdering rapist, to save his own skin," Bleddyn answered sadly.

"But he did not!" I protested brokenly. "He would never have done so willingly. He was about to go out to certain death. It was I who engineered his escape, for I could not bear him to be cut down with no possible chance. They bayed for his blood like hounds at the chase." I shuddered and drew my mantle closer about my shoulders. "Think you then that he does not care to meet me for this reason?" I asked the bard earnestly.

The blind harper inclined his head. "And jealousy of a sort, there may be also. But his infirmity is mainly that of a man who never having been guilty before of a cowardly act, now feels that he has committed an unforgivable one."

"What am I to do?" I enquired anxiously. Bleddyn considered carefully.

"Wait, I think my lady. Time the healer, may, God willing, enable him eventually to live with his conscience. Until he does that, he will never be able to live with you."

In order to pass the time, I began to ride in the surrounding mellow, well-cultivated countryside with Bleddyn and Philippe. It was a peaceful landscape, compared with the war-torn regions of the north. As time went on however, the estrangement with my husband seemed to grow even wider, and by early June my anguish over the matter grew daily. Gerald gave me no opportunity to discuss our problems openly and it seemed as though my cousin's evil interference in our marriage over five months before, had caused the kind of damage which could never be repaired. Bleddyn startled me one afternoon by his blunt exposure of my problems.

"Although I cannot see your faces," he began emphatically, as we sat together in the garden, "I can no longer bear this silent torture to which you subject one another. If this situation goes on for much longer it will destroy both of you."

"But Bleddyn, what can I do?" I moaned. "He will not speak of it to me."

"Then you must speak to him," he replied sternly. "First, however, I must tell you of some matter about which I feel you should know." In frank matter of fact tones, he began to unfold to me the most startling story – the whole tragic story of his life. I immediately discovered him to be a kinsman. By birth, he was a son of one of Cadwgan's brothers, an ap Bleddyn and as a youth he had excelled in all the physical accomplishments of swordplay and horse-manship. As was usual in our times, he had been placed in fosterage with Cadwgan, his uncle, to be trained in the arts of war as a youth should be. His looks, for he favoured his father, Cadwgan's favourite brother, his superiority in the field and his musical talents, had made him a ready favourite with Cadwgan and he was, he admitted with a wry smile, present on the Welsh side, at the siege of Penbroc in 1096. As Owain, Cadwgan's eldest son grew up, he became increasingly jealous of Bleddyn and eventually his hostility burst forth without restraint. Choosing a time when his father was away campaigning in the north, he accused Bleddyn of treachery against Cadwgan, and by using false witnesses, he achieved a swift judgement against him.

Bleddyn's voice did not falter as he related the punishment which Owain had personally meted out to him. "Taking me outside the castle bounds, he blinded me and deprived me of my manhood," he stated sombrely. "And then, having subjected me to a fate far more cruel than death could ever have been, he left me to starve by the roadside. For many weeks I staggered from village to village, barely sustaining life with the fragments of food I was able to beg." As his tragic tale unfolded, I found myself sobbing silently.

"Without realizing it," he went on, "I had gradually worked my way southwards. One day, as I lay weak and without hope by the roadside, a group of Normans approached on horseback. I expected them either to finish me off with a spear or at least to kick me out of their way. Instead, a young man, the knight in charge of the party, got down from his horse and came to kneel beside me. What answers I gave to his questions I know not but he lifted me gently in his arms and took me back to his castle on a packhorse." Bleddyn raised his blind eyes to my face. "That castle was Penbroc, the knight, your husband."

He leant towards me, speaking with considerable emotion. "Do you believe that Owain Cadwgan would have killed your husband that night, when he came to Cenarth Bychan, with the sole purpose of possessing you? No, for Owain, devil that he is, would never have been so merciful towards one to whom he bore so much envy." I cried out in distress, but Bleddyn was determined to drive his message home. "Your husband was saved by you, my lady, from a much harsher fate than either you or he could contemplate. Go now, and tell him so."

A faint sound of boot leather scraping stone swung my eyes from the harper to the figure of the man who stood in the gateway of the garden where we talked. Bleddyn, sensing his presence, cried: "Tell him now! Tell him everything!" And then with remarkable agility, he rapidly left the garden. How much of our conversation my husband had overheard I could not tell but composing myself, I addressed him.

"Sir," I implored. "I must speak with you!" He came to lean impassively upon the parapet, from where he viewed the westering sun as it gently gilded the Penbroc river. I paused, frantically searching my mind for the right words.

"You are now thank God, completely recovered from your sickness," he remarked with stiff courtesy. "If you have need of anything, Stephen and Branwen must furnish you with it."

I inclined my head. "I am indeed well, I thank you, sir, and my recovery is virtually complete, but I fear that neither Stephen nor Branwen could furnish me with that which my heart most desires." I was aware of a deep flush which instantly mounted his cheek.

"Do you really miss your cousin's company that much," he rasped harshly. I was bitterly conscious of the fact that in hurting me he scourged himself.

"If you mean my cousin, Owain Cadwgan, you must have a sadly distorted picture of his character," I replied, as evenly as my jerky pulse would allow. "I fear that men have no means by which they can comprehend the position of a woman placed as I was that night, at Cenarth Bychan. If I had resisted my cousin too strongly at the outset it would have placed my children's lives in instant jeopardy, and in a spate of vicious anger, he would almost certainly have sent armed men into the woodland to hunt you down also. It was only by complying with his wishes that I could in any way protect those whom I most loved." I was stirred to sudden anger by his curiously silent figure. "Never in your life have you had to subject your body as I subjected mine that night, to the abuse of its most sacred function. Men make love to whom they choose, when they choose, but a woman seldom enjoys such a privilege. It is useless to expect you to understand the feeling of revulsion which I experienced on that night, and all the others on which I was forced to share a bed with my brutish cousin." I drew a deep breath in an attempt to exert control over my shaking frame. "I, who had previously experienced the skill and consideration of a lover who — " I could not complete the sentence.

My husband's voice was low and full of emotion also. "I ask your pardon. My remark was as unforgivable as my cowardly behaviour which left you alone that night to combat such a situation."

"Do you consider," I cried, "that I should have been better equipped to combat such a situation with your dead body lying in the corner while he took me?" I steeled myself in order that I, as well as he, might face the truth. "Or even worse, with your blinded and mutilated body, sobbing in agony in the courtyard?" He swore profoundly, and I was amazed at the depth and feeling of his cursing in which Bleddyn featured prominently. "Bleddyn has more wisdom in his heart, than you will ever know," I wept, the tears coursing unchecked down my face. "Why do you think, that I was able to survive that nightmare journey home? Why do you think I fought so unreasonably for life, after you had brought me back here to die? Bleddyn knows, but you apparently do not. The one thing that sustained me was the knowledge that you had escaped from Cenarth Bychan that night, alive. Because on the night that my cousin Owain abducted me, I realized that I loved you, and if you had been dead, I should have had no reason to go on living."

Blindly, I fled across the courtyard, through the amazed and gaping throng who were gathered in the hall awaiting their supper, and gaining my chamber, I slammed and barred the door. Flinging myself upon my couch I wept as though my heart would break. Branwen came immediately to my side, but I refused all comfort. "It is nothing – nothing," I sobbed.

"For someone who has nothing at all wrong with them, you weep somewhat woefully," Branwen responded. She had however the tact to allow me to compose myself, and then she assisted me with washing, finishing by brushing out my long hair with soothing strokes. She carried me in some supper on a salver, but I left it untasted where it stood. "The master," she observed quietly, "also seems disinclined for food, for he has missed supper entirely, and ridden off in the direction of the Priory."

Many hours later, my husband came to my chamber door. He courteously requested privacy and Branwen left us hurriedly. "There is something that I must tell you," he declared in a strained manner, "for many years ago, when we entered our Pax and began to live together as husband and wife, I was not entirely honest with you."

"I feel sir, that I am too weary tonight to listen to a recitation of your infidelities," I managed, fearful of what he would say.

"There have been no infidelities," he answered in a low voice. "You see, Princess, from the moment that you rode into the courtyard here at Penbroc there have been no other women in my life. The spell which you cast over me then was such that I would never even have noticed them, had they prostrated themselves before me." I faced him with growing wonder. "My confession," he stated, "is that on the night we made our Pax, I did not dare to tell you of my love, for fear of frightening you, but now that you have told me – "

His reaction to my glance, to my utter consternation, was an anguished groan. "No, Nest, do not look at me like that,

I beg of you, for it is of no avail." He stepped backwards, away from me. "Why, all these last long weary hours I have been at prayer, in Monkton Chapel, attempting to reconcile myself — "

"What are you trying to tell me?" I gasped. "What ails you?"

"Cannot you see," he cried desperately, "that we can no longer live together, you and I. I love you too much to let you risk your life with another child. You have recently been so ill when you miscarried. I dare not let you risk yourself thus, again." His voice broke and the look in his eyes was such that I could not bear.

I crossed the room to him with great urgency. "But you do not understand," I cried. "There were many, very obvious reasons why I lost my cousin Owain's child. The vicissitudes of that harrowing journey in mid-winter, and on foot, would have slain many less strong than I. And in that condition, I became more and more vulnerable as the marauding hosts cut off one escape route after another." I threw my head back defiantly, and stated in terms of great clarity. "I was also quite determined that I should never allow that child to be born alive, imposed upon me as it was against my will. For I could not give it birth and forever after witness that living testimony to my shame." My eyes sought his and it became clear to me that it would take more resolution than he possessed at that moment, to resist what I hoped was a particularly potent plea. "With you to love and protect me, I shall not die," I told him, "but bear your sons joyfully."

Passionately, he drew me into the circle of his welcoming arms, and as the full impact of my words imprinted themselves upon his soul, he relaxed with a long, shuddering sigh. "Thank you Princess," he murmured unsteadily. "I shall cherish all that you have said, very close to my heart." The constricting emotional and physical restraints, which had shackled us both for so long, suddenly dissolved away. And the thanksgiving which re-united us both that night made precious restitution for the many abuses and abrasions which my mind and body had suffered at the hands of my perfidious cousin.

PART IV

A faint sound penetrated my consciousness fairly early next morning. Slowly, I opened my eyes. My husband stood beside the large oak chest, quietly completing his dressing. The warm early June sunshine, which filtered through the half opened shutters, bathed the room in a golden glow, which gave exact expression to my mood. Outside on the rampart wall a blackbird sang for sheer joy, of the morning. As soon as Gerald realized that I had awakened, he came over to my side. "I had hoped not to disturb you quite so early," he said softly, "but I have to go to inspect the guard and sit in at a court." I lay there savouring every detail as he deftly secured his girdle. Our reconciliation had wrought a stupendous transformation in him, erasing the taut lines around his mouth and relaxing him so that he no longer looked grim, but tremendously happy. He looked down at me with a humorous, half questioning smile that I found particularly moving.

"If you go out into the courtyard looking like that," I warned lightly, "everyone without exception, will know what you have been doing!"

He laughed, apparently delighted by my frankness. "I care not what they know," he declared, coming to kneel close beside me. "Do you mind if our love is visible for all to see?" he asked, with a hint of the old wistfulness. I shook my head.

"Nest," he murmured, pushing the hair back from my forehead and outlining my features with a gentle forefinger. "In what miraculous way did you come to me and what have I done, to deserve such an exquisite love as this?"

"The King sent me to you," I reminded him. "He chose you because he wished me out of his way, and you happened to live in one of the furthermost parts of his kingdom. And you cannot pretend, sir," I chided, "that you were in any way more enamoured of the situation at the outset, than I was."

"That only goes to show how little you appreciate your own beauty, or the power and fire of your personality," he rejoined. "I was less than overjoyed by the prospect of your arrival here, but once you had entered the Western Hall I was completely overcome. It was like being suddenly confronted by the brightest constellation in God's firmament. I was thereafter very hard pressed to retain my dignity and the coolness that you expected of me."

"I do not believe any of it," I replied, capturing his hand for a moment and holding it to my lips. "You behaved at that time for all the world as if I had been some irritating foreign body introduced into your neat and tidy world, with the sole purpose of upsetting it."

He leaned over to kiss me, in a way which made both of us forget that he had work to do.

"My heart persuades me to stay, but duty, the dullard, calls me away." He sighed regretfully, and then reluctantly got to his feet. "I will send Branwen to you anon, with food and wine," he promised. He engaged me with his most persuasive expression. "When I have finished my tasks, would you care to ride out around the manor bounds with me? We have not done so together for many months and it would please me greatly."

I agreed, readily, and after he had gone I lay back upon my pillows with a sigh, letting my new found sense of tranquillity and well-being wash over me like warm refreshing rain. The blackbird, as though inspired by my good fortune, sang an even more passionate refrain. It was useless for me now to pretend that I had not been deeply in love with my husband for many years, but it had required the brutal shock of my abduction to make me fully aware of it. When Branwen arrived at length with my breakfast, she was openly pleased with the turn that events had taken. It was evident that my reconciliation with the man towards whom she had once borne such antipathy, now met with her full approval. Of late, she had fallen into the habit of referring to "the master", in generous terms. She cast me a sideways glance as she began unasked, to prepare me a bath. "The master looks ten years younger this morning," she ventured boldly. "I have not seen him look so well since the days before Master William was born." I allowed her to chatter on uninterrupted, as she poured first hot and then cold water into the stone tub. My mind still dwelt in the private world which I shared with but one other – my husband. I was jerked out of this tranquil musing by a chance remark of Branwen's. "Thanks be to God," she asserted fervently, "that that just man, Walter of Gloucester, prevented him in time. It would not have been seemly for the master to have returned to you with the blood of so many innocent people upon his hands." Horrified, I rose rapidly from my couch.

"The blood of whom on his hands?" I demanded.

Branwen dropped her eyes. "The poor people of Ceredigion. Those who fled southwards when the Bishop of London sent the hosts of Llywarch and others to wreak vengeance on Cadwgan and that black hearted puppy of his, Owain."

"Because of my abduction?" I asked, in shaken tones.

Branwen nodded assent. "Cadwgan's people fled in many directions, but most of them escaped southwards into

Dyfed." She scanned my face anxiously. "You must not judge your husband too harshly, my lady. He was a man driven mad by anxiety and despair."

"But he decided to kill all those who fled into Dyfed?" I asked with great agitation. As if the poor folk of Ceredigion had not suffered enough for the sins of their chieftain's eldest son.

"But he did not, I swear to you," Branwen cried, frightened by the look on my face. "Walter, the High Sheriff, was in Carmarthen town at that time. When he heard that the Constable of Penbroc was minded to put Cadwgan's people to death, he met the master at Whitland, and there he persuaded him to spare them all." She eyed me apprehensively. "My idle tongue has distressed you, I fear my lady. I forgot that you did not know of it." I signified that I would bathe, the which I accomplished rapidly, engrossed the while with this new knowledge. How many times, I wondered, was Walter of Gloucester to act as my guardian angel? Perhaps though, it was right and just that I should realize even today, that the man I loved so profoundly was capable of so much human frailty that he could contemplate the massacre of hundreds of innocent people to revenge himself for the theft of my person.

Branwen helped me to dress and I submitted soberly, as she clad me in my most becoming attire. An hour or so later, when with quick and purposeful step my husband came in search of me, I was calm once again and outwardly serene.

"Come!" he directed, leading me out into the sunlit courtyard towards our waiting horses. "The day is far too beautiful to waste it by loitering within doors." With able hands he lifted me into my saddle. We rode slowly away from the castle, splashing through the stream to gain the gravel strand on the Monkton shore.

An hour later, as we rode around the sheltered southernmost tip of the Manor of Penbroc, we came across a small farmstead, half hidden in a minute valley. As we rounded a corner of the sunfilled courtyard which enclosed the cottage on three sides, I drew in my breath in wonder. Running the entire length of a drystone wall, was a riot of pale yellow blossom, which cast its delicate perfume freely into the summer air. Bees drowsily mumbled their appreciation of this bountiful feast. "Roses!" I cried with delight. "And such an abundance of them as I have never seen before."

"I thought that you would like them," he remarked in satisfied tones, "that is why we rode this way today. That bush is one of the most spectacular sights hereabouts." He got down from his horse to pluck a blossom from the bush to present to me. As he straightened up, with his prize held in his hand for all to see, a young woman in peasant dress with an infant slung upon one hip, came quietly around the corner of the small cottage. She said nothing when she saw the larceny which had taken place with regard to her rose bush, and seemed afraid to chide us for our theft. Gerald made her a courteous inclination and apologized with great gallantry for stealing from her garden. He only desired the one rose he explained, just one alone, to give to his wife as they were so beautiful.

The girl gave me a long searching scrutiny. I smiled at her cautiously. At last, as if mollified, she sank before me in a long and generous curtsey. She removed her gaze to Gerald and at length asked if he were not Constable of Penbroc Castle. Gerald agreed that indeed he was and that he had ridden this way many times before. The girl then addressed me, asking if I was that lady, the Princess Nesta, who had been carried off and who had returned to Penbroc mortally ill. I nodded soberly. Upon receiving this affirmative, the girl approached the rosebush and rapidly picked a generous armful of the fragile yellow blossoms. These, she handed with supreme gravity to my husband, who was considerably nonplussed. "I did not recognize you, sir," she observed solemnly. "For the gentleman who rode this way before was a grim man, full of sorrows. Your lady deserves these few flowers for she has wrought such a change in your eyes as I have never seen the like of in a man before."

To cover Gerald's extreme confusion, I thanked her kindly for her gesture, and enquired after the robust infant in her arms. "Would that his mother was as well as this child," the girl remarked. At my raised brow, she explained that she herself had only been married for a few months, to a Fleming. A good enough fellow, most industrious and worthy. From which, I gathered that she cared for him but little. This child, she explained, was her sister's son, and her sister had been forced to flee southwards, when the three hosts had recently ravaged Ceredigion. "My sister's man was killed by the host of Llywarch," she explained, "and so, after she knew that it was safe to come, my sister found her way here to me."

"Are you from the north, also?" I enquired in my own tongue. Suddenly, the girl's face became alive, and in Welsh she rattled off a quick animated resumé of her past. She was from my own country of Deheubarth, she confided, but from a long way farther to the north. Her sister had been so ill when she had arrived in the Manor of Penbroc, with her bad chest and deep harrowing cough, that the child she held was like to be left an orphan ere long. But the Fleming, her husband, was a good man, who would allow her to rear her sister's child along with any she might have of her own at a later date. My husband, sensing her unease, assured her in passable Welsh that he was sorry to hear of her misfortune. He declared that he would send the castle surgeon to look at her sister – if she so wished. She backed away, protesting that they could never find the means to pay him.

"You have paid in full, already," Gerald assured her, "with these roses. When autumn comes and the blooms have faded, you may send my wife a cutting of this wonderful tree of yours for her new flower garden. Meanwhile, we will do all in our power to save your sister, if that is possible. The castle surgeon has many skills." Overcome, she then vowed that we could have as many cuttings of the bush as we wished, and with this promise ringing in our ears, we slowly rode away. We rode in silence for a while, and then as we approached the castle bounds, my husband outlined a plan he had for a new building to be placed within the courtyard. The time had come, he felt, to build a chapel of our own, to serve our family and all who lived within the confines of the castle.

"I particularly," he declared, "need somewhere where I may occasionally express my thanks. For you – and for other, more sombre things." He looked at me closely, and all the joy of the morning had suddenly gone from his eyes. "You know why, don't you, Princess?" he observed soberly. "I could tell immediately from your expression, when that girl showed you her sister's child, and told of their journey from Ceredigion. How long have you known?" he asked painfully.

"Only since this morning," I replied quietly.

"This, of all mornings," he groaned. "And the love you hold for me," he asked unevenly, "can it endure this new knowledge?"

I assured him that it both could and would. "You once told me," I reminded him, "that we live in a brutal age. The most significant thing about your behaviour during my time with my cousin Owain is surely that Walter of Gloucester was able to persuade you against the violence which your anger desired. That you should feel this degree of acute shame afterwards is even more remarkable because not one single drop of blood was spilled by your hand. You are a man out of your time," I assured him. "Too good in many ways for border conflict." I saw him stiffen, then after a quick ebb and flow of colour he relaxed perceptibly. "And Philippe," I continued, "he has your susceptibility to an even finer degree. He will never make a soldier, that is sure. I asked him recently if he was interested in a career in the Church. He replied that he was not, as when he was of an age he wished to marry!"

My husband gave a delighted laugh. "And as he now begins to call me 'Father', in a very adult fashion," he declared, "we must soon decide what career Master Philippe shall follow." By the time we had re-entered the castle precincts, I knew that he had quite recovered himself. He dismissed the groom who approached, and gently lifted me down from my horse, holding me close for a minute before he let me go. "You are the strength whereby I live," he declared softly. "And when you were gone, I crumbled almost to the point of total extinction."

That autumn, Owain Cadwgan returned from his exile in Ireland. Bleddyn told me very quietly one day, that "our cousin Owain", had come back to settle illegally in Powys, which his uncle Iorwerth now held "of the King". Owain could persuade no man to take messages of good-will from him to King Henry, he added, so greatly did they fear that monarch's wrath. Old Cadwgan had also redeemed his lands in Ceredigion from the King, for the tribute of one hundred pounds, on the condition that he did not succour or support his eldest son, Owain, in any way. We heard little more save that, "that outlaw Owain now ravages and plunders the lands near to those of his uncle in Powys, with the aid of his cousin Madog".

In my new found happiness I was certain that my cousin could do nothing further to hurt me. A few weeks after my joyful reconciliation with my husband, I realized that once again beneath my heart I carried a child for him. This conception meant more to me than any that had gone before, confirming as it did, our absolute love. His present disposition to worry himself unduly about my health, which at that time could not have been better, made me cautious over advising him of my condition. Early on, I decided that if it were at all possible, I would not tell him of my pregnancy until I had overcome the first, vital three months of it.

From the outset however, the alliance which I held with this new unknown fitz-Gerald, proved to be both comfortable and reassuring. I secretly acknowledged that even if this present pregnancy should cost me my life, I would willingly have undertaken it, so precious had the weeks been that preceded it. Branwen, also sworn to secrecy, watched over me protectively. My new relation let me down eventually however, at a most inappropriate moment. Deciding forcibly and irrevocably one evening in late September that he could not abide the smell of eel pie, I was forced to beg to be excused, just as my husband was about to say grace at the supper table. With my kerchief firmly clamped over nose and mouth, I fled in precipitate haste towards my chamber. I had hardly reached the garderobe however, and begun to retch within its privacy, than firm hands came out to support my shoulders, and I realized that my husband stood behind me. The look on his face was so fraught with anxiety, that I gasped that he must not concern himself, as it was nothing. The others awaited supper I reminded him and he must go to them.

"Stephen will attend to it," he replied quietly. "He is quite capable." I took a damp towel and quickly rubbing it over my face, announced that I was completely recovered.

"It was the eel pie," I declared. "He did not care for the smell. It is often so."

"He?" he queried tersely. I nodded my apology.

"Yes, I am afraid that we have not been entirely honest

with you, your son and I." He pulled me to him convulsively.

"How long?" he murmured, anxiety making his voice low.

Gently I disengaged myself from his embrace. "Gerald," I said. "You cannot go on in this fashion for the next six months. Will you not believe me when I assure you, that I have never, ever, felt better in my life. The liaison between myself and this child, so far, has been eminently safe and satisfactory."

"But this present indisposition," he argued, a deep furrow creasing his brow.

"Almost the first time," I stated honestly. "Frankly, he just cannot bear eels – " Branwen bustled in at this moment bearing a small wooden trencher piled high with sweet custard. She curtsied to my husband and presented me with the custard and a spoon. As soon as my stomach became reconciled to this benign mixture, I immediately felt better. Gerald patted Branwen's shoulder gratefully.

"When you return to the hall for your own supper, would you be good enough to ask the butler to send a meal for two in here?" His features relaxed in a slight smile. "It might be best if we avoided the eel pie altogether. I will stay here and eat supper with my wife." Branwen disappeared readily to do her master's bidding and he remained where he stood, looking down at me with only a mere vestige of the anxious furrow, still evident across his brow. "Your colour has returned," he remarked in easier tones. I was considerably relieved to note that a humorous gleam had returned to his eyes. "Now what on earth are we going to do," he enquired, "with a son who cannot eat eels?"

"Enter him for the Church?" I suggested tentatively, for although I would never have laboured the point, I had a strong desire to give this child, should he himself be willing, to God and the Church.

"A bishop in the family," he mused. "It is an attractive thought."

Despite his father's acute and ill-concealed anxiety at the time of his birth, our third son, David, entered the world with the least possible discomfort or fuss. Throughout his infancy, he was to face life with the minimum amount of temperament and his bland assurance that the world was a place of peace and tranquillity, soon earned for him the title of "the little bishop", within the family. Philippe was particularly tender with this remarkably even-tempered newcomer who symbolised the successful re-union of his parents, for it had always been essential to the well-being of our eldest son that his father and I should be in perfect accord. Philippe was soon to go away to Gloucester where, under the wise influence and expert tuition of Walter, the High Sheriff, he was to learn the finer points of finance and administration. He looked forward to the freedom promised by his new career, and yet he was loath to leave us, and I secretly dreaded the day of his departure.

The attractive stone chapel, built by the Flemish mason who had fashioned my garden, was ready in time for the christening of our youngest son. This small but intimate fountain of tranquillity, built off an angle of the Western Hall, soon became a constant source of succour to all of us, and under the dedicated supervision of a young priest sent over from Monkton by the Prior, it rapidly became a focal point of the castle. There were many things at this particular time which conspired to drive us within its walls. Owain Cadwgan, driven out of Powys by his uncle Iorwerth, had recently come to settle within his father's lands, in nearby Ceredigion. Here, with many reckless young companions, he had begun raiding well within the borders of northern Dyfed. With ruthless indifference, he burned, killed and stole everything he could lay his hands on, carrying off large numbers of luckless captives, and shipping them over to Ireland into slavery. My husband and fitz-Richard sent many patrols and detachments to the north in an attempt to control this lawlessness, but as is the way with most guerrilla warfare, the raiders from Ceredigion struck and then disappeared over the border before our troops could reach them.

When an eminent Fleming, William of Brabant, was coldly cut down by the roadside, the King took swift action. He immediately dispossessed old Cadwgan from Ceredigion, and Gilbert fitz-Richard, having been given sole control of the area, marched in with a large enough host to quell the violence. Owain Cadwgan once again fled to Ireland, and for a short space we had peace. My husband at last decided that it was safe for Philippe to make the journey overland to Gloucester. Concerned that he would be unable to advise me of his safe arrival for some long time, and to allay my anxieties over the matter, I procured two doves, one white and one grey. I presented them to my eldest son on the day before his departure. I advised him to send the white bird immediately he entered Gloucester and then, when it returned to Penbroc, I should know of his safe arrival. "If there should be difficulties along the road, release the grey bird, and I will see that Papa at once sends more soldiers with all haste to assist you," I directed. Then I added softly: "We have been very close, Philippe, you and I. You were one of my first friends when I came here to Penbroc."

Philippe walked over to look at his youngest brother, who lay in his crib nearby. I was afraid for a moment that I had embarrassed him. "Soon, you may have sons of your own," I suggested tentatively.

"I sincerely hope so," Philippe replied seriously. "But I doubt that I shall find a woman for wife so much to my liking as you are to my father. Your relationship is unique. I know, for I have observed others far less happy."

"We have been extraordinarily lucky," I murmured. "For neither of us wished for our marriage, and it could have been such a disaster."

Philippe scanned the river. "There is only one thing I regret, mama," he informed me in even tones, so reminiscent of his father, "and that is, that you did not bear me, as you did 'the little bishop' there. You have always called me your son. Would that I was." He rapidly placed an arm around my shoulders to stem the approaching tide of tears which I could no longer contain. "I must see to my packing," he reminded me gently.

A few days after Philippe had gone, I heard that my uncle Cadwgan was dead. Bleddyn had been dolorously plucking his harp in the hall as I walked through. I stopped, restrained by the sense of deep tragedy present in the chords he played, for they awakened an echo from the time when as a child I had heard that my father had been killed in battle. "You play a lament?" I suggested.

"A lament for the old fox, your uncle and mine, Cadwgan," the blind harper replied. "The man who always wished to please everybody. He who was cut down so brutally last week in Welshpool, by the hand of his evil nephew Madog. For Madog, not content with the murder he perpetrated upon his uncle Iorwerth, has now doubled his crime with the slaughter of his other uncle, Cadwgan. He wishes to rule Powys in their stead. The King has sent for Owain Cadwgan from Ireland, that he may claim his own lands from his cousin Madog, and avenge his father's death."

It seemed but little time before we heard that Owain, on his return from Ireland had received Madog from his kinsmen in chains, and had blinded his former comrade as retribution for his father's murder. Owain once again began to rule Powys, but the tales from the north were ever those of turbulence and disaster.

Six days precisely after Philippe had left us, the white dove I had given him homed in to the dovecote below the rampart wall. Thankfully, I repaired to the chapel, to speak of my gratitude for the safe journey of the son I loved above all others. It was to be another three years before the King, advised by Gilbert fitz-Richard of the turbulent rule of the North Walian chieftains, decided to take action. A great host was gathered under the leadership of fitz-Richard, to march from Dyfed and Ceredigion, to meet the King's two other mighty armies in mid-Wales. Many men of our garrison were sent to join these troops, both horsemen and men at arms. My husband was anxious to march with them, but a messenger direct from King Henry bade him stay to hold Penbroc safe from the possibility of any retaliatory attack in the south. The King planned to lead one host himself, and he intended to march across mid-Wales, to join up with another of the contingents around Machynlleth.

I knew my husband well enough to realize that he would have welcomed this opportunity to march with our men to attack Owain Cadwgan from the south-west. For the temptation to settle old scores was particularly strong at a time like this, with three armies on the move. An army is not gathered overnight however, and during the early summer of 1114, we were startled one day by the arrival of a travel-stained messenger, who bore the King's colours. He reached Penbroc, as we sat at our midday dinner, and was ushered directly into the hall, where my husband received his dispatch whilst presiding at the top table. As Gerald cast a rapid eye over the parchment, I saw his expression change. "You come from Gloucester?" he enquired, in tones which told me nothing. The man agreed that indeed he had. "And the King plans to lie at Carmarthen tonight?"

The messenger bowed his assent. "If the weather holds

good, sir, His Majesty hopes to be with you tomorrow evening, at the latest." As the words sank in, I raised bewildered eyes to those of my husband. But in his face I was unable to read anything that could give me any comfort. From the moment he had received the King's brief letter, the shutters had come down so emphatically that I realized that I was looking at a stranger. Everywhere, the castle exploded into feverish activity. Bleddyn was the only person to whom I was able to gain access, and he had no more idea of why the King should suddenly strike south to visit Penbroc, than the rest of us. So unwilling was I to meet this man with whom fourteen years before, I had had such an intimate relationship, that I slept but little that night. Although Gerald endeavoured to mask his unease, I knew instinctively that he was every bit as tense as I beneath that outwardly cool exterior. Why should King Henry of England suddenly decide to visit a remote border fortress in order to make the acquaintance of a man whom he had never met before, and an ex-mistress whom he had not set eyes on for over fourteen years?

Penbroc Castle was every bit as neat and clean on the day that the King of England entered it as it had been many years before when I had stepped into its courtyard for the first time. It was apparent that the King was most impressed. "Your castle does you great credit, Sir Constable," he informed my husband, treating him to a brisk appraisal as Gerald made his liege lord a dignified obeisance. I immediately sank before my sovereign in a deep curtsey. As I rose he retained my hand, and as I raised my frightened eyes to his, I suddenly knew without any shadow of doubt why King Henry had chosen to come to Penbroc in the early summertime. He looked harsher featured, his hair was now almost entirely grey, but the expression in his eyes was the same as the one with which he had always viewed me when I had been a hostage at his brother's court. I felt a swift flood of colour invade my cheeks. "Incredible," he breathed, "quite incredible. It is as they say. The air of Penbroc suits you extraordinarily well, my lady."

"I thank you, Sire," I murmured formally, willing him to release me and pass on. At long last, he did so. Fearing to meet my husband's eye, I thereafter endeavoured with the utmost futility to merge into the background. After a cursory inspection of the guard, and a swift discussion with my husband on the fortification and manning of the castle and township, the King immediately sought me out and drew me to his side. To my utter consternation he took my unwilling hand, and tucking it firmly under his arm, suggested that I should show him the view of the river.

"The several Welsh bards who have recently come to our court at Winchester, tell us that from the rampart walk here at Penbroc the view is incomparable," he declared.

"But, Sire," I protested. "Surely my husband is better qualified than I to tell you all you wish to know about this castle." He brushed the scarcely veiled rebuff aside with good-humoured tolerance.

"I think not," he replied decisively. "Your husband, madam, is far too busy to find time to entertain his sovereign in the way that he desires." In a few well chosen phrases, the King had made the object of his visit to Penbroc eminently clear. An angry flush mounted my husband's cheek. With a stiff bow, he dismissed himself from the King's presence. With an agility that seemed quite remarkable in a man of over forty-six summers, the King rapidly led me to the most secluded part of the castle bounds. There, on the upper gravel walk, he turned impatiently to face me. He was not even slightly out of breath as a result of his exertions. He captured my hand. "Nest," he sighed. "What fools men are, to be persuaded against their natural feelings – Why did I let you go? The expediency of securing my northern borders seemed real enough fourteen years ago. Now, that advice appears to have been the utmost folly." He made to take me into his arms.

"Sire," I beseeched. "I beg of you – "

My dilemma was solved in the most unexpected manner by a small voice announcing. "Mama – Your Majesty, I am bidden to call you – "

The King released me with a sudden expletive, and I backed away tentatively. William, his face graver than usual, stood halfway up the bank beneath us. I scrambled down towards him, gratefully. "My son," I murmured. "Is aught amiss?"

"No mama," he gave a quick bob in the direction of the King. "It is just that I am bidden by my father's butler, to call you and His Majesty to supper."

"Supper!" the King exploded.

"Yes, Sire," the boy replied with cool dignity. "I fear you did not hear the bell." The King glanced at the lad as though he would send him away, but his eye then fell upon a splendid personage who wheezed and bowed at ground level.

"Very well," he rasped, rapidly descending to the lower walk where my husband's butler stood. The man dithered, obviously overcome by the awful responsibility of leading his monarch to a meal. "If the feast be ready," the King declared, passing the man with lengthening strides. "If it be ready, let's to it then, fool!" Had William been Philippe, I should have kissed him, so thankful was I for his timely interruption.

As supper progressed and the King drank deeper, my position became quite impossible. Acutely conscious of the murderous look now unmistakably present in my husband's eyes, I endeavoured with every wit I possessed, to foil the King's pressing attentions towards me. Wracking my brains feverishly, I vainly tried to think up some scheme whereby I could avoid the pending confrontation. As his impatience to possess me mounted and became obvious, I could feel the tension in the Great Hall build up to fever pitch. Never before had Penbroc witnessed a Norman King at play. A King could take whomsoever he wished, and no one could deny him. Not the lady herself, nor dare her husband thwart him in his ambition. I became increasingly aware of my husband's tense figure seated at the King's right hand. Driven to desperation by a fear that Gerald might attempt to physically injure him, I cast wildly about for means whereby I could escape from this cruel involvement. The thought of the King's person filled me with such revulsion that I dared not contemplate it. Surely a priest might reason with him? I glanced down the centre table to where our young resident cleric sat, stern and silent. He left his food untouched, his thin troubled face mirroring the horror with which he viewed this impending evil. But he, I immediately realized, was too young, and lacked the authority with which to argue such a vital moral issue, with his monarch. Suddenly, I knew with the utmost clarity, exactly what I must do.

The next time the King leant back to drink, I quietly asked to be excused. A few minutes only, I begged, for pressing personal reasons. "Ah," he smiled, "My lady cannot hold her wine. Just a few minutes then, for without you here the company would prove to be exceeding dull." He glanced at Gerald as he spoke, and I saw my husband's knuckles whiten as he tightened his grip upon his drinking horn. I avoided the nearest garderobe, off the Great Hall, but made as if I intended to visit my own chamber. As soon as I had escaped through the archway into the darkness of the night, I slipped quietly into the little chapel. One candle alone lit the dim interior, a slim, pure tallow candle, that burned continuously day and night before the statue of the Blessed Virgin. Without delay, I entered the small area within the altar rails and fell to my knees, before the table of Our Lord – I had been received into sanctuary.

It seemed but a little while before the search began. There was much muttering and bustling in the courtyard and above the other voices I eventually recognized the harsher tones of the King. At last the chapel door was thrown wide and I heard a few whispered words, as it became known that I had been found. Heavy footsteps approached the altar rails. "My lady," a courteous voice declared. "My lord King desires your company in the Great Hall."

I remained kneeling, and without lifting my head, replied. "Pray advise His Majesty that I am unable to join him, for it is required of me that I remain at my prayers." Without further parley the intruder retired, carefully closing the door. Some twenty minutes later, I again heard the latch click up and the door swung open. I recognized the muted cadences of the King's Chamberlain. The message however, was more peremptory.

"My lady," the Chamberlain announced, "The King requires that you should wait upon him immediately, in the Great Hall."

"I fear I cannot," I replied in low tones.

"Then I feel ma'am, that I must warn you, that the King's patience is rapidly becoming exhausted," the Chamberlain advised. There was a strong element of menace in his tone.

"I regret that I cannot attend the King," I replied with such finality, that eventually with a sigh, the Chamberlain also withdrew. The cold in the Chapel and my acute apprehension, made me shiver convulsively as I awaited the final outcome of my obduracy. When it came, it was from a totally unexpected quarter. Our own priest, Father

Honore, entered the chapel quietly, and before I could turn to meet him, he had come to kneel beside me.

"My lady, the King has sent me to bring you to his presence, but I beg you – " his voice broke. "In fact I beseech you, to remain where you are."

"Yes, Father," I answered. "You know well why I cannot obey the King's commands. Will you please go to him and advise him that I am in sanctuary."

The young priest bowed his head. "May God continue to guide and protect you, my lady," he prayed. "For your exemplary courage is without parallel."

A few minutes later the door was thrown open violently and angry footsteps approached me. "Madam, I demand an end to this treasonable behaviour," the King snarled. "You will accompany me at once!" He stepped over the altar rail, and I knew that he intended to defy the laws of the Church and drag me forcibly from sanctuary. To evade him I slid away from his groping fingers and snatching the brass crucifix from the altar, I fell to my knees in front of him, in trembling supplication. Then, thrusting the crucifix towards him, I cried that he could not, dared not for the love of God, take me from there. I saw him visibly recoil. His anger was overpowering, but like all Normans, I could sense that he was terribly aware of the mystery and sanctity of the Church. There was an awful moment of silence, then without taking his eyes from the crucifix, he slowly began to back away. When he had retreated beyond the altar rails, he cried one word. "Why?" It hung morosely between us, on the dank night air.

"Because," I replied in low tones, "although you sent me to this the farthest corner of your kingdom to be rid of me, it is here, strangely, that I have found my greatest happiness. This man, to whom you forcibly married me fourteen years ago, has proved above all others, to be the only man to whom I can truly give my love." His tone made no secret of the awful depths of his anger.

"Very well, madam," he spat. "If I cannot have you, I shall make certain that the Constable your husband shall not either!"

No sooner had the King left me, than the castle broke out into a veritable flurry of activity. I knew the sound well. The King's host was being prepared for the road. Terrified, I remained there irresolute. Dreading mightily the great personal injury to which the King might subject this man whom I loved so passionately, I waited sick at heart, wavering within my flimsy circle of safety. A rustling nearby made me hold my breath. As I listened, holding myself rigid in order to locate the sound, a familiar voice whispered close by. "Do not fear. It is I, Stephen. I dare not tarry, as the King's guards are everywhere, but I have a message from my master."

Something was pushed into my hands, and a few significant rustlings signalled his retreat. By the light of St Mary's candle, to which I crept furtively, I examined the articles which Stephen had brought me. There were two. One was an early pale yellow rosebud from our garden. It was a rose, grown from the cutting given to us by the girl who lived in the south of the Manor of Penbroc. She had presented us with it on the day after we had become forever reconciled. It was, and always would be, a symbol of our love. The other object which Stephen had pushed into my hand was a scrap of parchment cut from the edge of a ledger. Faintly scratched upon its surface, I could read three words in my husband's hand.

"Stay in sanctuary."

Holding these two precious relics closely, I crawled back into the mystical safety of the space between the rails and the altar. Now I knew his wish, all I could do for his safety, was to pray. Restlessly, I endured the cold of that long, poignant vigil. As dawn broke, I heard the King's guard call the soldiers to horse. Stiffly, I crept to the chapel door, just in time, to see the King's host disappearing out of the main gate. At the rear of the column, I saw with anguish, a prisoner being escorted by four of his own soldiers of the guard. It was my husband, and he was in chains.

I blindly groped my way back into the dim interior of the little chapel, to sink exhausted upon the altar steps. Some time after the King's troop had left Branwen came in search of me. She bore a jug of sweet mulled wine and the remnants of a loaf. Her eyes were red from weeping, and at the sight of me crouching there, her tears welled up afresh. "My lady, oh my lady," she cried. "Come you now and take a little portion of this bread and wine, for you surely must eat, or you will be grievously ill." My whole body was so stiff with the privations of the night that I staggered as I rose and was forced to clutch at the altar for support.

"Branwen," I begged brokenly. "Tell me that he is not – " She knew intuitively that which I seemed unable to put into words.

"Your husband is in no way injured, my lady," she assured me emphatically. "When they carried him from here I swear there was not a mark upon him, save that of the manacles with which they bound him." She caught me, supporting me upon her generous bosom. "I promise you that the master was in no wise mutilated, not even in spirit," she soothed, as I clung to her tearfully.

Whilst I dutifully forced down the bread and wine, my maid began slowly to relate the horrors of the past night. The King's wrath, when he had returned to the Great Hall after his interview with me in the chapel, had been monumental. For some long time, he had paced uneasily the middle distance of the hall, prowling like some caged wild beast. Then at last, raising his head, he had called upon his soldiers to seize and bind my husband. Branwen swallowed back a sob. "This they did, setting chains upon him and standing him alone in the centre of the hall." I cried aloud in anguish. "My lady," the woman assured me rapidly, "do not despair, for I swear to you that even thus, manacled like a common felon, the King failed to humiliate my master. Bleddyn declared later, that once your husband knew you to be safe, there was nothing further that the King could do to hurt him."

"Bleddyn said that?" I cried, grasping at any slender grain of consolation. She nodded, then with touching pride, related how my husband had stood erect, patiently awaiting his sentence, his rare courage making him a symbol of honour and respect to all his loyal people. It was clear that his brave bearing eventually affected even the King, who at first stormed mightily, threatening him with every dire punishment that the devilry of man could devise.

"The master, true soldier that he is, never flinched or changed colour," Branwen remembered. "While the King raged, my master kept such cool and steady eyes upon this monarch who would so sorely have wronged him, that it was far more telling than any spoken challenge. Almost as though some divine hand stayed him, the King hesitated, as if reluctant to carry out his evil threats upon your husband's person. When most of us could bear it no longer, Father Honore began to speak, quietly, but with forceful words. 'Sire,' he said. 'This man and woman have done no more today than defend the promises they made to our Lord, in this very hall, at their marriage ceremony.' " Branwen shuddered. "At first, it seemed as though the King would seize the priest by the throat, but instead he ceased his wandering and sat awhile in the great chair by the fire to ponder. When at last he leapt to his feet, it was merely to call the grooms to get his host ready for the road." My maid viewed me with concern. "The King took your husband with him and all of our own soldiers, including Stephen, the surgeon and the priest. He left behind a red-haired officer whose name I haven't heard, and a new garrison of his own guard."

Branwen sniffed and wiped her eyes upon her apron. "Only Bleddyn and I are left to succour you and your children in this evil hour, and that strange young man, Hait, who keeps the books and records. I think they only left him because they didn't notice him." She rose to her feet. "What would you have me do, my lady? It would be possible for me to send a kitchen boy into the town to discover if the King has really left the area, or is merely encamped a short way off." I agreed to this suggestion gratefully and she departed. At length, a large red-haired man with a military bearing, stalked into the chapel. Confronting me with curious eyes, as if he could not understand why I should make so great a stir over mere women's work, he informed me curtly that his name was Wilfred of Worcester.

"I am the King's officer, left to hold this fortress while His Majesty subdues the trouble-making Welsh tribesmen of the north," he declared, with an incivility that made me bite my lip. "After he has accomplished this end, he will doubtless give me orders with regard to the future of this castle. Meanwhile, you may retain your own personal chamber off the Western Hall," he stated. "But I am to inform you that under no circumstances may you leave this castle. Those are the King's orders." He left, as abruptly as he had arrived. Branwen crept in cautiously.

"The King's host has departed from thence," she indicated the town, "in the direction of the mountains. They hope to reach fitz-Richard's new castle at Aber Teifi by nightfall, but it is a long ride and I doubt they will."

I hastened to my chamber, determined to attend afternoon dinner as usual. As I entered the Great Hall to present myself for this meal, there was an anticipatory hush. It was immediately apparent to me that the man who now held Penbroc for the King, was determined to humiliate me in every way he could devise. Accompanied by Branwen, I began to traverse the length of the hall. Long before I reached the top table, I realized that every place there had been deliberately filled before my arrival. Without any obvious hesitation, I proceeded to glide into the nearest vacant space at one of the lower stations. Once there, I stood with as much dignity as I could muster, bowing my head in reverential posture to await grace. There was an audible sigh as my intention became clear and then after a lengthy pause a voice began to intone the grace. From the corner of my eye, as I settled myself with apparent composure to begin the meal, I caught the reassuring sight of the King's new officer, Wilfred of Worcester, in full blush. His calculated snub had rebounded upon him, to my complete satisfaction.

After this episode, the new chief officer at the castle left us strictly alone, ignoring me wherever possible. It was a better situation by far, than I had come to expect. I quickly gathered the children around me, and assured them that as soon as the King's summer campaign was over, Papa would return to us. "Until then," I advised, "be tactful, and do not unduly annoy Master Wilfred and his soldiers."

Bleddyn seemed totally lost and subdued, and I realized with a pang that like me, when my husband was removed in such a way from his world, he scarcely lived. Try as he would, the blind bard was unable to gain any knowledge, either from his colleagues in the town, or from those other sources whereby he sometimes foretold the future, that could give us any comfort.

A few days later I realized that I had used up the last of my meagre store of silver pennies. "Now we are totally dependant upon the doubtful generosity of the King's garrison," I informed my maid anxiously. "I have no money left."

Branwen looked thoughtful. "Do not distress yourself, my lady," she said. "I think that I know of someone who will help us." She returned fairly rapidly with a small leather bag of money which she bade me keep upon my person. "I applied to that strange young man who sits behind the screen, continually writing in his big ledgers," she declared. "Hait, your husband's chief clerk. He really was most helpful."

I was certain that I had never previously exchanged more than a few polite words with my husband's secretary. "I must see the young man at once," I said. "So that I may thank him." My husband's clerk sat in his usual place behind the wooden screen in the Great Hall. He was industriously reckoning up a sum, with the aid of white counters, upon his chequer board. As soon as he realized my presence he leapt to his feet, nervously upsetting the board and spilling the counters all over the floor.

"What interesting things these are," I declared, "I vow that I had no idea that they were carved of deer antler." I picked up a counter and held it in my hand to examine it the better. My innocent observation sparked off the most remarkable flow of words I had ever heard the young man utter. In a few minutes I had had a full history of the uses of the chequer board and of the materials commonly employed in its manufacture. It proved an uncommonly fascinating discourse. No wonder my husband held this young man in such high esteem. A thought suddenly struck me. "Did you furnish my husband with a piece of parchment cut from one of your ledgers, on the night that the King was here," I asked rather painfully, "so that he might send a message to me, in the chapel?" My husband's secretary bowed his head, solemnly. "You will forgive me, if

I do not offer to give it back?" I suggested unevenly, "but I – "

He tactfully averted his gaze. "All of us who have lived within this castle with you both, would like you to know of our sorrow over the events of that night," he declared stiffly, but sincerely, nonetheless.

"Thank you," I murmured, quite recovered now from my weak moment.

"If I may venture an opinion, my lady," he began tentatively. "Your husband the Constable, will I am sure, eventually be able to redeem his position with the King, by patience and quiet service with the army, during the ensuing summer campaign. If the King had it in his mind to physically punish your husband, I am certain that he would have done so during his first flush of anger, while still here at Penbroc." I was touched by his obvious loyalty.

"You have been most reassuring," I murmured, "at a time when I sadly lack for those with whom I can converse and I thank you for it." He politely escorted me as far as my chamber door.

"It is useful to know that we have at least one friend near at hand," Branwen declared when he had gone, a sentiment I was to echo in the next few weeks, for Hait was often to pour comforting phrases into my willing ears over this difficult period, and I came to rely more than a little on his restrained but able presence.

I was sitting in my garden at my tapestry frame one early afternoon, listening to Bleddyn's most soothing folk music, when our peace was rudely shattered. Wilfred of Worcester burst suddenly upon us, propelling a disreputable looking pedlar in front of him. The pedlar, who seemed terrified at suddenly finding himself in such surroundings, was quite incoherent at first. "This man has news of the King's armies," the chief officer muttered abruptly, prodding his unwilling agent into speech. My heart suddenly leapt in fear – I rose to my feet. "Well go on man – " the chief officer prompted. Haltingly, the pedlar began his tale. It appeared that while crossing a narrow bridge over the Dyfi river, King Henry's vanguard fell victim to an ambush. A handful of Owain Cadwgan's archers, concealed behind rocks on the farther bank, let fly their arrows as the King's host appeared. One archer, bolder than the others, took aim at the King himself. Realizing the danger, the King's prisoner Gerald of Windsor, threw himself between the bowman and the King, and taking the full force of the arrow, fell at the King's feet, while the King remained shaken, but whole. Wildly, I grasped the pedlar by his ragged smock.

"Tell me," I shook him urgently. "The Constable of Penbroc, Gerald of Windsor, was he gravely injured or no?"

"Why of course," the man squeaked, rolling his eyes in terror, "didn't I tell you, he lay at the King's feet, dead as mutton – "

Violently shocked and only half aware, I heard the chief officer murmuring trite, insincere phrases of condolence and then his words. "Until I receive confirmation by the written hand of the King, I shall continue to administer the castle and the town as at present." I heard, as if far away, his boots receding and the patter of the pedlar's bare feet on the stone flags of the garden walk as they retreated. I became aware of Bleddyn weeping from his sightless eyes. He begged me to go with him, within doors, to Branwen and the comfort of my children.

"No, just leave me, I beg of you," I insisted. "I want no one, need nothing." A phrase began to beat slowly through my brain, words which my husband had spoken on my arrival at Penbroc. "What are either of us my lady, but the pawns of Kings." 'The pawns of Kings', and now he had given up his life to save that of the most cold, unlovable King of them all. I grasped the stone parapet which edged the small garden, and gazed with eyes as unseeing as Bleddyn's into the farthest distance. Now that he was dead, my whole being died also. Branwen came, and tragically begged me to go with her. I must lie down for a while until I felt a little better, she implored. I shook my head, hardly moving my eyes from the river as it flowed like a trickle of life, ebbing away towards the sea. Well then, Branwen suggested, should she send the children out to comfort me in my sorrow? In a strange voice that I did not know, I told her that all I wanted was my warm cloak, to shelter me from the cold. She brought it at last and left me unwillingly, when I said quietly that I wished to be there in the garden on my own.

Eventually, dusk came, to fold itself around me. I gained a little comfort from its unquestioning anonymity. The supper bell tolled, but I could not move to answer its summons. Light showed, flickering through the slits of the Great Hall, as the rush dips were lit, but neither chill air nor darkness touched me, for nothing could equal the ice which lay around my dead heart. I was only partially aware that someone came at last. Someone who stood silently beside me, keeping with me the timeless vigil. At last he spoke – It was Hait. "My lady," he said quietly. "You must come into the hall out of the cold. The night air is chill and you shiver continuously." When I made no answer he placed a compassionate arm around my shoulders, and drew my body closer to his for warmth. I did not resist, for I could feel nothing, knew of nothing, save that he had taken me into my private chamber, for I heard him directing Branwen to put me into bed.

He must have returned later, for I again recognized his voice. "Go and take some rest, it is long past midnight." As I sank between consciousness and oblivion, I was aware that someone sat close by my side. Sometimes the covers were pulled up more firmly around my neck. Someone moved and went quietly to the door. "Branwen" a voice whispered, close by me. "Branwen", "Branwen", "Branwen", came the echo from my fevered brain. Slowly, I felt a delicious torpor come over me, a generous warmth penetrated my wracked frame at last, and as the beneficent rays of this summer sunshine gave me new life, I lay content within a warm cocoon. Some time later, I came back slowly to semi-consciousness and as I stirred, I felt gentle fingers pushing the damp hair back from my brow. Frightened by I knew not what, I started up in alarm, but gentle hands drew me back within that inviting circle of comfort and warmth, and a compassionate voice soothed me with tender phrases. Too weak to resist, I sank back submissively onto the pillows.

It was a voice I knew. Haltingly, I called his name. "Hait!"

I awoke at first light, disturbed by an unfamiliar movement, and for a long second, I stared at the man beside me before I recognized who he was. Then with my eyes full upon him, I remembered – everything. Silently, he climbed out of bed and donned his clothes. His eyes trapped by mine.

My maid hearing someone stirring hurried into the chamber, full of anguish, asking herself the while how she could have slept in my hour of sorrow. Hait moved towards the door. "Your mistress is greatly improved," he volunteered. He viewed Branwen uneasily. "I will leave her in your hands if you are rested, and try to snatch a few hours sleep myself." Then avoiding my eyes, which watched him lifelessly from the pillows, he hastily left the room.

Gradually, automatically, I began to resume the outline pattern of my previous existence at the castle. The life I had been forced to adopt since the coming of the King. Branwen and Bleddyn did their best to guide me, for I walked as one in the dark, not having any place to go. Hait was there too, quiet and resourceful. Neither he nor I made any further reference to that first night of my bereavement, and he assiduously avoided being left on his own with me.

Three days later as we sat at dinner in the afternoon, a loud commotion rent the inner recesses of the courtyard. I paid little heed as the guard on the gate made his challenge. After a minute or two of parley, three men entered the Great Hall. The man in the centre leaned heavily upon his two companions. Wilfred of Worcester rose to his feet, to be confronted by none other than Stephen, the foremost of the three. "I have here a royal pardon for my master Gerald of Windsor, from the King himself," Stephen cried, in ringing tones. "He is to be re-instated here, as Constable of this castle, forthwith." With startled eyes, I viewed the man who leaned so heavily upon his fellows. As he raised his head, and his eyes met mine triumphantly, I rose trembling to my feet. A cry was drawn from my lips at this unprecedented miracle. I ran towards him, and he struggled to stand free of the others in order to greet me.

"It is nothing," he assured me hastily, as I rapidly approached, "a mere scratch, nothing for you to be alarmed over. Just an arrow in the shoulder – " His voice tailed off as I reached him, and he collapsed in a heap at my feet. Throwing myself down beside him, I drew his head into my lap. Stephen swiftly knelt down and felt for the thread of life which coursed through his wrist.

"He is quite correct," he stated quickly, shocked by my reaction. "It is a flesh wound my lady, that is all, but we have ridden far and fast to get him home. He has lost rather a lot of blood and will need good nursing and much rest." I looked up at Stephen, barely able to comprehend. "But they told me he was dead," I cried and the full tragedy of it all smote me at last. "Stephen, swear to me that he will live," I beseeched him.

"As I live and breathe," Stephen vowed, "your husband is in no danger of his life, my lady. The surgeon is a good man and he has been in constant attendance upon him." Then stooping low over my husband's unconscious body, I was able at last to give up those tears which had been locked within me since the pedlar had brought his ill-fated news, four days previously.

PART V

In spite of Stephen's protestations that my husband's wound was not serious, I had many an anxious hour before I could be entirely sure of his recovery. He lay in the big bed in my chamber, delirious for many days with the high fever that raged as a result of his hasty journey south. In his delirium, much of the anguish which Gerald had so carefully hidden from view during the King's attempt to publicly disgrace him, became apparent in his half coherent muttering. From the small truckle bed on which I lay, placed across the foot of his sick bed, I re-lived those agonizing hours with him many times. When I could bear this torment no longer, I would go to him with towels steeped in cool spring water, and compassionately sponge the fire out of his pain-wracked limbs. When the fever finally left him, he was pathetically weak. Branwen, whose nursing skills were of an absolute excellence, was far more successful than I in persuading him to take the nourishment which the surgeon deemed necessary for his full recovery. As I saw her dedicated concentration to her task, I understood the manner in which she had snatched me back from the void, not so many years before. My husband was aware of it too. "How would we survive without such folk as you, Branwen?" he asked her, as childlike, he lay passively obedient to her every whim, in the calm which mercifully follows such turbulent fevers.

I could see her gratified face, as she answered gruffly. "You sir, and my mistress, were born to survive. Aye, and those lusty sons of yours with their straight limbs and handsome heads, full of a strange mixture of book learning and the arts of war. Take Master William now, since your return he has aided Stephen with the sureness of a grown man. In a few years he will be quite ready to occupy his inheritance," my maid assured us, as she rapidly collected a pile of used dishes and departed in the direction of the kitchens.

"William wants not for a standard bearer, while he has Branwen to watch over him," I announced with a smile.

He caught my hand as I came within reach, and kissed it poignantly. "It is almost as if he were Branwen's first born, and not ours," he mused quietly. "But she is right, on the subject of the boy's ability. I think that I shall only send William to de Barri of Manor Pyr for a couple of years. He is too useful to me here, and as soon as he is able, you will wish him to have Carew."

I nodded. "Yes, William must have Carew. It may perhaps be the only portion of my father's lands that our eldest son will ever inherit." I corrected myself at once. "Our first born son, for our eldest, Philippe, continues to enjoy Gloucester." I searched the top of the oaken chest amongst my wools, meaning to read him Philippe's latest letter.

"Read it to me after dinner," he suggested drowsily. "I tire somewhat rapidly these days, just stay there so I may see you – " I reached for my frame and quietly commenced work upon the new tapestry that the children and I had just designed. It was an epic scene, depicting the ambush at the ford over the river Dyfi. I was determined that my grandchildren should know in years to come of the way in which their grandfather, Gerald of Windsor, had with outstanding courage saved the life of the King. As my husband dozed intermittently, I examined his well-loved features carefully. This last campaign, with its initial strain and dishonour, had aged him considerably. Although his wound was healing at last, his eyes were sunken with the recent fever and shone far too brightly, denoting that he was still a sick man. Across his remarkably distinguished brow the grey hairs now outnumbered the fair ones. He was still however, a potent force, a fact which even this present great physical weakness was unable to mask, for he had lost none of his dignity or power to command. He opened his eyes as I minutely examined him, and the smile I received, was one of complete contentment. "Tell me what work you do?" he begged. "I like your pictures; they contain such colour and drama."

"This one certainly does," I replied, showing him the canvas. "See here is the Dyfi flowing strongly beneath the bridge. Later, bowmen will be visible on the far bank here, amongst these bushes. The King stands thus, and here – " my voice softened as I beheld the spot on the canvas which was to hold his prone figure – "Here lies the lord of Penbroc, having received the cruel arrow designed by Fate for the King of England!"

I saw him flush abruptly. "The Constable of Penbroc," he corrected with great deliberation. "You know well, Nest, that I shall never be aught else." He caught my eye sternly as I was about to intervene. "No," he assured me with constraint. "The King made that eminently clear when he gave me my pardon, and permission to return to Penbroc, after I had received my injury." He removed his eyes from mine. "I know what you feel, that that is the least he could do, but he had already made his intentions known to me when he interviewed me so pointedly that night, in the Great Hall – 'You could sir, have been Earl of Penbroc, had you been more ready to accommodate your King,' were I think the words he used, on that momentous occasion." I got up and went swiftly to the bedside. He caught my hand again and pulled me towards him until our eyes were level. "Better a Constable with honour," he declared, "than a corrupt Earl." I buried my face in his linen shirt. His good arm encircled the only part of me that he could reach, my shoulders. "Fear not, my beloved," he whispered, "and it were a choice such as King Henry offered, I would rather remain a commoner." His grip tightened. "For if I had become Earl of Penbroc that night, you could by now, be carrying another child for the King."

A sudden spasm of grief shook me, and I was unable to look up to meet his eyes for a very long time. Later, I left the chamber, and finding Branwen in the hall, asked if she would please send my husband's secretary to speak with me. Hait joined me at the abutment. "My lady," he said anxiously, "your maid said that you wished to speak with me." I felt that I could only recourse to absolute frankness. The gravity of the situation demanded it.

"My husband has just informed me," I told him seriously, "that he gave up an earldom to save me from becoming pregnant by the King of England. How do I then break to him, that instead of the King's child, I now carry within me the son of his secretary?"

"My lady – " he faltered. "It cannot be so."

"Then if it cannot be, can you enlighten me as to the child I now hold. It is most assuredly not the King's, for both I and my husband fought King Henry almost to the death to prevent it. Neither can it be my husband's child, a fact of which he will be only too painfully aware. For a month he was away campaigning in the north as the King's prisoner, and latterly as you must know, he has lain gravely ill." I turned away to hide the depth of my fear and distress. "You are the only man who could possibly be father of this child and I beg you to advise me of the means whereby I can confess my grave deficiency to my husband." Hait no longer dissembled, he merely began to search his mind for ways whereby I could be saved from the certain wrath which we both knew was bound to follow such a disclosure.

"You were too sorely grieved that night to know what was toward," he stated grimly. "I and I alone am responsible for your present condition, but we must find a way of advising your husband of it, which gives the whole story. I fear that because of his great love for you, his anger will be so swift that he will not hear me out." I gasped as his meaning became clear. So sure was Hait that my husband would kill him, that he was more anxious for time to explain my innocence, than to propound his own. "I will offer it as a case on which I wish him to pass judgement for one of the courts," he decided solemnly. "In this way he will be bound to listen to all the evidence." Voicing once more his bitter regret over his behaviour towards me, he asked when my husband would be well enough to receive such unwelcome news.

"When he is strong enough I will send for you," I declared, inwardly aware of the pain which I knew would be my lot as soon as we had made our disclosure – for I had no illusions about remaining at Penbroc once my husband had discovered my shameful secret. I was however, determined upon one thing, that his recovery should not be put in jeopardy by my confession. I had to wait, but not too long, for I knew also, that I could never allow him to come to me again, holding as I did, another man's burden. As my husband rapidly recovered his lost strength, I, in some tragic way, began to lose mine. At last even Gerald began to notice it.

"I must soon become wholly well and then we can get out of doors, around the Manor lands together once again," he said, his eyes viewing me with perplexity. "Being confined to a sickroom for so long with a fractious invalid has sapped your strength. You dwindle and become thinner every day. It will not do."

"You are far from fractious and I only become thinner in your imagination," I protested quietly. My new pregnancy had reached its seventh week when he finally decided one morning that he was fully recovered.

"I think," he remarked dreamily, as I cleared away his breakfast things, "that I would like you to throw away that ridiculous small bed, for it offends me." The look in his eyes as he deliberately held mine, made me exit rapidly with the dishes. I became aware of the rising note of exasperation in his voice as I did so. "Nest," he called, as I slid out of the door. "You don't have to run away from me in that way, like a startled hare!" I went immediately to the Great Hall. Hait was writing when I arrived. As he noted the look on my face, he said but one word.

"Now?" I inclined my head. "I will come at once," he said quietly, putting his quill pen onto the rack above the desk.

When I opened the chamber door, Gerald stood by the bed. He had managed unaided to don a tunic. As I drew near, he caught me to him urgently.

"I shall have to teach you that it is not possible for you to evade me any longer," he began, and there was an amused gleam unmistakably present in his eyes. "I am no longer a cripple." Before he could kiss me, I breathlessly murmured that Hait wished to speak to him. "Hait does? Can't it wait?" he asked.

"I am afraid it can't," I replied, in such serious tones that he released me, and turned towards the half opened door. Hait gave a discreet knock and entered quietly.

"Well?" my husband asked, a trifle impatiently.

"It is a court case over which I feel that I must have your judgement, sir," Hait advised him in a cool detached voice.

My husband sighed. "Very well, but make it brief will you?" Hait inclined his body in a courteous bow. In clear measured phrases, he began to tell of the singularity of the case. It was unique, he thought, in legal terms. My husband remained standing and I grasped the back of the settle staring in embarrassment and dread at the clean rushes with which Branwen had restored the room that morning. It did not take long for Hait to sketch out a fair picture of our tragic dilemma. The woman, he stated was a victim of cruel circumstance. Believing her husband to be dead, she had grieved so sorely that when the man in question came to her, she scarcely knew anything, other than her total solitude. She was in an acute state of shock, and appeared to have taken a severe chill. In impassive tones Hait went on to tell of the way in which the man, fearing for the woman's life by reason of the acute shivering which beset her, sat with her for hours, until finally in a desperate bid to warm her, he had entered her bed. My husband eased himself onto a nearby bench at this moment. "Your case Hait, begins to adopt all the pathos of a major tragedy," he declared, "but pray proceed." Hait quietly related how, eventually, because of his love for this woman, whom he had secretly admired for years, the man became overcome, and forgetting his integrity and her infirmity, made love to her.

"In my opinion," he stated, "this poor lady hardly knew what was toward."

"Come now," my husband remonstrated, "are you trying to tell me that this – this lady, was unconscious?"

"Virtually so, sir, or so the accused claims."

"Then what is your case Hait? Surely there is no problem. They must marry." Hait assured him that there was indeed a terrible and tragic problem, for the lady's husband had not been dead, merely badly injured and he now brought a case against the accused.

"His wife," Hait stated in sombre tones, "is to bear the other man's child." There was a long silence during which time the only sound was the chirping of a grasshopper, which had been carried in with the fresh rushes.

"What did the jury have to say on this matter?" my husband asked at length.

"They could come to no conclusion sir."

"A difficult case," my husband agreed. "And what is your verdict, Hait?" he asked simply.

"Mine sir, would be that the lady should be exonerated of all charges. She was merely the innocent victim of an unscrupulous man. For him, I would show no mercy. Either death – or the loss of his members – " His voice faltered, at last. Gerald eyed him shrewdly, and my heart, like Hait's voice, faltered and almost stopped. My husband knew, of that I had no doubt.

"You are over harsh in this matter," he told Hait and his voice showed no emotion whatsoever. "I feel that perhaps you do not view this problem dispassionately enough. This man and woman are I am certain, victims as you have said, of cruel circumstance. I agree with you also, that the woman was more of a victim than the man. He infamously took advantage of her tragic grief, to satisfy his own appetite, but even he could be telling the truth, when he said that he feared initially for the woman's life. The need for physical comfort between men and women is a very human predicament. This man may also truly love this woman, his defence of her points to this. I would banish him for his crime and when his child is born, he should take it and with the aid of a nurse, rear it at his own expense. An interesting case, as you say. When am I to hear this in the courts?"

I fell to my knees with a cry. "You have heard it," I wept. My husband got slowly to his feet.

Hait stood before him bravely, although his voice shook.

"I am that man," he said with great feeling. "I pray that you will have mercy on your lady, for she knew not what she did. Now, you must make fresh judgement upon this case." My husband's hand moved towards his sword, where it lay on the table close by. For a moment I watched paralysed, as fury and blind emotion wracked his whole being, giving way eventually to reason.

"Get out of my sight Hait," he rasped, "and don't come within it again, lest my resolve snaps and I resort to violence. You may retain your post in the cantrefs, but your deputy will in future be in charge of the Shire. When your child is born, you will receive it and see that it is raised decently. Did you think that where a King failed to walk you could vainly go? Now leave us, before I do you mortal injury!" White and shaking, Hait left the chamber and I heard his feet echo across the Oriel.

After a pause, I realized that my husband stood above, silently looking down upon me. "Put me away," I begged brokenly. "The sisters of mercy at Whitland will take me. I am no longer fit to live with you."

He raised me gently. "What, should I then put you away and thereafter spend the rest of my life in loneliness and misery, because I cannot be with you?" he asked, and his voice was infinitely kind. "Why, that would be utter foolishness."

"But now, the shadow of Hait's child will forever come between us," I moaned. "To fight the King so, almost until death and now this – I cannot bear it!"

He drew me to him for comfort. "I doubt that the little fitz-Hait will get in our way for some long time to come," he observed calmly. "And by the time he does, my anger will have mellowed, I do not doubt."

I looked into his eyes and knew that nothing could destroy the emotion I sought for there and readily found. The wonder of it almost broke my heart. A sob suddenly choked me. "Come away to the garden," he said simply, "and there let us look at the river, and from it, regain our strength."

In a short while, I was fairly certain that almost everyone who lived within our close knit community knew of, or had guessed at, the true reason for Hait's hasty departure. The screened off desk in the Great Hall lay unattended for some days, its bare top surmounted only by neat piles of unopened ledgers. Then suddenly one morning, a short fat youth took up its many challenges and fairly soon, speculation as to the fate of its previous incumbent died down to a flicker of mild curiosity.

It was only a week after my husband had learned of my guilt however, and dismissed his secretary, that Stephen also informed us that he was to leave Penbroc; fitz-Richard, when they had met one another with the King's armies during the summer campaign, had once again invited him to join his retinue. "He has asked me to accept the post of Constable at his new fortress in Cardigan," he explained, "and I feel at my age, that I must take it." It was obvious that Gerald would feel this loss keenly, for they had worked together in great harmony for many years. As William was also about to leave Penbroc to train as a knight with de Barri, at Manor Pyr, the deficiency would be all the greater. Stephen was not so much a member of staff as one of the family.

I tried to explain this to him one afternoon at dinner, without being too sentimental, but his mood seemed so taciturn that I eventually gave up my attempt, adding lightly, to cover my confusion. "Of course now that you will have your complete independence, you must marry. I am sure that one of those attractive girls, that we see you with so often in the town, would be only too pleased to settle down with you in Cardigan. It is a pleasant spot and it is high time that you began to have some sons of your own.

Our boys will certainly miss you, but you have spoiled them for long enough. Maurice will hardly allow you to stir a step without that he is by your side." To my utter astonishment and consternation, Stephen flushed, and abruptly turned the subject. I was even more confused that night, when I was told by my husband as he prepared for bed, that I must not harangue Stephen further on the subject of marriage.

"He has his own very good reasons for not taking a wife," he said shrewdly, "and it will be best if you do not press him unduly over the matter. He feels sick enough at the thought of leaving us. Penbroc has been his home for almost twenty years. He was with Lord Arnulf as a lad."

"Then why does he go?" I argued. "I just don't understand him, for fitz-Richard has tried many times before – "

Gerald came around the bed, and took me into his arms with the gentleness that had particularly characterized his treatment of me since my disgrace. "We all have our ambitions," he said enigmatically, "and Stephen is no exception." He sighed. "But I shall miss him greatly for all that, young de Cogan is not nearly so enterprising." A few days after Stephen had ridden away, en route to Cardigan, we received a number of dispatches from the King's Chamberlain. One of them was calculated to humiliate us and I wondered just how long it would be before the King tired of such ploys. The letter informed us that His Majesty's hosts were now on the long march back to Winchester, having entered into a state of peace with the North Walian chieftains, whom the King had ridden north to subdue. 'Sir Owain Cadwgan', who had recently been knighted by King Henry, was to accompany the King upon his next campaign in Normandy, the letter concluded. Some quirk in the King's nature had made him ennoble his arch enemy and ours, the Prince of Powys, who now rode with the English King as his companion and friend. The snub to my husband was inescapable. He, the gallant knight who had saved the life of his ungrateful monarch, had been passed over as a rebuke because of my refusal of the King's favours.

My husband acknowledged the slight with an amused shrug, but Branwen waxed exceedingly garrulous upon the subject. "King Henry and Owain Cadwgan are like and like," she pronounced contemptuously, with a complete disregard for the laws of treason. "For never before did two such villains walk together, one with the other." Both Stephen's and Hait's departure, rapidly increased the amount of work which fell upon my husband but he remained unfailingly cheerful, never once showing his hidden hurt during this wearysome period, when we both endeavoured to wait patiently for the birth of Hait's child. I quite expected and indeed would have readily understood that he should take another during this time, but all the indications were that he diverted himself as usual with extra work.

A quite unexpected diversion occurred for me however, during this seemingly endless period, and one which even in my wildest dreams I could scarcely have contemplated. I was in the garden one morning, feeding the birds which Bleddyn regularly encouraged with sweet words and generous helpings of grain, when Branwen came hurriedly through the gate. She was in a great state of excitement and from the way she was forced to snatch her breath, it appeared that she arrived in some haste from the farthest corner of the castle. "My lady," she began, with uncharacteristic hesitation, as though she was anxious not to anger me. "My lady, a young man has arrived and he is most desirous of seeing you. I – I took the liberty of bringing him straight to you here in the garden." I puckered up my forehead in a quick frown, for I wore my oldest kirtle.

Before I could object however, a young man stepped politely past Branwen and made me a profound genuflexion. His dark expressive eyes were bright with some hidden excitement, and as he raised his handsome head and smiled at me, I knew him instantly. With a hand across my breast, I endeavoured to quell the racing of my heart as the child within me jerked and leapt in panic. The face I beheld was that exactly of my son William, as he would be some fifteen years hence. "Gruffudd?" I murmured, the ready tears cascading down my cheeks. My brother, whom I had not seen for over twenty years, caught me before I fell and holding me in a firm embrace entreated me not to weep.

"You must not cry thus, sister of my heart," he begged. "I would not have come upon you with such haste had I known of your condition!"

"But you should, you must," I sobbed into his shoulder. "How I have longed to behold you, this many years."

He had landed farther up the coast, from an Irish boat, at dawn and had ridden to Penbroc immediately. "I had to wait for some time," he informed me diffidently, "until your husband the Constable had ridden away southwards with a number of his company."

The words made me raise my head to examine him, as his full meaning became clear. "My husband," I said slowly. "Oh – " I stopped, and he finished the sentence for me.

"Yes, I had to wait until it was clear that he had gone for some hours. He and I are traditional enemies. He is Norman, the agent of the French King, Henry, and I am the eldest son of Rhys ap Tewdwr, Prince of South Wales." He threw back his head proudly as he stated his rank, and deep within me I realized that he had not returned from Ireland at last, thus boldly, only to visit me.

"Do you hear aught of us here, in the court of the Irish King?" I ventured.

He nodded solemnly. "Many bards from Wales and

many exiles also, continually throng the court there. They
have told me much about you, over the years. The bards
still sing at great length of the beauty of the Princess Nesta,
daughter of Rhys." He smiled with wicked charm. "They
also tell me that the Norman knight, your husband, a man
of exceptional gallantry and command and a most able
administrator, latterly defied the King of England, no less,
to keep you for himself alone. It was said that he risked
death and displeasure, and even worse, for his great and
abiding love of you. "Is this so?" I bowed my head, then,
feeling weak from excitement, I sat down upon my garden
bench. I needed time in order to think clearly of this
momentous change which had suddenly come upon me,
with the reappearance of my brother. This young man of
twenty-eight, had been a mere lad of seven years old when
our father had been killed by renegade Norman marauders
in Brecheiniog. Indeed, I myself had been scarcely eleven
years old when we had last met.

At length, I felt constrained to explain to him my present
predicament and the tragic circumstances that had led me
into my present pregnancy. Gruffudd drew in his breath in
awe, as I outlined my husband's generosity over the matter.
"Most men would have killed you both," he cried. "To
think that you should have found such rapport, with one
who is not of our own blood or race. I marvel at it," he
pondered.

"Yes," I agreed simply. "Had our father not perished
when he did, and had his kingdom of Deheubarth
flourished, I should probably have had either Owain
Cadwgan, or his equally evil cousin Madog for husband." I
shuddered. My brother looked up sharply.

"I know well what you suffered at the hands of that
scoundrel, Owain, the son of Cadwgan," he told me. "He
bragged of his exploits continually in Ireland, both in war
and with women. The High King deliberately kept us apart

after he learned of your abduction, lest I should do Owain an injury. 'Our cousin' waxed highly sentimental over you however, whenever he was in his cups," he observed soberly. "You made a considerable impression upon him."

"It is a nightmare that I should be grateful to be allowed to forget," I replied, a little brusquely. "In view of my present delicate situation," I added seriously, "I feel that I cannot approach my husband with a request that you should stay here at the castle. However, I have many Welsh friends in the town and I am certain that you may lodge with one of them with the greatest of safety, until my confinement is over."

By the time my husband returned that evening, no trace of my brother Gruffudd was visible, either in the castle, or in the town. Branwen and Bleddyn with their many contacts, had placed him in a safe retreat, where I prayed that he would remain until after the birth of Hait's baby. On several occasions I managed to visit him, on the pretext of purchasing fabrics from the merchant with whom he secretly lodged. It came to me after the second of these visits, that my brother was quite incapable of inaction for any length of time, and that by various means, through itinerant traders who visited the town, he had been sending numerous messages to those of our kinsmen whom he thought he could trust. I was far from happy with the situation and Bleddyn, who was always acutely aware of political danger, even as it fermented, was plainly troubled also by these covert overtures to the chieftains of the North and mid-Walian heartlands. The New Year broke cold and uncompromising, and in all of my fifteen winters at Penbroc, I had never before known the winds from the Irish Sea to carry so much ice on their breath. I was increasingly grateful for my new fur-lined mantle, and the small charcoal brazier in my chamber, which my husband ordered the servants to light for me every day. One of my favourite pastimes during these inclement days was to listen to my son David, as he struggled heroically to read works far beyond the capacity of a four-and-a-half-year-old, even one as erudite as he. "You try too hard," I chided him gently. "I fear that your tutor forces you on too fast. You must enjoy your childhood while you may."

"Oh no, mama," the child insisted seriously, "Brother Thomas feels as you do, and he begs me to go outside to play with my brothers. He tells me that such weighty matters ill become my extreme youth, and that I shall grow feverish with the strain." The small pale face lifted to mine, and the easy going maturity in the dark eyes, reassured me. "Indeed mama, I do not tax myself at all and I dearly love to read the Scriptures." I kissed him fondly, and extracted a promise that he would continue to ride his small cream pony with the Serjeant at Arms, for at least one hour every day in the fresh air. "Even if it rains mama?" he asked obediently. I nodded emphatically.

That particular day proved to be so harsh, and the wind so searching, that it was out of the question for me to venture outside, even around the upper rampart walk. With a sigh I settled to my tapestry, although it quite failed to engage my interest. My husband, I knew to be upon some business in the outlands of the Manor. I had hardly completed fifty stitches when the door of my chamber opened furtively and I looked up to discover to my horror, my brother Gruffudd shaking the powdered snow from his cloak. I struggled to my feet. "Gruffudd!" I gasped. "Are you mad that you must come here so openly in broad daylight?" He stepped over to me and gave me a quick embrace.

"Tush, Nest, cease your chiding. It is perfectly safe, your husband has been gone this last hour, and seems quite unlikely to return before nightfall. Idwal, the merchant with whom I lodge, watches the castle for me," he explained. "Do not frown in such perplexity, dear sister," he coaxed. "I was bored, and just had to talk with you. Why, we have not met for two whole weeks." He leaned back fractiously, upon the bench beside the charcoal brazier. "God, how I long to hunt, the days drag interminably," he grumbled.

I put my frame aside and went to him urgently. "That, I understand only too well in my condition but that you should venture here in broad daylight," I repeated, full of apprehension.

"Why, would you have me attempt to visit you at night and risk the righteous anger of your husband, who might mistake me for a lover?" he asked, with a gleam of interest. "That would be folly indeed. He has a stern eye, this husband of yours. I saw him sort out a minor riot on the market square last week – " He patted my arm, as I viewed him anxiously. "It is all right, no one saw me; I watched the fight from a darkened doorway." His eyes adopted an appreciative light. "The first quarrel was between two drovers, neither of whom would give the other right of way. One was forced into the ditch that spans the farther side of the square. His fellow, and the cooper from the far end of the street then began another brawl in the mud and before you could count ten, almost every passer-by had joined in, on one side or the other. Suddenly, there was a cry of – 'the Constable! Take care friends, the Constable!' "

My brother looked at me with hardly veiled amusement. "Within seconds, the street began to clear, and 'everyman' picked himself out of the ditch, and wiping his bloody nose attempted to creep away, secreting his cudgel as best he might. There was a ringing command. 'Hold! I will need an explanation of this,' and everyone froze where they stood. I was most interested," my brother confided. "It was my first opportunity of examining your husband at close quarters." He flashed me a charming smile. "Most impressive," he allowed. "Still remarkably handsome, for all that he must be forty. I compliment you, Nest," he said, "for now I understand your weakness, and why he has managed to hold your interest for so many years." He got up, and began to pace the chamber with restless energy. "At all events, he had very soon got the measure of his offending townsmen. The instigator was soon upon a horse, with his hands bound, ready to be taken into custody. He had the right man too, for with a few pertinent questions thrown out to left and right, to men who realized that honesty was the only policy when fixed with such a forbidding eye, he soon got at the truth. He then rode away, leaving the mopping up operations in the hands of a burgess of robust proportions called Humbert or Hillbert – "

"The name was Hubert," a crisp voice advised him from the doorway. "Hubert the tanner, to be precise." In utter dismay, we both swung to face the speaker. My husband stood on the threshold, and he wore his most inscrutable expression. As my brother turned to face him, I saw his hand move towards the sword which swung at his hip. He was still in full mailed shirt, as if he came prepared for any eventuality. At first, I was certain that he did indeed believe that I entertained a lover in my private chamber. His eyes slid over me speculatively, and I could sense the tautness in his every movement. Gruffudd met his gaze boldly, a half smile evident on his youthful features.

Unable to bear the tension any longer I moved tentatively towards the man who stood in the doorway. "Sir," I began haltingly. "I would like – " He was at my side in two strides. Gently he drew me towards him.

"Now Princess," he suggested quietly, "would you care to introduce me to your brother – "

I let my head sag against his shoulder in relief. "How did you know?" I asked weakly. He laughed.

"Well," he announced in appreciative tones, "Rhys ap Tewdwr left a very fair impression of himself, wherever he went, but none more so than in his eldest son and daughter. You are as alike as twins, the eyes identical, noses almost so, hair the same hue – " He quickly looked again, from one to the other of us, and his arm gathered me in closer as he did so. "Lips identical also. My advice to you both, is that one day you should gaze into the same pool, or if you can find a mirror that dare encompass you both, to examine carefully what you see in it." His voice altered subtly. "It was also a little naive of you both to believe that I should not somehow learn that the eldest son of Rhys ap Tewdwr had landed in Dyfed many weeks ago." He smiled down at me. "It would have been unduly careless of me as the commander of such an outpost as Penbroc, not to have learned of such a fact almost as soon as your brother had set foot in the lands under my stewardship." He relaxed his grip on me and held his hand out towards Gruffudd. "Welcome to Penbroc, brother, so long as you come in peace," he declared, and there was a wealth of meaning in his words. "I have no doubt that you will be far more comfortable here at the castle in such freezing conditions, than lodged at Idwal's house in Well Street."

He laughed once more at our bemused expressions, but Gruffudd, recovering himself rapidly, took the extended hand and bowed deeply. "Your generosity is well known, sir," he replied, with a reciprocal smile. "I shall do my best not to betray your trust." My husband's eye was searching, as he acknowledged the underlying tenor of these remarks.

"I feel that I must make my position quite clear at the outset," he stated seriously. "I am, and will always be, a loyal vassal of His Majesty King Henry of England. As brother of my wife, I gladly welcome you and extend all hospitality to you. But – " he paused significantly. "If ever you come out in open rebellion against the King, who is my liege lord, I shall not hesitate to pursue you, and if necessary capture you and bring you to the King's justice.

Do I make myself plain?" Gruffudd sighed, but his eyes still retained their brightness and fervour.

"You make yourself infinitely clear, sir, and I thank you for your words of warning. If I decide to take the necessary steps to regain my father's old kingdom, I shall endeavour to put myself at least a day's ride from your territory. I have no great wish to compromise your position with King Henry, or that of my sister." It was the nearest that I ever heard my brother Gruffudd come to giving his word, and his intentions with regard to Deheubarth were eminently obvious. Gerald secured my arm within his and suggested that my brother should send a servant as far as Idwal's house for his belongings.

"Meanwhile," he declared easily, "let us see what the cooks have prepared for our dinner, this piercing cold makes me uncommonly hungry."

The restless nature of my brother Gruffudd made it impossible for him to remain settled in one place for any length of time. He found the winter weather irksome and wished to be off and doing, amongst his many other relations farther north. What it was exactly that he wished to be doing, he was tactful enough not to specify, but at the end of seven weeks he left us, to visit some cousins in Ystrad Tywi, saying that if we had no objection, he would return to us later. His relationship with my husband during his stay at Penbroc had been remarkably cordial and on more than one occasion, Gerald had gone out of his way to provide an exciting day on the hunting field for his energetic brother-in-law. Although their conversation was usually guarded, it was at times like these, when they returned weary but stimulated from the chase, that they really seemed to enjoy one another's company. Gruffudd had a great deal of ready charm, and he would exert himself considerably to gain the eye and ear of this new brother, who was so much older than he both in years and experience.

It was only too obvious that my younger brother, in order to escape from what seemed to be the perils of too great an affection for his traditional enemy, had decided to move on far sooner than he had intended. His feelings became eminently clear on the night before he left us. He drank rather more than usual and just before he removed from the supper table to retire to his bed, he raised his drinking horn in tribute to his host. His bright dark eyes were full of expression as he murmured. "Would that we could love our enemies less, and our friends more!" I looked quickly at Gerald and read in his face an acknowledgement, humorous though it was, of the frustration of his purpose. He had deliberately set out to woo my brother from his warlike designs, and knew that he had failed. He raised his horn to drink the toast and I felt the sadness of the occasion deeply. If only the power of my husband's considerable personality could have triumphed over my brother's ambition to repossess the lands of our father. Sympathetic as I was to the Welsh cause, I feared that the joint might of the King and his many magnates could bring suffering and death to many innocent people before peace came.

Gerald rose to his feet and extended a hand towards me. "Come," he ordered gently. "We men in our selfishness forget that you are so near your time, that you need your rest." He bade a courteous good night to Gruffudd and the assembled company, and quietly escorted me to my chamber.

Gruffudd had not been gone many hours when I began to labour to bring Hait's baby into the world. It was with a great sense of relief that I experienced the first pangs. At last my long wait was over. There is very little that I remember of the birth. As usual it was remarkably easy.

When the child drew its first breath and gave its first cry, Branwen gave me to drink from a draught that stood on the chest nearby, and I fell into a deeply induced sleep. I did not see Hait's child, neither did I have any wish to do so. My husband returned soon after the birth and while I slept, he and Branwen had dispatched the child immediately to its father, who waited with a nurse at a convenient place in the nearby town. It was a strong healthy boy, I was assured by my maid. More than Hait deserved. As if he feared that his judgement with regard to the banishment of Hait's child had been over harsh, my husband was particularly tender with me at this time.

"You do not have to be so kind to me," I pleaded. "I had no wish to retain this baby here at Penbroc. I am almost ashamed that I felt nothing for it, no love, just emptiness – "

He moved around and sat close by the side of the bed. His hand gently traced my features as he contemplated me in silence for a moment.

"Supposing," he suggested softly, "just supposing that I deal with you thus because I cannot help myself. For when I look at you, my love is such that I can never cease to wonder, how so much feeling can exist between two human beings. Would you question my 'kindness', as you call it, then? Or would you accept my love gladly, as I do?"

I caught his hand impulsively. "Gerald," I cried unsteadily, "are you ever afraid, really afraid? So many things and people have endeavoured to part us, and we have overcome them all – but there is one thing which will assuredly part us, and I fear it greatly."

He looked down at me with serious eyes. "You mean death?"

I nodded miserably. "Whenever we are truly happy, then I fear it most. For then we have the most to lose," my voice faltered and stopped.

He sighed and his hand tightened over mine. "As a

soldier, death has stalked me all my life, since I was a young squire in Lord Arnulf's army. We have faced it squarely a number of times, you and I. Particularly so on the night that your cousin Owain broke into Cenarth Bychan, and then again, I faced the possibility for many weeks when Stephen brought you back to me at last and you hovered on the brink so perilously. Perhaps it was never nearer than on the night when the King came to Penbroc." His tone softened even further. "And you would not lie there now, in childbed, if you had not experienced such an acute sense of bereavement when you ultimately received news of my death from the King's armies. Can it hurt us any more than it already has?" He stooped to kiss me. "Live now my beloved while we may, and be thankful." I reached up and pulled his head down onto my breast, too full of emotion to weep.

Within a few weeks we had once again achieved that closeness which had blessed our reunion in the summer of 1110, after my abduction. Even the sudden reappearance of my brother Gruffudd in the early springtime, did nothing to mar my happiness. He brought with him a most pleasant surprise. When he arrived I heard him murmur something to Gerald which I did not quite catch. Then he came towards me, wearing his most engaging smile. "See, I do not return empty-handed," he cried. "In the chapel, sister, is someone who has journeyed from on far to visit you. I believe that young David is already entertaining your guest handsomely for you." Suddenly, I knew.

"Hywel?" I said emotionally, and then as I turned towards the chapel door a terrible memory smote me.

"Nest," Gerald advised me quietly. "His scars are not visible to the world, either mentally or physically, and you must not remind him of them. It was a long time ago."

"Yes," I replied simply. "It was a long time ago." Composing myself rapidly, I ventured into the semi-darkness of our little church. By the light of Our Lady's candle, I could see two figures seated companionably side by side on the Prior's sedilia. They were discussing theology.

"Mama," my five-year-old son cried with great animation, as I appeared within their magic circle. "My Uncle Hywel has been telling me of many miracles – " The young man by his side rose to greet me and his reassuring smile contained such serenity that my anguish for his person was immediately stilled.

He did not catch me up impulsively in his arms, as Gruffudd had at our first meeting, but he grasped my hands with unmistakable warmth. "Nest," he said, as though it was only yesterday since we had sat together in our hollow tree on the moorland. "Nest, you haven't changed at all."

I returned his clasp affectionately. "Can you really remember me that clearly?" I asked in wonder. "Why you were no older than David here, when we last met."

"Ah yes," he claimed with feeling. "I remember you vividly, a flash of red against the uplands where we played. You often wore a kirtle the colour of holly berries. Many was the time that you gave me comfort when I fell and bruised my knees, and we used to take turns to swing from a stout branch of the ancient hollow oak tree on the moor. And on dark winter evenings we shared the hearth in our father's hall, while the scent of burning apple wood mingled with the wonderful music of the bards."

I laughed happily at the memory. "Come, David," I cried, "I am sure that the Good Lord would be happy for us to say our thanks in my garden by the river, which I am sure that your uncle will enjoy."

"Mama," the child asked simply. "Would you prefer me to withdraw so that you may speak privately together, with my uncle?" I caught my brother's eye over the head of this, the most adult of my children. Hywel shook his head.

"Your uncle enjoys your conversation, my son," I assured him. "You may stay." The garden was beginning to rouse itself from its long winter sleep. The extreme cold of the first few months of the year had goaded the spring blossoms into a frantic wish for life. Their scent mingled with the salty tang which rose from the seaweed which lay strewn along the river's edge. My youngest brother strolled contentedly about, discovering many varieties of plant and herb half hidden between the stones.

David solemnly described how the garden had come into being. "The year before I was born," he declared, "my mother was very ill during the winter time and when she recovered, she discovered that my father had fashioned for her this beautiful garden so that she might sit and regain her strength in the sunshine." He pointed out the minute rock pool. "Only last year, mama filled that with some small, but very attractive fish." The child's face lit up. "But the very next day a greedy heron came and stood over the pool. He rapidly ate all the small fish for his breakfast. Mama called him King Heron."

Hywel turned speculative eyes upon me. "King Heron," he mused. "He who is supreme, and consumes all the smaller fish. It is an apt parable."

I knew exactly what he meant. "Hywel," I begged, "cannot you prevent our brother from instigating this insurrection? Many innocent people will die and even more will be hurt."

"Yes," he agreed soberly, "many will be hurt." He, better than most men, knew how bitter that hurt could be. "But I cannot in all conscience stop him in his attempt to regain our father's old kingdom of Deheubarth," he declared. "It is his true inheritance and did not our father Rhys ap Tewdwr, die, an old man of eighty summers, defending the family lands? If Gruffudd does not succeed for himself, it may be that he will one day have a son, who in his turn might inherit our father's territory. No, Nest, I cannot prevent him, and though I would be far happier as a scholar in holy orders, I must do all within my power to aid him. Please try to understand."

I clasped his extended hands and bowed my head. "I have infinite sympathy for his ambition," I cried, "but it is the slaughter and destitution, the burnt out valleys and the hungry people, that I cannot bear to contemplate. But I shall feel easier if you are with him – he needs a little restraint."

"I pray that it may not be as bloody a battle as you fear," he said quietly. He examined my face carefully. "We received news this morning that King Henry now knows of our presence and guesses at our intention. Gruffudd plans to move tomorrow. We shall approach the chieftain of the far north, ap Cynan for his support."

"Tomorrow!" I murmured, "and you have but come today."

"I had to see you first," Hywel said simply. "I wished to refresh my memory. Now, I shall always remember you as you are at this moment, in this beautiful garden, fashioned for you by the noblest of the King's magnates. I find his love for you both genuine and reassuring. Your happiness sustains me."

A few weeks after the departure of my two brothers for the north, to seek aid from Gruffudd ap Cynan, we heard that that chieftain, for fear of King Henry's wrath, had refused them all help. Moreover he had planned to capture them, and deliver them up into the King's hands. My brothers, being warned in time of his intent, had fled southwards, being forced initially to seek sanctuary in the church at Aberdaron. Bleddyn informed me that they were now hidden in Ystrad Tywi not so far away and that he knew with certainty that Gruffudd had managed to gather around him a substantial war band.

"My husband must be informed of this at once," I told the bard.

"My lady, he already knows," the blind harper replied sadly. "See!" he walked me as far as the ramparts. In the water meadows below the castle bounds, flocks and herds were already being gathered together. Outside, on the hill yonder, beneath Monkton Priory, I could see the archers practising slavishly at the butts, and within the courtyard very obvious preparations were being made to make the castle ready for any eventuality. The apparent goodwill of my brothers had not prevented my husband from attending assiduously to his duties as Constable of this the main fortification in the west. "It will never be put to the test," Bleddyn assured me, as he noted my mounting unease. "I know, deep within me, that your brothers will not turn their eyes towards Penbroc. Stephen however, at Cardigan, is in a far more vulnerable position," he added in sombre tones, "and a messenger left early this morning to warn him of the situation."

When my brothers had first departed from Penbroc to make their journey to the north, I had revelled in the rare privacy thus afforded, for there were no visitors for once at the castle. For a few precious weeks we had lived together my husband and I, in almost unprecedented harmony, fully recapturing our youth and all of our previous passion. The first days of summer had been warm and mellow and we had wandered about the Manor hand in hand, enjoying fully the complete unity of our minds and bodies. For once, we had been able to live quite untroubled by any alarms or interruptions from the outside world, for Gerald had at last taken a well-earned holiday. When Bleddyn told me that morning that we were unlikely to be besieged, I knew already, that once again I held a child for my husband. I longed to give him another daughter, to spoil him in his old age, and I entered into my long enslavement to this latest fitz-Gerald with great tranquillity and joy.

My brother Gruffudd, however, when he made his first move, struck far closer to home than either of us had expected. The first inkling we had of any danger was the long line of refugees who fled towards our town walls for protection. My brother had attacked and burned Arberth Castle, a bare fifteen miles to the east of us. When my thoughts turned to that delightful valley with its green bower of nut trees and distant view of the blue mountains, my heart cried out in anguish. I could not envisage it raw and bleeding. With bated breath we waited. One by one, the patrols and scouts from our garrison came back with news. No sooner had Gruffudd ap Rhys sacked Arberth and seen it in ashes they said, than he had headed eastwards, away from Penbroc. It was a declaration of war. I could never be sure in my mind whether Gruffudd's regard of Penbroc was due to his finer feelings towards us, or because of his awe of the might of such a fortress and his fear of the strength and ability of its commander. At all times Gerald spoke comfortingly to me of his conviction that Gruffudd intended to leave us in peace, but summer drew on and the uncertainty remained.

My brother attacked Llandovery Castle and Swansea, but their garrisons held out with the tenacity with which my husband had held Penbroc, in the siege of 1096. All Gruffudd succeeded in doing was to burn the outer castle in each case, and in doing so, he lost many men. After hearing of these feats however, many young men and hotheads gravitated to him from all over South Wales, and they continued to plunder and carry off spoils, until that year's end. Eventually Gruffudd attacked Carmarthen Castle boldly, and its commander was slain. Skirting Stephen's stronghold at Cardigan, for reasons best known to himself, my brother then began to attack and ravage Ceredigion. It was only when he attempted to take the castle at the mouth of the Ystwyth, that his amazing run of luck finally petered out. Here, he had to contend with a well-trained Norman garrison, which had brought in reinforcements under cover of night. Gruffudd's unruly band of mercenaries began their attack without mobilizing their men to the best advantage. "Like a furious rabble without a ruler," so the bards sang afterwards.

The Norman Constable, Ralf, angry because of previous losses at another castle farther south, fought savagely and long. My brother Gruffudd was forced to flee in haste back to Ystrad Tywi, leaving many of his men dead and dying. Amongst the dead, lay my brother Hywel. It was to be many months before I learned of this loss, for Gerald, fearing my grief, kept the knowledge from me until after the birth of our child. Angharad, our second daughter, was born in the springtime of the year 1116. She was small, but very beautiful and her father took her immediately to his heart. By the time I learned of Hywel's death, Angharad was four weeks old. In tending her, my grief for my gentle brother was in some strange measure mitigated, and indeed, I was thankful in many ways that he did not live to be hunted down by the King's men.

With an uncanny streak of self preservation, Gruffudd dodged his pursuers through the length and breadth of Ystrad Tywi. Because of its difficult terrain, King Henry astutely put several of his loyal Welsh chieftains to harry my brother and his followers through the wilder woodlands of Carmarthenshire. One of the men he employed to do this evil work was his new knight and henchman Owain Cadwgan, Prince of Powys, who had returned from Normandy in the autumn. It was with a great deal of trepidation therefore, that I learned that the King's son had taken up residence at the freshly repaired Carmarthen Castle, and that my husband was required to go with a large force to meet him there, to swear fealty to the young

Prince. Gerald departed with a grave face and an immense host of both Normans and Flemings. My only consolation was that William, with a contingent of the de Barri family of Manor Pyr, was to join my husband's force at Whitland. William, a knight already at fifteen years old, had a very cool head. Together, I felt that they might be more than equal to the task of a meeting with Owain Cadwgan.

Bleddyn was full of cautious optimism. "You worry too much, my lady," he chided softly. "It is a large force which rode from Penbroc, and the Flemings are obdurate when they are called upon to face danger."

"I have concern for my brother also," I admitted. "Although I do not always agree with Gruffudd, I love him, I cannot help myself, and I could not bear that he should fall into the hands of my evil cousin."

"The Prince Gruffudd will live to have many sons," the bard declared enigmatically. "Do not grieve for him, my lady."

I had just left the dinner table early the next afternoon, when a small troop of horsemen rode into the courtyard. From the way that the leading rider vaulted from his horse, I knew instantly that it was William. With him was the eldest de Barri boy. My son, seeing me standing by the archway, came straight towards me.

"Do not fear mama," he declared, "my father is well, and will return to Penbroc by nightfall. It is other news that I bring." His eyes were bright, with a strange light that I could not easily interpret.

"You saw the King's son?" I asked, although the matter did not interest me greatly.

"Yes," the lad answered, "last night, and I swore fealty. He is scarce as old as myself. They say that he favours his Scottish grandfather, Malcolm Canmore." I could tell however, that this was not the burden of his message. He introduced his patron's son and the young de Barri kissed my hand with a considerable flourish. William viewed me a trifle uncertainly. "We left Carmarthen before dawn had broken, the matter was urgent; I felt that I must see you before my father reached home. Mama, a little before dusk last night my father killed Owain Cadwgan, Prince of Powys."

I steadied myself against the massive door jamb. Somewhere, from within the inner recesses of my mind, I could hear once again, a voice. "I swear that I shall kill Owain Cadwgan with my own hands, before I die, so help me God." It came booming back to me now, with all the clarity and resonance of a funeral bell. I glanced up at my son and was able at last to understand the strange light that illuminated his whole face. It was a blaze of triumph.

"Perhaps," I suggested in uneven tones, "you had better tell me the whole story." His tale was vivid, and I knew without doubt that the scene had become indelibly printed upon his mind.

"Yesterday, at about the time of nones, three o'clock in the afternoon, our host, with my father at its head, drew near to the walls of Carmarthen," my son began seriously. "As we came up, almost to the castle walls, we found a small group of refugees, who had fled thence from Ystrad Tywi. They were weary and terrified and they carried with them many dead and wounded. When we approached and they realized who we were, they cried out to us bitterly, that they had been attacked and robbed by none other than Owain Cadwgan, who had chased them right up to the castle gates. Purporting to carry out the King's commands he had vowed to spare none of the folk from Ystrad Tywi, claiming that they had hidden and succoured that 'petty thief', Gruffudd ap Rhys." My son paused momentarily to draw breath.

"The Flemings," he asserted, "were at once righteously indignant, calling Owain both murderer of their bishop

William of Brabant, and the scoundrel who had carried hundreds of their fellows off to death and captivity in Ireland. My father immediately asked these poor refugees where Owain Cadwgan could be found, as they had been so recently pursued, and they said, 'See yonder! He withdraws in leisurely manner with his spoil, our goods and our cattle, which he has stolen from us.' At once, my father quietly advised the Flemings that he had an old, very bitter score to settle with the Prince of Powys, and that he would follow until he came up with him. He said that they were at liberty to join him if they wished. William's eyes were alive, as he added. "With a loud shout, they said to the last man, that they would follow him.

"A few miles north-east of Carmarthen town, the two rivers, the Cothi and the Tywi, entwine, to make their joint way to the sea. It was at the confluence that we caught up with Owain Cadwgan. His force was small, far less than ours. At first, he did not appear to appreciate our intent, but then, realizing that an alien host greatly outnumbering his own was rapidly overtaking him, he withdrew across a ford over the narrower course of the Cothi, onto a tongue of land which divides the two rivers as they converge. This slender strip of turf was no wider than fifty yards, at the place where we faced him. He was virtually trapped, with the wider, faster flowing Tywi in full spate at his back. With great boldness, he turned to face us. It was then that he saw my father upon his war horse, well to the front of our column.

"My father called to him in a loud voice: 'Owain, son of Cadwgan, knowest thou me, for I am determined that you shall know me before I kill you.' Then the Prince of Powys called upon his archers and they took aim at us, letting fly their arrows. My father using his great shield, fended off these barbs with great dexterity. Before Cadwgan's archers could muster a second volley, my father snatched a bow from our nearest bowman, and took aim at his enemy."

William glanced at me quickly. "Do you remember, Mama? When we were in hiding at Carew, how my father used to hunt food for us with his bow and arrows? Philippe used to say that Papa could fell a stag at the full distance that an arrow will fly. It must have been so with the arrow with which he killed Owain Cadwgan. It was a superb shot. The Prince of Powys fell immediately. Arrows flew then on both sides, but after a few minutes, realizing that their leader lay dead, all but two of Owain's followers fled. My father held back his host, allowing those who wished to escape us, and then he forded the Cothi, dismounting at the other side. The two men who remained at the feet of their dead Prince were terrified, but they did not move. My father bade them fear not. When he was certain that his arch enemy was indeed dead he allowed the two men to carry away the remains of their leader, to be buried in his own country — "

My son's voice tailed off, for he had heard as I had the trumpet which signalled that the Constable had returned to Penbroc. Instinct made me refrain from running towards my husband as he dismounted. Without a glance to left or right he stalked through the waiting throng of men and women, and on past the door which led to my chamber. Before any of us could move or speak, his gaunt figure had been swallowed up within the dark recesses of the little chapel. William came quickly to my side. "Go to him, Mama," he pleaded.

"No, William," I replied firmly. "When your father needs me, he will come to me. Until then, I too must respect his privacy."

A few hours later when my husband sought me out he was outwardly calm, but I understood him too well to believe that this was more than a veneer, a disciplined facade, in time of need. I waited for him in our private chamber, pretending that there were various duties required of me by our small daughter which kept me there, out of the public eye. At last, he stood in the doorway. "I hear that William has visited you today," he remarked adopting a casual tone.

"Yes," I replied, "He and the eldest de Barri boy called here to see me as they rode home from Carmarthen."

"Our son will have informed you, I do not doubt, that Owain Cadwgan, the Prince of Powys met his death yesterday, just outside Carmarthen," he declared soberly.

I bowed my head tactfully. "William was of the opinion that the world had been saved from much evil by his death," I answered softly. "At least, many lives in Ystrad Tywi will have been saved."

"Perhaps," he agreed, with a restraint that alarmed me.

Overnight, he had suddenly become a much older man. It was as if, from the moment that his most hated adversary had died, Gerald himself had begun to wither. Much of his own spirit seemed to have flown with the arrow that pierced my cousin Owain's evil heart. This black period was to persist for many months. Outwardly, always competent and dignified, the Constable of Penbroc continued about his duties as usual. But, privately, I had to exert all my ingenuity and compassion to prevent a total breakdown in this man I most loved. There were times, in the quiet middle of the night when I held him to me closely, that the barriers would fall, and he would bury his head, his whole body becoming wracked by uncontrollable grief. "Why?" I would ask, soothing him gently. "What ails you so, husband of my heart?" He did not know, could not tell me why he wept, or why such weakness should assail him.

Gradually, the tension would relax, and that sure confidence which had never before deserted him, would sweep back, returning his weary soul to some semblance of normality. During this most difficult time our smallest

daughter Angharad became an unfailing source of delight
to him, and as she grew, the bond between them
strengthened. She did much to speed his recovery. As soon
as she learned to walk they could often be seen together,
hand in hand, inspecting the castle compound. But the
rebuilding of Carew Manor was perhaps the challenge that
finally dispelled the ultimate depths of depression, and gave
my husband an all-abiding interest in his later years.
William had returned home from Manor Pyr, with his eyes
firmly set upon the lush green meadows of his inheritance.
He had also begun to take great interest in a winsome
fifteen-year-old, the eldest daughter of a neighbouring
magnate, and although he realized that her father would
not consent to her removal from his care for some years, he
was determined to woo and win her. Maurice, who had
taken his elder brother's place at Manor Pyr, as his own
training grew and developed, urged both my husband and
me to reclaim the lands which we owned in the north of
Dyfed, in the cantref of Emlyn. Our previous experience at
Cenarth Bychan made us unwilling at first to take any steps
which might put us and our family into so vulnerable a
position again. Bleddyn was always unwilling for us to
return to the lands beyond the Prescelli Mountains. "Why,
Emlyn," he declared with feeling, "is as poor a piece of land
as a crow ever flew over. You would do best to forget it
entirely."

Maurice who was a second son, was nevertheless most
persistent. Everyone knew, he stated, that the meadows
along the Teifi river were as good as any we had in the
south of Dyfed, and as far as trouble went, both Cadwgan
and his son Owain were now dead, and none of the others
of that breeding counted for much. Added to which, his
uncle, Gruffudd ap Rhys, was only strong enough these
days to skulk quietly within the bounds of Ystrad Tywi,
and raise sons out of the King's sight. Altogether, he

insisted, we should be guilty of criminal negligence if we did not develop all the land under our jurisdiction. After much coaxing, and Maurice had a way with him very reminiscent of his father and Philippe, we at last gave consent. We raised a small but strong outpost in the cantref of Emlyn, which was re-named Cilgerran. The Teifi gorge was still ås breathtakingly beautiful as it had ever been, in spite of our bitter memories of my abduction. Moreover, the hunting and fishing in that area, my husband and sons soon decided, must be the best in the world.

Another very pleasant aspect of Emlyn was its close proximity to Cardigan. Stephen soon began to meet us regularly there, and we gladly picked up the threads of our friendship, which seemed after a few months to be as closely woven as it had been at any time during the past twenty years. The last few years had been good to us, but my husband was ageing fast, a process I watched with foreboding. Outwardly, he still managed a far more active day than most men of half his years, but like many of his contemporaries, he was terrified at heart of a debilitating sickness taking him in its ruthless grip, or of creeping old age which now watched him wherever he walked. After two years away Maurice came back to Penbroc, and he and his father began to spend more time in the north organizing the cantref of Emlyn, for William now occupied Carew and there was little left there for them to do.

When the blow eventually fell, I was totally unprepared for it. During the winter of 1120 the sharp weather again brought a number of wolves down from the mountains. Deciding that these voracious packs were causing far too many losses amongst the deer parks in Emlyn, Gerald rode north as soon as Christmas was over, and the weather permitted. William, enticed away from Carew by the promise of a wolf hunt, went with his father and younger brother and a number of our best huntsmen. "For who knows," he cried, "when the opportunity for such sport will arise again?" Fearing that I should fret at this rather more lengthy absence than usual, Gerald had been particularly attentive before his departure. We had had a memorable Christmas that year, with all of the family present at Penbroc except Philippe, who sent many messages from Gloucester from himself and his young bride. He hoped, he concluded gaily, that we should enjoy the responsibility of being grandparents ere long.

"The only problem with being a grandparent," Gerald remarked thoughtfully, "is that most of them creak at the joints. How can one accept the prospect of old age with the stoicism with which one faced youth? I fear that I have not got it in me to fall into decay gracefully."

I went to him quickly. "You are not old," I insisted. "Since fitz-Richard died, you have dwelt overmuch upon the subject. You once told me to live now while we may and be thankful." He pulled me to him and kissed me with all the fervour that he had shown in youth.

"This is one thing that never stales," he whispered. "You come to me still, with all your infinite variety and I marvel at our good fortune, as I have never ceased to do." I raised my eyes to his and smiled, as I remembered.

"My father," I declared proudly, "Rhys ap Tewdwr, sired me when he was almost seventy and my two brothers at an even greater age. Never tell me again that you are old at forty-six, you founder of the fitz-Geralds." I rested in his arms comfortably. "What is so strange," I mused, "is Stephen at half that age, with no wife and no child to come after him."

Gerald viewed me soberly. "There is still time. He has many years yet, but if he does marry, I don't doubt that it will be after my days." I asked him to explain himself, but he refused entirely to be drawn on the subject, and after we had retired, the matter went completely from my mind.

On the next day, my husband with his two elder sons rode away north for the wolf hunt in Emlyn. As they were likely to be away for some time, I settled myself patiently to wait. The weather was crisp but fine, so I made a point of walking at least once a day, for exercise, around the castle perimeter. Young de Cogan my husband's lieutenant, seemed these days to manage the castle when he was in sole charge with the same brisk efficiency that Stephen had always done. He was a handsome rogue and it was visible for all to see, that my elder daughter found him immensely attractive, although she had scarcely seen more than fourteen summers. I made a resolution, when I came upon them whispering intimately by the stable door, to discuss the matter urgently with her father when he returned. She was far too young. It might be a good thing if she visited her godmother in Tenby for a few months in the springtime.

By some strange chance, I found that habit had led me into the little walled garden. I seldom visited it during the winter months, though I spent long hours there in the temperate summer weather. It bore a stark cold aspect now, in January, with the plants that lived through the cooler weather huddled in screwed up uncomfortable heaps around the rocks that allowed them scant shelter from the wintry tempests. I leant on the parapet, and gazed at the half frozen river. Momentarily, the sun peered at me with forlorn watery rays, lighting the countryside with a fleeting brilliance and then suddenly, as if in eclipse, there was a darkening of the landscape as the light was withdrawn. An eerie sigh swept up the river, and a few dead leaves swirled and rattled around my feet. A great sadness descended upon me, and I shivered in anticipation of I knew not what. As I stood there, caught up for a moment inescapably in time, a bell tolled from the distant Priory calling the monks to their devotions. It was the hour of nones, the ninth hour of the day.

With dragging feet, I made my way towards the warmth and shelter of the Great Hall. Throughout that evening I could settle to nothing. At last, restlessly, I retired to my bed, but sleep came infrequently to me, until almost dawn. I had just fallen into a deep refreshing slumber when I was disturbed by activity in the courtyard – If only they could change the guard less noisily. As I turned over, to resume my broken dreams, I heard a sound which immediately banished sleep. It was a sound which I had seldom heard before, that of Branwen, weeping piteously. I rose swiftly from my couch and went in search of her. She was hunched on a bench in the Oriel, rocking miserably back and fore in her grief. I did not have to ask – "My husband is dead," I said, as she lifted her tear-stained features to mine.

"Oh my lady," she cried, coming quickly to my side. "My lady – God have mercy on his noble soul."

"How?" I asked in dull tones – "And where?"

"By an arrow, swiftly," she sobbed. "Thanks be to God. An arrow shot from the bow of a solitary archer, sent by one of the younger brothers of Owain Cadwgan. Master William says that he must have been stalking them for days, to get a clear shot at your husband." She turned anguished eyes upon me. "It was along the path that runs beside the Teifi river, as it winds through the gorge, beneath the mound on which once stood your castle of Cenarth Bychan."

"Is he – ?" I asked, unable to finish.

"Your sons carried their father's body home immediately," my maid told me quickly. "They are even now laying him to rest in the chapel, with the aid of Father Honore."

"Then will you please take me there, Branwen," I directed.

A profound hush had fallen over the castle, men went about their business, taking and giving their orders in whispers. They parted uneasily to allow me through to the chapel door. Inside, a few extra flickering candles burned around a makeshift bier, rapidly erected from boards and trestles. Upon this they had laid him. His large military cloak was as yet his only pall. My two sons conversed in low tones with the priest. "I will go to her immediately and tell her," William declared.

"There is no need, my son," I advised him quietly, "I am here."

"Mama!" The boys turned to me with one accord. Even by that dim light, I could see the dread which dwelt in their eyes, at the thought of my sorrow. William caught my hands urgently. "Mama, he did not suffer; it was instantaneous. Quite a wonderful way to go. You know how he could scarce bear to think of infirmity and old age. It is as he would have wished."

"Yes," I agreed sorrowfully. "It is exactly as he would have wished. Now will you go, all of you. I wish to speak with my husband alone."

"Mama!" Maurice cried, the tears running down his cheeks. "We cannot leave you thus."

"Please," I insisted gently, "you can and must. For I wish to be left on my own with him for a little while." With a few quiet words Father Honore, understanding my need, drew my sons and Branwen away from the makeshift bier and out into the courtyard. I raised one of the candles in my hand, holding it where the light most illuminated his features. His expression in repose was of the utmost serenity.

"My love, you are at peace," I whispered softly. Raising his hand, I kissed it gently. It was quite cold. Later, I allowed them to remove me temporarily, from his side. When they begged me to eat, I forced down as much as I could obediently consume, and when they bade me rest, I did my best to comply. The boys were adult and businesslike over all the arrangements for the handing over of the castle, and the funeral itself.

On the second day before we buried him on the hill which overlooked his beloved fortress, Stephen came. I was in the chapel keeping a silent vigil, when the door to the little church opened quietly and someone entered. I did not raise my head, thinking it to be Father Honore. There was a strangled sob, choked back and a few whispered words, as the newcomer paused by my husband's body. Two hands then came upon my shoulders from behind, as I knelt at the altar rail. I braced at the compassion in their touch. "I came as soon as the messenger arrived," a well-known voice assured me.

"Thank you, Stephen," I replied simply. "You were the best friend he ever had."

"Yes, and he himself, was the truest friend a man could ever have had," Stephen replied soberly. "He knew my innermost secret and yet still forgave me and continued to be my friend, without restraint. Few other men could have done so."

I raised questioning eyes to his. "You have never had a secret, that other men could not share," I objected. "I doubt there was anything to forgive."

He held my eyes with an intensity that hurt. "Ah yes, there was," he insisted. "Your husband knew, that for the last ten years I had loved his wife, to the point where little else mattered, and yet he trusted me to keep my bond – and I did so, faithfully." I gave a cry of distress. "Forgive me," he begged, "but I kept my vow to him that I should never speak of it, whilst he still lived."

I struggled to my feet and backed away from him. "Oh Stephen, not now," I sobbed. "I beg of you, not now, I cannot bear it."

He dropped his gaze. "Forgive me, Princess, for those unforgiveable words, but here, by these altar rails seemed

to me, to be so right – and openly thus, in front of him. You
see he asked of me that I should care for you and your
younger children, if he should die before me, and this I
swore to do. I will not distress you further." He bowed with
humility. "If you need me, I shall be with Maurice and
William. The son of fitz-Richard is at Cardigan, keeping
the castle. I do not plan to leave here until your future is
settled according to your own wishes."

An unnatural strength possessed me until my husband
was buried and I had removed with my children to Carew,
into the care of William. The King sent a new chief officer
and extra men to garrison the castle as soon as he received
news of my husband's death. Gerald's lieutenant, young de
Cogan, had expressly wished to be allowed to leave the
King's service, to join that of William, at Carew. He was a
servant of the fitz-Geralds, he declared, rather than that of
the King of England. Stephen stayed for a week, until our
move to Carew was completed. He returned to Cardigan
sadly, not daring to speak to me further of his hopes of
becoming the family champion. The worst hurt I had to
bear was the sight of my youngest child, Angharad. She
had adored her father. At four years old, death was quite
incomprehensible to her. Piteously, she searched hither and
yon for Gerald, beseeching anyone who came near, "to find
Papa," for her.

It was only when Stephen came down to visit us that she
relaxed, taking his hand when he appeared and not letting
him out of her sight until he rode off again in the direction
of Cardigan. The sight of her curled up on his knees,
sucking her thumb contentedly at the hearthside, as she
had done with her father, was almost more than I could
bear. Stephen found his way to Carew frequently during
those first few months after Gerald's death.

"It is a long journey for Stephen to make so regularly,"
Maurice remarked wistfully one day, as he had bidden

adieu yet again, to his old friend. "He does so wish to look after you, mama," the lad ventured, not caring to meet my eye. "I am sure that he appreciates fully the great attachment you and my father had for one another. Stephen does not expect you to love him exactly. All he really wishes for is that you should accept his protection."

"Then you, as well as I, know that such a thing cannot be unless I marry him," I declared shortly. "And I have no intention of ever marrying again." We carried on in this wise for some months. Bleddyn and Branwen, now both ageing fast, kept silent, but were eager to greet Stephen whenever he came to Carew. I also looked forward to the diversion of his visits. The boys had their own lives and I was anxious that my widowhood should not in any sense mar their youth. William was full of his forthcoming marriage. His devotion to his first love had never wavered and the girl's father, impressed with both his ability and fortune, had at last given his consent to the match. My children were just beginning to live, whereas the larger part of me lay dead and buried on Monkton Hill. In many ways, I felt that I could not bear to cast my shadows upon their early joys. Carew brought back many memories of the years that Gerald and I had spent in hiding there at the mill. Jean and his wife were both dead and another miller now operated the new improved tidal mill, a little further downstream towards the river mouth. But in every corner of the lane, every twist of the mill stream, there dwelt some sign or other of my husband's presence. I never really settled down at Carew and Angharad was always disturbed while we remained there.

Three months after my husband had been buried, I agreed to return to Cardigan with Stephen. He had difficulty in restraining his great joy. He knew the nature of the love which Gerald and I had reserved for each other he declared, and he expected nothing from me. All he wished for was that he should be allowed to give me and my youngest children a little security. The two elder boys were quite capable now of managing Carew and they had de Cogan, who was an extraordinarily able chief officer. We were married very quietly at Cardigan, at the end of Lent. To my surprise, Bleddyn as well as Branwen volunteered to accompany me to my new home, and for this I was thankful. Angharad, delighted to be in residence continually with this new father figure, reverted to her former relaxed, happy temperament, as Philippe had done twenty years before, when I had first arrived at Penbroc to mother him.

Although I continued to mourn Gerald with an acute pain that could never be removed, Stephen helped me also to bear my loss with greater fortitude. He diffidently assured me on our wedding night, that he expected nothing from me, in return for his love and protection. I quietly replied that I intended to be his wife in every sense, for he was no longer a young man and although he never discussed the matter, I knew that he desperately wished for a son. His devotion to me made him gentle and kind, and he was by no means a novice in the arts of love, for he had had many women, over the long years which he had spent at Penbroc. That which I had most dreaded, in time, became a comfort and a solace for my deepest loss. I became pregnant almost immediately. Stephen found it difficult to conceal his jubilation, and I prayed that I might give him a son, healthy in mind and body.

Despite his loving care, I felt tired and weary of the world. Now that Gerald had gone my reason for living gradually seeped away, for our love had been something quite unusual in this world. Branwen sensed this, for her old eyes watched me carefully, as summer changed reluctantly into autumn and then eventually doffed that flaming mantle for the sober vestments of winter. I feasted my eyes on all that had previously pleased me, knowing full well that the singing river and the curlew's cry heralded the end of earthly existence. For winter had come, and I waited but to fulfil one further duty, before I too could sleep, like the trees that lined the flowing Teifi. I was brought to bed with Stephen's child in January, a year to the day since I had lost my soul, with the arrow which had killed my beloved. With rigid determination, I clung to life for the time which God required of me, to bring my second husband's son into the world, alive and well. It was a difficult labour, making the fight hard, and distressingly long. At last, I heard a resolute gasp and a determined wail, then Branwen's triumphant voice declaring. "A strong, strong lad my lady, every bit as healthy as the others."

"Please tell Stephen," I begged weakly, "that his son 'Robert' wishes to make himself known – "

Epilogue

When I knew for certain that the child was safe and well a glorious warmth began to assail me. I became dimly aware of Stephen's excited tones as he viewed his coveted son. "Yes, yes, he is like Maurice, the same shape to the mouth. He is perfect." Wearily, I opened my eyes and smiled at him. He grasped my hand strongly. "You are tired," he said gently. "Our son was in no hurry to get here and he has wearied you. Yes, I like his name, it has an authoritative ring – Robert fitz-Stephen."

"I am delighted that he pleases you," I managed with difficulty. "Bleddyn must enter his birth into the annals of Cardigan – ." I smiled again and closed my eyes.

"Nest!" Stephen cried. "What ails you?" Over my head I could hear a whispered dialogue between Stephen and Branwen and then Branwen's cry of distress.

"Oh sir, sir, I can do nothing. She will not respond. See, she slips away from us!" Suddenly the warmth which I had enjoyed became dispersed by a cold breeze which blew in from the sea. I shivered and drew my garments more closely about me. From far away I could hear Stephen's voice calling, calling me –

"Nest, Nest," he beseeched in agonized tones. "Don't leave me. Nest, you cannot leave me now. We have had so short a time – You cannot leave me – Nest!"

It had become pitch dark, and I could not see the way

upon which I walked. The path was very stony and then suddenly, I knew the place – It was the gravel walk that I traversed, at Penbroc. Before me, I could just perceive a distant light. As I approached the little wrought iron walking gate which gave onto the garden, I realized that the light came from within. The gate swung open before I could do more than lay a finger upon it, and then as I entered, I understood at last what I had seen – the garden was full of the most wonderful sunlight. Someone stood there, by the parapet wall, and I knew that he waited for me. He turned as I approached and held out a hand towards me, with the old disarming gesture, that I knew so well. The tunic he wore was the whitest that I had ever seen, gracing the form of a mere captain of the guard. His face was that of the young man whom I had married, twenty-two years before. Joyfully, I reached for his outstretched hand, and he grasped mine eagerly.

"I thought that you would never come," he murmured softly, drawing me within the circle of his waiting arms.

WOLVERHAMPTON
PUBLIC LIBRARIES